10 MAY 1 6 2002

The Redemption of
Sarah Cain

Also by Beverly Lewis
in Large Print:

The Shunning
The Confession
The Reckoning
The Postcard
The Sunroom

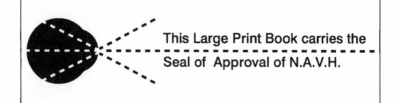

The Redemption of Sarah Cain

Beverly Lewis

Thorndike Press • Thorndike, Maine

Published in 2001 by arrangement with Bethany House Publishers.

Thorndike Press Large Print Christian Romance Series.

The tree indicium is a trademark of Thorndike Press.

The text of this Large Print edition is unabridged.
Other aspects of the book may vary from the original edition.

Set in 16 pt. Plantin by Christina S. Huff.

Printed in the United States on permanent paper.

Library of Congress Cataloging-in-Publication Data

Lewis, Beverly, 1949–
    The redemption of Sarah Cain / Beverly Lewis.
        p. cm.
    ISBN 0-7862-3113-0 (lg. print : hc : alk. paper)
    I. Title.
    PS3562.E9383 R44   2001
    813'.54—dc21   00-051216

In fondest memory of
my teacher and friend,
Dr. Mary Bainbridge Vyner.
Concert pianist, composer, teacher,
and the director of the
Lancaster Conservatory of Music
since 1958,
Dr. Vyner instilled in generations of
young pianists
a passion for great music.

Dear Lord and Father of mankind,
Forgive our foolish ways!
Reclothe us in our rightful mind,
In purer lives Thy service find,
In deeper reverence, praise.

O Sabbath rest by Galilee,
O calm of hills above,
Where Jesus knelt to share with Thee
The silence of eternity,
Interpreted by love!

Drop Thy still dews of quietness,
Till all our strivings cease;
Take from our souls the strain and
stress,
And let our ordered lives confess
The beauty of Thy peace.

— John Greenleaf Whittier from
The Brewing of Soma (1872)

Prologue: Lydia

Mamma slipped away to Glory one week ago today. The People laid her to rest on Glendorn Hill in a simple poplar coffin next to *Dat*'s grave, under a stand of sycamores. The January sky sagged, gray and low, like an eternal sigh. Had there been a speck of azure in the heavens, I might've thought the Good Lord meant it as a sign of hope.

I stood tall and silent with my four younger siblings: Caleb, Anna Mae, Josiah, and Hannah, ranging in age from fourteen to six. We watched as the men from our church district shoveled the hard, cold dirt into the gaping hole. My throat ached, yet I did not so much as shed a single tear as little Hannah sniffled next to me at the graveside service.

Following the burial, I remained mute at the shared meal held at Noah and Susie Lapp's place — some of our closest friends amongst the People. Susie's plump face looked ever so concerned as she caught my gaze across her crowded kitchen. Still, I kept my emotions in check.

'Twasn't till much later, when the house was dark and hushed, that I embraced my grief freely. Alone, and in the privacy of my room, I trembled with the sorrow of our loss. Mine, and my younger brothers' and sisters'.

Mamma had drilled one thing into me before her passing: *"Be strong and courageous. Keep the family together, Lyddie. Will you promise me this?"* These were to be the last words on Mamma's lips. And, indeed, I gave my word. I was bound and determined to do this thing. For dearest Mamma.

The next morning, the children and I gathered in the front room for Bible reading and prayers. "Remember, we're strong . . . *together*," I told them.

Caleb, tall and blond, had accepted the substitute headship of the house when Dat passed away three years ago. Confidently, he carried Mam's old *Biwel* to the nearest rocker, his frame almost too lean for the wide girth of the hickory rocking chair. Still, he sat erect and determined as could be.

Turning the pages, he located the familiar passage. He began to read in a clear, strong voice, just as Dat always had, from the Twenty-third Psalm: " 'The Lord is my shepherd; I shall not want.' "

Redheaded and chubby, Anna Mae, eleven,

held hands with petite six-year-old Hannah as they sat on the large rag rug, eyes fixed on Caleb. Josiah, a stocky eight-year-old, slid next to me on the sofa, a bit closer than usual, his flaxen hair *schtruppisch* — tousled — as always.

" 'He maketh me to lie down in green pastures: he leadeth me beside the still waters,' "Caleb continued.

My mind wandered back to many-a springtime day, when Mamma packed us picnic lunches — after morning chores were through — letting us romp in the thick meadow grass out behind the barn. Robins and whippoorwills flew low overhead, chirping private messages back and forth, while cool blades of grass refreshed my callused bare feet. Once, when no one was lookin', I pressed my face into the lime-colored fronds, holding my breath ever so long, lest the *wonderful-gut* moment slip away all too soon.

" 'I will fear no evil: for thou art with me; thy rod and thy staff they comfort me.' " Caleb's youthful voice intruded on my carefree thoughts, reminding me that the Lord was with us, indeed. Almighty God had promised never to leave us nor forsake us. I'd learned from Mamma, through the years, to cling to that promise with all my might.

Truth be told, I *did* harbor fear inside me.

9

Had nothin' whatever to do with *fearing evil*, like the words of the psalm. Yet I was worried. With Mamma gone to heaven, I wondered whatever was to become of us. I was fretful, too, 'bout my chances of marryin' the sweetest, kindest — and most handsome — Plain boy in all of Lancaster County. *Jah*, my hopes and dreams were wholly bound up in Levi King. Best of all, he loved me, too. Said so a year ago, when first I started goin' to Sunday night Singings.

At almost seventeen, I'm no longer a child; 'specially not in a community where young people start pairin' off come sixteen. Many-a girl is hopin' to marry at my age and to be bearin' her first little one nine months after. Might be happening to me soon if Dat hadn't had the farming accident that took his life. And now Mamma's gone, too.

" 'Surely goodness and mercy shall follow me all the days of my life: and I will dwell in the house of the Lord for ever.' " Caleb finished reading the Scripture, yet as we all knelt for prayer, I wondered what *goodness* could ever come of us bein' orphans.

God's sovereign will was not to be questioned, I knew. Still, I felt for sure and for certain He must be lookin' down from on high, seein' our fresh and bleeding heart wounds. Surely the God of heaven and earth

10

was weeping right along with us.

Nearly every day now, I go and stand quietlike between two cemetery plots high on the hillside of Grasshopper Level. 'Tis freshly blanketed with snow, and acres of rich farmland spill down toward the valley, a panorama of beauty far as the eye can see. Truly, a promising sight. And if I'm very still, a sheen of sunlight seems to whisper through stark trees overhead. I gaze over the wintry ridge, and I glimpse what must be Glory lights, playing off dormant fields below.

In my mind's eye, I recollect last summer's long, humid days when first I suspected there was somethin' wrong with Mamma's heart. Dozens of birds flapped their wings, preening in the birdbath behind the house, while moss spread over the springhouse, turnin' it a musty green. Anna Mae, little Hannah, and I did our best to help Mamma with the inside chores. One way we helped was by hanging out the Monday mornin' wash all by ourselves.

Ancient frogs brooded in the well, yet creeks shriveled up nearly dry, and flaxen cornstalks stood high, burstin' with the sweetest ears of corn the Lord God ever made. The white tips of the neighbors'

11

wheat rippled in the breeze, reminding me of the bay waters off the shore of Watch Hill, Rhode Island, just a few blocks from Grandpa Cain's weather-beaten Cape Cod cottage. A place we loved to call home when Mamma, Dat, and I visited in the summer, years before we ever became Amish.

Leaning on Mamma's simple grave marker now, I let my eyes roam a bit farther, down past the Amish schoolhouse on Esbenshade Road, then east and beyond to Rohrer's Mill Road where a working mill, powered by an old-fashioned waterwheel, grinds grain for Amish friends and neighbors. Facing back toward the northwest, I looked hard in the direction of Strasburg Borough — population: 2,950. Quaint and warmhearted Strasburg, where it all began. Our Plain life, that is.

I can never stop thinkin' about the first day we came here from bustling Bridgeport, Connecticut, with only two suitcases in hand. *"In shedding nonessentials, one sheds vanity,"* Dat had said, though at the age of five, I scarcely understood any of it. Still, those words became my father's motto, and I sensed our lives were about to change.

Seeking a closer walk with God, my parents went in search of a covenant community — a people set apart. 'Course, not a single one of our city friends thought we'd ever last as Plain folk, 'specially since none of us back then had been born into the Amish culture. But, honestly, it took hardly any time at all learnin' the customs of our Anabaptist neighbors and church family.

Promptly, my parents joined church as soon as they could be baptized. The People welcomed us with friendly smiles and open arms. Noah and Susie Lapp took to us right off, as did their grown children and grandchildren — an enormous clan of about two hundred souls — almost enough to form a church district all their own. They, along with the preachers' and bishop's families, must've sensed our earnest spirit, that we could be trusted in the fellowship of the believers.

Often Dat would say, all smiles, as we sat 'round our supper table, *"I'm glad we came to Lancaster County when we did."*

Mamma's reply brought out her deep dimples. *"We sacrificed near everything."*

Here, Dat might glance 'round at the kitchen and the bounty of food. His words still rang in my ears. *"We've never been happier in all our born days, jah?"*

Mamma's sweet answer brought reassurance to my soul. *"God brought us here. I know it sure as I'm Ivy Cottrell."*

Never happier?

I let the question tumble over in my mind. If only Dat and Mamma hadn't died so awful young. 'Cause now five of us are left to look after our small farm, unless Aunt Sarah comes and takes us away, that is. Hopefully, we'll get to stay put, biding our time till Gabriel's trumpet blows. Staying put — that's what *I'm* hopin' for, yet who's to say if my wish counts for much.

"Nary a promise for the morrow," Dat used to say, his blue eyes shining with conviction. *"Live ev'ry day as if it's your last. . . ."*

So I must learn to trust God for our needs, each and every day. 'Course, our Plain friends are just as kind as can be. There's even been some talk of the brethren and their families dividing us up and takin' us in as foster children. That's what happened to the seven Glick brothers over in Northumberland County, here recently. 'Cept *they* were sent off to English — non-Amish — homes for a while, and how terrifying for them. Mamma never would've wanted us separated, not even amongst her closest Amish friends. She had her heart set on a much different plan.

Hannah, Josiah, Anna Mae, Caleb, and I are mindin' our business now, waitin' for our mamma's sister — a fancy *Englischer,* of all things — to come fetch us and cart us off

14

a continent away. Away from the close-knit community of the People. *Our* people. Ach, the Plain life's all we know or dare to remember.

What life will be like with Aunt Sarah, I care not to guess. She lives out in Oregon — at the opposite end from where we are now, in more ways than one. She was a schoolteacher for a few years in Stonington, Connecticut, but something soured her on teaching — don't know exactly what, really. Anyways, next thing we heard, Sarah Cain had headed out west right quick and become a real estate agent. Only the Good Lord knows why she gave up passing on knowledge to bright young minds in favor of making money hand over fist, hiding her teaching talent under a bushel.

All in all, it was Aunt Sarah who gave us the sharpest tongue over our goin' Plain. Poor, dear Mamma suffered so, saying her sad good-byes and a-frettin', trying to explain such a decision to her friends and to her only sister, too.

Guess I shouldn't be worried 'bout things, 'cept Sarah's voice sounded ever so hollow at the news of Mamma's heavenly homegoing. If I hadn't known better, I'd think she was sore vexed at Mamma for up and joinin' Dat over in Gloryland. 'Course, now thinking on it, being named guardian for a houseful of children might come as a big surprise to any single woman. Fancy or not.

I doubt Mamma ever told her sister 'bout the last will and testament she and her lawyer drew up several months ago. Guess she was smarter than to tell Aunt Sarah such a thing. Why *did* Mamma have to go and appoint her younger sister to be our second mother, anyways?

Ach, Sarah Cain or no, I fear we've got some awful big changes ahead. Sure as daybreak, we do.

Chapter One

Sarah perched on the edge of her king-sized canopy bed, thinking ahead to her day as she did each morning, before she ever skimmed her pedicured feet into lush slippers and plodded across the bedroom suite of her urban town home.

Still drowsy, she turned up the volume on her clock radio, preset to Portland's premier classical station. She reveled in the music of Schumann's Piano Concerto in A Minor, never tiring of the piece — especially the Intermezzo with its colorful, refined harmonic language. She allowed the fantasia-like work to sweep over her. As she did, she focused on a brass picture frame on the round bedside table. A doll-faced child with wide blue eyes and an eternal smile gazed back at her.

Sighing, she ran her fingers through her shoulder-length hair, staring hard at the youngster's angelic face. No matter the pain the picture evoked, she must keep the memory of this child alive. Because, at twenty-eight, Sarah fairly flew from one appointment to the next — morning, noon,

17

and night — never sitting still after this one brief retrospective moment each day.

Bright and unseasonably warm, the day was marred only by occasional clouds dotting the western horizon. The local meteorologist declared the noon hour "shirt-sleeve weather." Unusual for Oregon in winter.

Sarah was glad she'd worn a rather subdued, yet regal, gold blouse under her tailored brown vest, because by midafternoon she'd had to shed her suit jacket. Thumbing through a file marked "Hughes," she placed it neatly into her leather over-the-shoulder briefcase. Eager to be punctual for her next appointment — an important visit with a wealthy client — she waved a fleeting goodbye to Heidi Norton, the desk receptionist.

The doors of Alexander's Realty would remain open a few more hours, but she — the star real estate broker — would be absent. Last year's top-selling businesswoman was heading toward the area of Washington Park to meet with a new client, Willard Hughes. She held within her professional grasp the potential sale of luxury town homes on the city's prestigious west side, making the prospect of meeting Hughes all the sweeter. If she nailed the deal today, Sarah could literally beat out the realty owner for monthly sales. All competition aside, Bill Alexander would be more than elated. He would be amazed at the strength of her numbers. Late January, to boot.

The drive across town was a relatively short one, and the meager flow of traffic was in her favor. Catching her reflection in the rearview mirror, she scrutinized her naturally blond hair before turning the ignition key. She had purposely made the decision to book the upcoming appointment prior to rush hour.

Excellent planning.

The sun had moved across the sky, unyielding yet invigorating. As she drove, she relaxed in the driver's seat, enjoying the leather comfort. Having suffered through her youthful years of lower-middle-class living, she was still surprised to be able to afford such luxury.

Pure extravagance.

She gazed at the intricate dashboard and stroked the leather-covered steering wheel of her new BMW. Pricey, though she'd negotiated a good deal for herself as always.

Scanning the radio, she stopped at the easy-listening jazz station. The gentle lament of a saxophone soothed her, and she settled into a mellow and relaxed awareness. While she'd never thought it possible, her emotions had actually resumed a fairly even keel in the past year.

Just as she turned off Route 26 at Capitol Highway, her cell phone rang. "Sarah speaking," she answered.

"There's a long-distance call for you." She recognized the bright, melodious voice of Heidi, the receptionist. "Can you take it?"

She glanced at the digital clock on the dash. "I'm running late. Who's on the line?"

"A young woman . . . she says her name's Lydia Cottrell — your niece."

Sarah felt the crease of her brow. Hesitantly, she said, "Go ahead, put her through."

While she waited, Sarah recalled a recent letter from Ivy, Lydia's mother. Older than herself by six years, Ivy — and her out-landish husband — had chosen a completely foreign life-style, against the better judgment of their family and friends. Even Sarah, at the young age of seventeen, had been mystified when her sister joined the Amish. But that was a long time ago and "plenty of water under the bridge," as Ivy liked to say. Yet, to Sarah's constant frustration, Ivy seemed to seize every opportunity to justify the impulsive move, perhaps in hopes of making a convert of Sarah. Ivy's most recent letter, however, had a strangely different tone. Not so moralizing as tender, even compassionate.

"Hullo?" A fragile female voice came on the line. "Is this Aunt Sarah?"

Having not seen Ivy's daughter in twelve years, Sarah scarcely knew what to say. "Lydia, what can I do for you?"

"I'm awful sorry. Honestly, I don't know how to break this news to you." The girl paused, saying no more.

"What is it, dear?"

Nearly breathless, Lydia continued. "Mamma's gone . . . passed away this morning. Her heart gave out."

She winced. *Ivy, my sister — dead?*

Sarah's hand steadied the steering wheel as she grappled with the reality. At last, she managed to speak. "I . . . I'm terribly sorry." Struggling to gather her thoughts, Sarah said no more as the shocking news pierced her soul.

"Mamma's funeral will be at Noah and Susie Lapp's house, three days from now . . . Friday morning," Lydia went on. "The burial's to be on Glendorn Hill, next to our father's grave."

Her niece's words struck a dissonant chord. Sarah had no idea where Glendorn Hill was located, having not made the effort to attend her brother-in-law's funeral. And

21

now, as her thoughts were in a turmoil, she was uncertain as to whether she would attend Ivy's services, as well.

"Mamma's lawyer will be callin' you real soon," Lydia said gently, her voice quavering.

She wondered what the attorney wanted but would not question her niece about legal matters. It was obvious Ivy's daughter was suffering deep grief. "Is someone there able to help with the funeral arrangements?" she asked.

"Oh my, yes," Lydia replied. "No worry 'bout that."

They said hurried good-byes, but only after Sarah offered obligatory inquiries about the other children. Then, clicking off the cell phone, she drove several miles before steering the sedan toward a parking lot. She stopped the car and leaned her head against the neck rest, forcing the air past her lips.

"Mamma's gone . . . passed away this morning."

Lydia's dismal words persisted in Sarah's mind, echoing again and again. Yet she shouldn't have been too surprised, aware of the fact that heart disease ran in her family on both sides. With that knowledge came a new realization. As far as her immediate family was concerned, she was now alone in the world.

22

Lowering the visor, she shielded her eyes, pondering Lydia's indication that Ivy's lawyer would be calling. What could the Lancaster attorney — any legal counsel, for that matter — possibly wish to convey to her?

The remaining hours of the day passed as if in slow motion. Sarah managed to close the coveted deal with Hughes, but the details of the transaction seemed nearly surreal. In fact, every movement, every thought, every word was colored by the recent news.

Ivy was dead.

Much to Sarah's chagrin, Ivy's attorney phoned her at home that evening just as she was updating paper work for the future closing of today's sale. He introduced himself as Charles Eberley of Lancaster County. "I don't believe we've met, but your sister certainly spoke highly of you."

Ivy spoke highly of me? His comment surprised her.

"Perhaps we'll have an opportunity to get better acquainted at the funeral."

"Oh, well, I'm sorry to say . . . I don't know if I can see my way clear to make it." Her words seemed flat, even to her ears.

"It's imperative that you come to Pennsylvania, Ms. Cain, and as soon as possible. It's important for you to be on hand for the official reading of Ivy's last will and testament."

"When is the reading?" she asked.

"Next Thursday, two o'clock in the afternoon."

Sarah could not imagine making the long trip. Not for the mere sake of hearing that she was to be the recipient of one or more of Ivy's handmade Amish quilts or doilies. "Please, Mr. Eberley," she spoke up. "Anything belonging to Ivy should — *must* — be passed along to her children."

"Are you saying you won't be coming?"

"That is correct."

He was silent briefly. "It seems you've made up your mind."

"Anything my sister wished for me to have ought to go to her children," she insisted again, hoping to conclude the conversation. "My sister would not have wanted it any other way."

Eberley paused again. Then — "Listen, Ms. Cain, Ivy specifically requested that I not reveal the contents of the will unless you were physically present. Which is precisely why you must come to Lancaster." He continued. "Besides Ivy Cottrell's children, are you not her only living blood relation?"

"Yes."

"Then you *will* come, won't you?"

Sarah was surprised by his persistence, but she refused to commit to anything. She truly intended to put him off. For how long, she didn't know.

An absurd possibility crossed her mind. What if Ivy had named Sarah the legal guardian of her five children?

"I'll have to get back with you, Mr. Eberley," she said tersely. "Good-bye." She did not wait for his reply. She hung up, feeling the heat in her neck rise to her cheeks. What an unlikely and ridiculous notion — the acquiring of her sister's ready-made family. Sarah chuckled at her own rampant imagination. Surely that was not the reasoning behind Charles Eberley's urgency.

Regardless, she had no intention of returning his call.

Chapter Two

Friday morning, January 21

It's ever so unsettling to realize just how closely bound up we are in each other's lives. Mamma's passing has knocked the wind clean out of me. Every so often I catch myself startin' to cry, then there are moments when I feel stronger again. These feelings come in waves each and every day.

But there's one thing that will not change. I will not fail to keep my promise to Mamma. Her children, all of us, will stay together, or I'll die tryin' to make it so.

Susie, Mamma's dearest friend, gently chides that I ought never to make such negative comments. "What's confessed aloud affects a person more than we know," she says.

'Course I don't want to say wrongful things. But, then again, I believe God sees my heart. He knows I don't mean to make rash statements or say things displeasin' in His sight.

I 'spect I should be more careful, yet I'll move heaven and earth if need be to make sure all us Cottrells stay together.

Oh, Father in heaven, I will fear no evil. . . .

Traffic was somewhat congested as Sarah made her way toward downtown Portland. She skillfully weaved in and out of the lanes, pushing the speed limit slightly. The stoplight turned red prior to her final turnoff.

A token glance in the rearview mirror revealed not her own reflection but a misty vision of a snow-covered school playground. A thick gray fog shrouded the clapboard houses that lined the quiet street across from the school yard. Her memory stirred and she heard a distant chain on a flagpole clanking steadily. Intermingled with the faraway sights and sounds were the screams of a little child and other children running toward her. Flinching, Sarah attempted to reject the poignant memory, pushing it back into that dusky alcove of years. Thirty-eight long months had come and gone since that cruel day, yet sorrow and guilt continued their reign.

Behind her, a driver blared his horn. She jumped a bit, then noticed the traffic light.

Green.

Accelerating slowly, she moved forward, keeping pace with traffic.

She located a parking spot two blocks down from her favorite doughnut shop, then hurried inside for a cup of coffee. Spying a small table near the window, she snatched it up by placing her briefcase on the booth seat.

A waitress came quickly. "Cream or sugar?"

"Neither, thanks. I like my coffee black and hideous."

The petite waitress cocked her head. "Have it your way."

Sarah smiled to herself. She'd had it *her way* for quite some time now. Actually, much longer than that. The period of the placid years, the teaching years prior to coming to Oregon, had been some of the best of her life. After the tragic playground incident, though, everything changed. Life's pulse ceased to beat. Life's color turned ashen gray.

Abruptly, she'd terminated her teaching career to appease a small-town uprising, overzealous types who preferred stone-throwing to articulating reason. All this in her own close-knit hometown.

Sarah took a sip of her hot bitter coffee and opened her briefcase, reviewing the day's schedule. She would not allow random thoughts of the past to derail her. Not today.

The waitress circled the tables again. "Is

there anything else I can get for you?"

Sarah assumed the young woman was anxious to finish out her bill.

"Coffee's all I need," she said, noticing the hint of relief and scrutiny all mixed together on the woman's face.

She's glad I'll be on my way, she thought.

Sarah recognized the all-too-familiar look and recalled an earlier time and place. A moment of lasting pain. . . .

"I'm going to have a *dozen* babies," Ivy had coyly boasted at age eighteen, just six months before she was to be married to her high-school sweetheart.

"Better wait and see what your husband says about that," young Sarah retorted. "*If he shows up for the wedding!*"

Ivy ignored her comment and gave her an inquisitive, yet sarcastic look. "How many children do *you* want?"

At age twelve, Sarah had never considered such a thought. She *had* secretly wondered which boy in the seventh grade she might end up marrying someday. There was one very handsome redheaded fellow three desks from hers in science class. . . .

"Never mind," Ivy shot back, irritated. "There's no way to have a reasonable discussion with you. You're too into yourself,

Sarah. Besides, anyone can *see* you'll never be the 'mother hen' type."

Sarah shrugged off Ivy's snide remark. Who cared? Her sister couldn't see inside her. *Nobody* could!

Mother, it seemed, never made any attempt to put a stop to their seemingly innate bickering. How clashing the discordant blend between siblings. Any seeds of rapport that might have existed had long since been replaced with strife. Sarah and her sister had been rivals from her earliest recollection. She often thought it was because she'd spoiled Ivy's only-child status, a position Ivy held for six years before Sarah's arrival. But the sisters' conflict had more to do with a tussle of temperaments than their birth order. From her earliest recollections their personalities had never jived.

Always in the limelight during high school, Ivy had been voted "Miss Congeniality" her senior year and was commonly seen on the arm of one handsome boy or another. Sarah, on the other hand, had to force a jovial face in public, though everyone said she was "as pretty as a picture." She much preferred playing classical piano or shopping at the mall with her girlfriends rather than going out with boys. When it came to men — young or old — she was far more reticent than Ivy. Especially at that time in her life, boys and dating made Sarah nervous. Not until her college years did she branch out, feeling more comfortable with the opposite sex. And it was while she was teaching school that she joyously began to "find her voice," cautiously freed to emerge from her shell, away from the confines Ivy's shadow had cast on her rather cloistered world.

A few months into her first semester, the principal stopped her in the hallway. "I believe you've discovered your calling in life, Miss Cain." She was surprised but genuinely delighted at his observation.

Obviously convinced, he added. "Not many young people possess a genuine teacher's heart these days. It's truly refreshing to see it in you."

The comment put a renewed spring in Sarah's step. She felt, at least for the moment, that she might actually perform well as a classroom teacher. She would sincerely try. The principal's remarks had given her something that Ivy — *poison* Ivy — could never offer. Confidence in her future as an instructor of primary age children. And faith in herself.

Once a teacher, always a teacher, Ivy had written in a letter after she and her husband had gotten religion and uprooted themselves and their youngsters, replanting and starting over on Pennsylvania soil. *You're good with children, Sarah, when you want to be.*

When you want to be . . .

Ivy's tone reminded Sarah of her sister's ever present condescension. Being told to "pull yourself up by your bootstraps" meant you might fall forward and smash your head. And if you weren't careful, your heart, too.

She'd tried; oh, how she'd yanked those tethers on her illustrative boots after that icy, snow-slick day of morning playground duty, but to no avail. The great tragedy of her life and its aftermath of horror-filled days left her guilt ridden and exhausted. Along with it came increased agitation between herself and her sister.

The principal's ongoing admiration and support in the midst of acute trauma — even the prospect of tenure — could not convince Sarah to remain. At the end of the school year she resigned, cutting short her teaching career after four fleeting years. Her own recurrent yet irrational fears ultimately dispelled her measure of hope. She left Connecticut, moving as far from her home as possible.

The family tie between the wayward sister

and the "redeemed" sister began to unravel further. By the time Sarah fled the East Coast, she had written off her and Ivy's relationship as irreconcilable.

Yet over time, she had become highly efficient, sometimes forceful — even bluntly outspoken — but extremely successful in her newfound career. In the process she had cut Ivy, *everyone,* out of her life, not allowing herself to care for or about anyone. Disconnecting from family, she clung only to herself. The path of least resistance.

Gathering up her briefcase, Sarah paid for her coffee with a five-dollar bill. The waitress could keep the tip in spite of her visible eagerness for Sarah's departure.

Just then she caught sight of the waitress, who just happened to be glancing over her thin shoulder. "I'm going, I'm going," Sarah muttered.

Later in the week, Sarah agreed to set up an appointment with a young couple referred to her by a well-to-do client. More than likely the twosome were unmarried, though they didn't divulge the fact during the hour Sarah spent with them. She discreetly eyed both their ring fingers. Bare. Yet they seemed in a big hurry to purchase a

33

town house together.

"A condo would be cool," the young man said.

Sarah went out of her way, professionally at least, to walk them through her usual systematic approach to finances and housing needs. In this case, though, a place to call home was more than likely a *desire*. Not a necessity. Her guess? These two merely wanted to play house, break free of over demanding, restrictive parents. Such was the lot of many of society's young people these days.

Doesn't anybody get married anymore? She shrugged off her temporary disgust, happy to move ahead with her afternoon.

Now she was on her way to meet with an upper-middle-class client and his wife. They were interested in "moving up" to a more expensive house. "A preexisting home would be perfect — no older than five years," the new client had indicated over the phone, explaining that they were in need of four "good-sized bedrooms," three baths, a separate, *elegant* dining room, etc., etc.

A house like that would push them into a higher sales bracket and earn Sarah more money for the same amount of Realtor work. She could easily imagine the chic new outfits, complete with accessories, she would purchase for herself with part of her sales commission. Maybe it was time for an up-graded computer, as well. And why not throw in the latest color printer while she was at it? A vacation cottage somewhere would be nice, too. So much money — too little time to spend it.

The sky was overcast as she drove to the Summit Point sales office just south of Port-land proper. Her spirits began to droop the closer she got to the designated meeting place, though not a soul would have known by the looks of her. She had taken extra care to apply her best makeup that morning, choosing a particularly well-tailored suit — turquoise virgin wool — with a cream-colored blouse. She slid her fingers across the pearl choker at her throat, enjoying the feel, smooth and sumptuous. Her earrings matched her neck jewelry, and she played with first the right, then the left, as she waited for her clients inside the temporary building.

Staring at the sky, she thought of Ivy and the possibility of her last wishes. It was be-yond ludicrous to second-guess her de-ceased sister. Besides that, Sarah had no solid evidence that such a last will and testa-ment even existed. Ivy had never been the type of woman to plan too far ahead, except, of course, for a year's worth of fresh canned goods, dried meats, and fruit preserves she often wrote about "putting up." No, Ivy Cottrell, Amishwoman by choice, placed far too much stock in God's providence to do any such estate planning. But nagging thoughts continued, and Sarah tried to no avail to force them away.

She spotted the well-dressed couple as they walked arm in arm up the steps to the sales office. Over the next two hours, she showed them four different house options. All the while her thoughts were entangled with unanswerable questions. Questions that related to her sister's children and the possibility that Ivy had made her a beneficiary of something — or someone.

By nightfall, she had worked herself into a subconscious frenzy. To help absorb some of the shock of the past day's news and to avoid the madness of insomnia, she turned to her finances and checked off her credit card expenditures, reconciling last month's statement with her checkbook. As usual, the management of her income gave her great comfort.

Chapter Three

Lydia stared at the wooden lamp on the table across the room, her eyes drawn to the light. More than a few of her Amish girlfriends — back when she attended the one-room schoolhouse — had been Old Order. Each night their fathers brought in the gas lamps from outdoors. Younger brothers and sisters gathered like bees to a honeycomb, sittin' under the golden circle to read or sew or color, as grown-ups talked over the day's events near the ring of light.

She had spent many-a night at one particular girlfriend's house, down the road a piece. Fannie Flaud, one of Noah and Susie Lapp's numberless grandchildren, was her best friend in all the world.

Fannie had gone with Lydia to their first Singing ever, back nearly a year ago. Both sixteen at the time, they sat side by side on the same bale of hay, watchin' the boys come strutting into the barn. Levi King and all the other boys wore their *for-gut* black trousers and long-sleeved white shirts and tan suspenders. 'Course, Lydia and Fannie acted disinterested, like they weren't *really* payin' the fellas any mind. That's how it was at Singings and whatnot. Girls weren't s'posed to let on they liked any one boy.

"Levi's sweet on ya." Fannie had been the first to say it. She'd whispered it to Lydia just minutes after the fast songs had started.

"No . . ."

"Ach, you just wait and see."

Her heart was beating too fast. "Do you think so, really?"

"I *know* so, Lyddie."

Turned out, Fannie was right. Quick as a wink Levi had asked Lydia to ride home with him in his new courting buggy.

All these months later, and now she was really and truly Levi's *Aldi* — girlfriend. Whether or not she would end up Levi's wife was another thing yet.

Sarah was thumbing through a home decorator magazine when the phone rang. Because it was late in the evening, she let her answering machine screen the call.

Bryan Ford's familiar voice came on the line, and quickly she picked up. "Hey, stranger."

"Great to hear your voice, Sarah." He paused. "Any chance I can entice you to have supper with me tomorrow night?"

The ever spontaneous Bryan.

"Maybe, if you'd called me two weeks ago. I'm back-to-back with appointments." *And my sister just died,* she thought.

"Must you always be so busy?"

She ignored the question. "So . . . what're you doing in town?"

"Research."

She didn't press for more. Fact was, Bryan seemed to enjoy popping up at the most unexpected times, despite his busy life as a computer systems analyst based in Boston.

"I'm here for two days, then you won't hear from me again."

"That a promise?"

He chuckled. "I'm attracted to spunk, which, I suppose, is why I'm here." His voice had softened to a more serious tone, but there was a definite hint of jest.

"You're impossible."

"Look who's talking."

Their bantering took her back to college days. Dark-haired, witty, and terribly good-looking, Bryan Ford had declared her to be his one and only soul mate, the woman destined to complete him. At the time, she'd scoffed. *"You're a dreamer,"* she'd told him, meaning it.

But he was more than earnest about starting a romance. And they'd had a whirl-wind of camaraderie and affection. Nearly two years' worth. *"Never forget who loves you best,"* he always said, walking her up the dorm steps.

Without question, she had believed him. Yet they'd parted ways after graduation.

Her decision. Due, in part, to Bryan's dogged tenacity — his obsession with having been an only child and wanting a wife who also longed for many children. Overwhelming to Sarah at the time. Now, as well.

"I could meet you somewhere Sunday morning — fifteen minutes over coffee," Bryan suggested. "How about it?" He hadn't given up on her over the years. Apparently, he wasn't backing down now, either.

"Sunday morning — *any* morning is next to impossible. Ditto for tomorrow supper." She knew how heartless it would be to encourage him, though she did enjoy his company more than she cared to admit. Spending time with Bryan often made her feel as if she were missing something quintessential in life. Yet their mutual esteem had suffered from the marked disagreement, the one enormous wedge between them, separating two friends, keeping them a continent-length apart — she, in Oregon; Bryan, in Massachusetts.

"I'm told you do eat breakfast sometimes," he taunted.

"Rather infrequently."

"Then will you have an infrequent Sunday breakfast with me?" He was being terribly polite, not at all pushy as he had been years before — the singular, too-enterprising push that had ended their romance. Today he was merely asking permission to have breakfast with her. It *had* been months since his work had brought him this far west.

The urgency in his voice piqued her curiosity. She sighed, careful not to exhale into the phone. "Oh, Bryan. I just don't know. . . ."

"It's *only* breakfast."

Most likely, he had come all this way to see *her,* though she was fairly certain there was also a client waiting somewhere in the wings.

Legitimately, she couldn't refuse. "All right, but we'll have to make it short."

"And sweet?"

"Whatever." She laughed.

"Hey, don't overdo it with the enthusiasm."

She wondered, *Is he impervious to pain?* Why did Bryan keep coming back? Not that she disregarded him; on the contrary, Bryan Ford was as likable as any of the men she'd dated. But he was more than good-natured

41

and fun-loving. He happened to be devoted to her, for a reason that she herself had yet to discern.

"Seven-thirty too early?" she asked.

"Name the place."

She did. He promised to be prompt.

"See you soon," she said and hung up.

Returning to her magazine, she pushed thoughts of Bryan out of her mind. No time to analyze whatever relationship they did or didn't have. She struggled to read, but after a few minutes of distracted effort, the decorator magazine soon lost its appeal. Sarah placed it under the glass-topped coffee table and headed for bed, ignoring nagging thoughts of Ivy . . . and Charles Eberley.

Sarah still hadn't decided what — if anything — to do about the attorney's pointed request. One thing for sure, she did *not* want to wedge valuable time out of her schedule merely to travel to Pennsylvania to hear the inconsequential details of Ivy's last will and testament.

Too much work to be done here. Too much living to do.

Sarah thought of her deceased sister's children. What would happen to them?

"They're not my problem," Sarah whispered to herself. She brushed her teeth, flossed, and headed off to bed.

Friday night, January 21

I feel compelled more than ever to write down my thoughts several times a day. 'Least for a while I will. Maybe just till things settle some inside me.

Fannie says it's a good idea to get my feelings on paper. "Helps clear your mind," she told me today when she and her mamma stopped over for hot cocoa and sticky buns midmorning. The Good Lord surely must've sent these dear friends to me while my brothers and sisters were at school. I felt ever so lonely till I saw them coming.

Every now and then, without warning, I see Mamma's face clearly before me. Never will I forget how beautiful she was, inside and out. Heart-shaped face, cinnamon brown eyes, soft strawberry blond hair nestled in a thick bun under her prayer cap. And her smile, ach, *it nearly takes my breath away just remembering.*

How I miss her! Sometimes, when the house is dark and my brothers and sisters are fast asleep, I'm tempted to have a look-see inside the family chest in Mamma's room. The deep drawers tempt me so, to do more than just look, really. I 'spect there must be letters, lots of 'em, hidden away inside the wide bottom drawer. Some from old friends

43

in Connecticut, I'm perty sure. From Grandma Cain, too. Others from Aunt Sarah herself. And somewhere safe, Mamma's own journals are tucked away.

Truthfully, I'm afraid I might yield to the Tempter and read such personal writings come one of these days. Almighty God knows it takes more than simple willpower to steer clear of my mother's empty room altogether — takes downright grit. Still, it irks me to think of our worldly aunt comin' and rummaging through Mamma's private things, simple as they are. Just doesn't seem basslich *— fitting — somehow.*

So what'll become of us? I lie awake worryin', this same tormenting question swirling 'round in my head. Standing at my window, I pray often, staring down at the sleepy fields around Grasshopper Level, all white and silvery in the moonlight. God will hafta do something and right quick, I'm thinking. 'Cause, no telling, Aunt Sarah won't wanna stay here in Amish country. If she does, she'll be more than befuddled by our ways: horse and buggies and three-hour Preachin' services. Thank goodness we're the sort of Plain folk who are allowed electricity and telephones — even running water. Otherwise, there's no telling what Aunt Sarah would think. Backwoods urchins, *she'll prob'ly call us, when what we really are is God-fearing Amish.*

After everything our parents went through to join the Amish and live the simple life before God and the People, I truly hate to think of leaving Lancaster County. It's a mighty good thing my brothers and sisters don't remember modern ways. They'd be scared something awful, I fear.

Chapter Four

Saturday's farm chores were the same as any other day — sweeping out the barn, feeding chickens, and milking three cows to supply milk for themselves and a good many payin' English customers.

"Fresh raw milk is a wonderful-gut source of income and makes for healthy English bones as well as Amish," Mamma often said if any of the younger children fussed over having to crawl out of bed in the dark.

Along with everything else, there was forever a growin' basket of mending, hand stitching, and other sewing to be done, 'specially with youngsters like Hannah and Josiah in the house. Anna Mae wasn't nearly so rambunctious, though, and for that, Lydia was grateful.

Plenty of cookin' and bakin' needed to be done, too. Caleb was a lanky boy, nearly as tall as Dat was before he died, though sometimes it was hard to remember just how tall without any pictures to jiggle her memory. Lydia often wondered how it would be to own just a picture or two of her deceased parents. Even black-and-white snapshots would be awful nice. But she never questioned the unwritten rules of the *Ordnung,* nor Bishop Joseph and church members who passed down the centuries-old blueprint for the People. This was the life Dat and Mamma had chosen for themselves and their children.

Forgetting those things which are behind . . . I press toward the mark for the prize of the high calling of God in Christ Jesus, she recited mentally as she stirred the batter for blueberry pancakes.

Tomorrow, the Lord's Day, would be another story yet. There'd be no extra chores, just what *had* to be done in the barn — milkin' and whatnot. She would be cookin' food ahead for her siblings today. A right-gut baking ham was just the thing. She'd slice and serve it with other cold cuts tomorrow, along with strawberry-banana Jell-O, cup cheese, and homemade bread. Josiah had been beggin' for Apple Dapple cake here lately, so she'd prob'ly go ahead and bake some for the whole family.

She'd never been tempted to cook or bake on Sundays. It never crossed her mind to do such a thing. Mamma was always so careful to follow the ways of the People when it came to food preparation. Lydia sometimes fretted that if Sarah Cain *did* come to stay, they'd be forced into doin' things the fancy way, the English way. She shuddered to think they'd have no choice but to go back on their parents' solemn vow to the church and to God.

'Course, if she had her way all 'round, she and her brothers and sisters would just continue doin' the things they were doing each and every day. Really, there was no need for Sarah Cain to come. Not at all. And by the looks of it, with no hide nor hair of Aunt Sarah yet, she must be feelin' the selfsame way.

Wiping her hands on her apron, Lydia moved to the utensil drawer. "Come now, Anna Mae . . . Hannah. Time to set the table," she called.

Hearing the pitter-patter of scurrying feet — helpin' hands on the way — she thought how appreciative she was to the Lapps and Fannie's mother, Emma Flaud, too, for havin' kept a close watch on her and her brothers and sisters all week.

Still, she couldn't help but wonder how long before the Children and Youth Agency might come a-calling, knockin' on their door, inquiring of them, possibly escorting them out to a waiting police car and whisking them away to strangers. The what-if visions in her mind made her shiver sometimes.

If Aunt Sarah did come and they could talk her into settlin' down here — look after them the way Mamma wanted — at least they'd be spared bein' split up. And Lydia's promise would become a reality. It was the one and only reason why she ever pleaded with the Lord God heavenly Father. "Please, Lord, change Aunt Sarah's heart, if it needs changin', that is. And . . . if it's not too much to ask — and in your divine will — won't you send her to us real soon?" She'd prayed this every single night now, for over a week.

Quickly, Lydia dipped out one-fourth cup of batter from the large mixing bowl and onto the black-iron griddle. She watched as the sizzle ceased to sing on the griddle, the tiny air bubbles beginning to appear.

Lord Jesus, take my hand and lead me through this day, she prayed silently, squeezin' fresh oranges for their juice. *I trust you always, puttin' a smile on my face for those 'round me to see your grace at work in me. I'll keep on lovin', workin', and prayin'. For as long as I live. Amen.*

The fragments on the horizon had amassed, steadily growing into a partial cloud cover. The sun would be sinking into the great sea to the west a few hours from now.

Bryan had often referred to the Pacific Ocean that way, especially after Sarah first moved to Portland. *"The great sea beckons,"* he liked to say with a glint in his dark eyes. His way of enticing her away from the office for a few hours . . . he was well aware of her weaknesses. Walking barefooted along the shore, the tide tickling her toes, was definitely one of them. *"Come with me, Sarah, let's go beach combing."*

Sometimes, especially if the day was a sky-blue Saturday like today, she would give in and allow him to take her to the ocean. Their impulsive getaways rarely occurred more than once or twice a summer. They weren't actually dating, but Bryan called whenever he was "in the area," which, in the past eighteen months or so, had been rather sporadic. She had even wondered if he was losing interest in her. Maybe he had found another love interest, someone to return his affection, the way she had at first, before the subject of their fierce disagreement emerged toward the end of their senior year in college. The great debate had been to blame for their demise. Ultimately, Sarah blamed Bryan.

"We can work things out," he had declared repeatedly. "I know we can."

She was unyielding. "I don't think so."

"We should try, at least." His eyes searched hers, desperate for answers.

Bryan's stubborn stance — his reasoning askew — coupled with Ivy's ceaseless sermonizing letters collided in a colossal reaction in Sarah's mind. "It's a pointless discussion."

"Please, Sarah, help me understand why you feel this way."

She had never brought herself to reveal the truth to him — the reality of her debilitating fears coupled with her inability to get past his unreasonable insistence on wanting so many children. She felt he was hung up on the idea, and his position continued to annoy her.

Yet he attempted to woo her, repeating her name sweetly, obviously enamored with her.

To no avail.

Sarah . . .

Over the years, she had taken issue with her mother for assigning her a name with obvious religious overtones. Sarah with an "h" had automatically linked her in primary school, if only subconsciously, with the Hebrew spelling. That old-fashioned spelling used by so many conservative types these days.

Sarah coupled with Cain was pure misery. She could hardly forgive her parents for this unseeming and unnecessary blight on her persona. There had been ample opportunity, back before her parents' deaths, to change things. Often she had considered altering her names, at least the spellings, though she'd never followed through with the legal contacts. Changing her last name to *Kane*, she'd decided months ago, would be far better suited for an auspicious real estate agent.

She wouldn't have admitted to being preoccupied with name changes, though the association with two rather unserving ones tended to push yet an additional thorn into her psyche.

Stopped in rush-hour traffic, Sarah became restless and reached for the glove compartment. Opening it, she located a card from Bryan, sent months ago. She dared not reread the amusing verse and the familiar signature.

Sarah, please help me understand. . . .

The past was too far behind her now. Had she accepted his marriage proposal instead of sashaying out of his life, her last name could have changed rather effortlessly.

She laughed softly. Their romance was neither here nor there, yet Bryan continued to hang on. Why?

Just as the traffic jam loosened up a bit, her cell phone rang. Shaking her head, she was exasperated to see that it was the real estate office calling. She reached for the cellular phone. "Sarah speaking."

"Sorry to bother you, but a long-distance call just came in . . . for you," Heidi informed her.

She felt her throat muscles tense. "Long distance?"

"Charles Eberley from Pennsylvania. Can you take the call?"

Sarah was frustrated, staring at the clock on her dashboard. It had been days since she'd first heard from Mr. Charles Eberley. She'd hoped he wouldn't call back.

"Can you handle this for me?"

"Get rid of him, you mean?"

It wouldn't be wise to stonewall any longer. She couldn't put *this* man off forever.

"He asked specifically for you," Heidi urged.

Most assuredly, the call was urgent. Sarah felt as if she had been plunged into a vast tide of formidable responsibility, against her will. She needed more time to ponder, to plan. Her personal and professional future was in peril.

"What should I tell him?" Heidi's voice

penetrated Sarah's thoughts.

"Give me a second." Inhaling, she held her breath long enough to mentally replay the initial call from the Lancaster County law firm of Chatwyn, Dunlap & Associates.

Signaling, she made a right-hand turn onto the exit ramp and headed for a coffee shop. She sensed that a larger circle of time and space was about to encompass her life, demanding immediate attention. Torn between career and conscience, she waited for the receptionist to put "Amish country" on the line.

Staring through the windshield, she focused on a complex of office buildings in the distance. She'd dreamed of — *coveted* — managing her own real estate office someday. For the first time in her life she felt prosperous in her own right, entirely fortuitous.

Certainly, the news of Ivy's death had been unsettling. With both her parents deceased, and now her only sibling, Sarah assumed she might start to feel alone in the world. But she hadn't actually mourned. Not yet. To think of sitting down and shedding tears over someone who had merely shared the same genetics seemed a travesty. Not that she was heartless. Simply put, she and Ivy had never clicked. Not as sisters.

Certainly not as friends.

Charles Eberley's voice came on the line. "Hello, Ms. Cain. I'd hoped to hear from you by now."

"Yes . . . things got hectic here."

Without skipping a beat, he continued. "Ivy — your sister — had specifically requested that you be present at the formal reading of her will —"

"I realize that, but —"

Charles Eberley continued. "I have no choice but to relay her wishes over the phone."

Sarah listened silently.

"Your sister appointed a sole legal guardian for her children prior to her death. You, Ms. Cain, are her first and only choice, as stated in Ivy's last will and testament."

Sarah's worst fear.

By dying prematurely, Ivy was putting Sarah in a bind. Unquestionably, a noose of sorts. What reasoning was behind such a preposterous choice?

"You'll have to excuse me, but this makes no sense," she replied.

"Well, it's quite simple. Mrs. Cottrell wished for you, her only sister, to care for her children. Makes perfect sense, Ms. Cain."

"I don't think you understand . . ." She stopped short of revealing their rocky childhood and all the adult years of disputatious conversations, not to mention Ivy's persistent God-filled letters, which were most offensive of all.

"You're quite right. I *don't* understand the relationship you had with your sister, but I do respect your unwillingness to accept guardianship. You are under no obligation to do so. You must know, however, that if you choose not to take custody, the state of Pennsylvania will step in and make decisions on behalf of your nieces and nephews."

You are under no obligation. . . .

Sarah thought of Ivy's Amish friends and neighbors, the various women her sister often mentioned in her letters. Ivy had never minced words when it came to her community of "sisters" or the camaraderie they shared. *We're one in the unity of the spirit,* she would write. If that were the case, then perhaps some of those "spirit sisters" could pitch in and care for Ivy's offspring.

"What about an Amish family?" she asked. "Why isn't that a workable solution?"

He sighed audibly. "There are few Amish foster homes available, and even fewer who are able to take on *five* children. Social Services will step in, separate the children, and place them in state-authorized foster care — more specifically, non-Amish homes."

What's wrong with that? she thought.

"Ivy was adamant about *not* wanting her children separated or raised by strangers," he added.

Sarah shrugged, thinking how *she* might've welcomed such an idea as a girl, even benefitted by such an intrusion by outsiders when her own mother passed away. Living separate from Ivy as youngsters? Why, the thought was positively appealing.

"Ivy named *you* the legal guardian. She wanted you to live with Lydia and Caleb, Anna Mae, Josiah, and Hannah in Lancaster County, preferably."

"And this is stated precisely in Ivy's will?"

"I drafted the will myself" was the less-than-cordial reply.

Considering everything, she felt overwhelming hostility toward Ivy, who — even from the grave — was still trying in her overzealous way to connect. The audacity, Ivy insisting that Sarah summon whatever maternal instincts she possessed to take charge of five nieces and nephews!

Such a decision would thoroughly complicate Sarah's lavish life-style.

Yet she was torn emotionally over her dilemma. *Are the children being cared for properly?* she wondered. *Are they frightened at the loss of their mother?*

Quickly, she dismissed such thoughts. None of this was her responsibility.

She simply wouldn't accept guardianship for Ivy's children. Her sister would not have the last word — again!

She recalled a letter Ivy had written to her weeks prior to Thanksgiving. *If I should fail to recover from this affliction, if the Lord God should choose to call me home, I'll need someone to care for my dear children. . . .*

Sarah had ignored the comment, disinterested in volunteering her services in the event of her sister's death. Instead, she encouraged Ivy to take care of herself. *Why don't you see a good cardiologist? Please don't put it off any longer,* she'd written in a letter, knowing, most likely, that bullheaded Ivy would not heed her advice. No, Mrs. Cottrell was deep into herbal home remedies — the original Earth Mother. That Sarah's sister had breathed her last, trusting the "Great Physician," as Ivy liked to refer to God, yet failing to follow a doctor's strict recommendations, was another thorn in Sarah's side.

The fact remained, Sarah had ceased corresponding with her sister after that final letter, and because of this and for other reasons, she was puzzled why Ivy hadn't considered one of her Plain friends as a guardian. Someone like the amiable Susie Lapp or

Emma Flaud or any number of other women whose names frequented Ivy's letters. Someone *similar* to Ivy herself, perhaps, who had birthed a number of children, who was comfortable around little ones.

Someone . . . *anyone* else.

The attorney's voice pierced the cloud of her musing. "I need to know if you plan to come, Ms. Cain."

Cradling the cell phone in her hand, she felt cornered. Literally. It never entered her mind that she had an indisputable choice. And there was no need to contemplate her Day-Timer. Her schedule was solidly booked weeks ahead. "I'll phone my niece Lydia tonight . . . check in with her," she said. The truth was, she scarcely knew *of* her sister's children, let alone felt comfortable dialing the phone and chatting *with* one of them.

"These matters simply cannot wait another week."

These matters . . .

She shivered despite the sun's fading rays, grateful that Mr. Eberley had not inquired as to why she hadn't attended Ivy's funeral. No need for him to probe the issue. He'd probably sized her up accurately — self-assured, wealthy younger sister, caught up in her own world. No doubt, this was his impression of her.

Gripping the steering wheel, she wished the nightmare away, selfishly wanting her sister well again. She'd wanted Ivy out of her life, of course. But not *this* way — with Ivy dead and the awesome intrusion facing Sarah head on.

The well-spoken attorney had not a clue as to the nature of her disheartening relationship with her sister. How *could* he? It was impracticable to undertake an explanation of why she had not immediately flown to Grasshopper Level — or wherever the location of her sister's children — and gathered them up in her figurative arms. No words could rationalize her behavior.

"I'll make travel arrangements tonight," she heard herself say as if in a dense fog. Impenetrable.

"*When* may I expect you?"

He was pinning her down. There was no escape.

"Tomorrow, early evening, if at all possible." Sarah's world orbited crazily, tipping off its axis. Sighing, she backed out of the parking spot and sped back to the real estate office.

Chapter Five

Saturday evening, and still no sign of Aunt Sarah. And nobody but nobody in the Amish community wanted local authorities aware of the Cottrell children's "in limbo" status, waiting for validated adult supervision, so to speak. Not after the dreadful thing that had happened with the Glick family in Northumberland County a while back.

"Outrageous." That's what Lancaster Amish folk were still saying of the whole mess. In silent, stoic terror, seven young Amish brothers had been removed from their home and placed in English homes, of all things. Two of the younger children — five-year-old twins — didn't even speak a word of English yet. So for sure and for certain, that was prob'ly one of the reasons the Lapps and Flauds had come so often to look in on them.

Lydia stopped her speculatin' and went to the kitchen sink to wash her hands. "Who wants pumpkin pie and ice cream?" she called.

From all over the house, her brothers and

sisters came running. "*Geb's mir* — give me some!" Josiah called, slipping on the checkered linoleum and nearly losing his balance.

"Careful, now, and say 'please,' " she scolded gently.

"*Sei so gut* — please." Her youngest brother grinned from ear to ear.

Lydia gave him a spontaneous hug. "You're somethin', now, aren't you?"

"Jah, he *is*," little Hannah said, wagging her pointer finger. "Guess what I seen Josiah doin'."

"What you *saw* him do," Lydia corrected her wee sister, seeing the smudges of chocolate in the corners of Josiah's smile. "And I do believe I'm a-spyin' right this minute what Hannah's talkin' about."

Turning back to the sink, she ran the cold water, then proceeded to wash Josiah's face clean with the flap of her apron. "There, now, much *besser*."

With his white shirttail hanging out of his trousers, Josiah stood there lookin' at her. "Can I have two dips of ice cream?"

"Don'tcha mean *may* I?"

Hannah smiled, showin' the gaps where her front baby teeth had been. "Lyddie would make a gut schoolteacher someday, jah?" she lisped.

Lydia hadn't thought of it, not recently,

anyways. What with the months of Mamma bein' so awful sick and doublin' up on chores and whatnot all.

Josiah asked more politely this time. "*May* I have three dips of ice cream with my pie, please?"

She had to laugh. "Looks like the amount of sweets goes up with the askin', ain't so?"

Caleb unfolded his long lanky legs beneath the kitchen table, nodding his head in agreement. "Josiah gets his sweet tooth from Dat," he said, waiting his turn for a hefty slice of pumpkin pie.

Lydia was mighty glad she'd made three pies this morning, after everybody left for school. Scooping up homemade ice cream, she turned her thoughts to Mr. Eberley's phone call. She wasn't sure if she liked the idea of him callin' when she was home by herself. A man's voice over the phone sometimes made her downright jittery. Sure, he was Mennonite and all — awful nice of Mamma to pick someone sympathetic to their ways. Still, her toes curled in her black high-top shoes, hearing Mamma's lawyer say, "Your aunt lives a long ways from here, you know." This, his explanation for Aunt Sarah staying away this long.

But Lydia was no fool. She knew Mamma's sister lived far away. She just didn't understand the holdup. Why on earth had Mamma picked such a woman for their caretaker anyways? 'Specially if this fancy lady wasn't gonna budge an inch and get a move on?

I will fear no evil: for thou art with me. . . .

Lydia stopped her stewin' and took two long, deep breaths. *"Fillin' the lungs with air is wonderful-gut for the soul, too, don'tcha forget,"* Mamma would say if a body was out of sorts. Lydia often had to do such as that, tryin' her best to keep herself calmed down over one thing or another.

"Tell us a story, won'tcha?" Josiah asked from the table, his eyes blinking to beat the band.

"First, I want you to take two deep breaths," she told her youngest brother. "Try 'n relax now, jah? Your eyelids are nearly blinkin' off."

Caleb grinned silently, keeping his peace.

She looked down both sides of the table. Caleb, at the head of the table where Dat used to sit, kept an eye on spunky Josiah to his left. The girls — tiny Hannah and red-headed Anna Mae — sat together to Lydia's left.

What with the pie-eatin', the kitchen quieted down right nice, 'least for the time it took to gobble down dessert.

"I'll tell y'all a story when sticky fingers are

clean," she said, repeating Mamma's constant bidding.

Hannah and Josiah licked their gooey hands. And without being asked, Caleb reprimanded Josiah and Hannah. "Licking your fingers clean is *not* what Lyddie had in mind, I daresay."

Josiah, his blunt-cut hair all rumpled up and blue eyes downright sincere, volunteered an apology. "Sorry, Lyddie," he said.

"*Es dutt mir leed* — I am sorry," Hannah squeaked, brown braids wrapped 'round her head.

Anna Mae had remained silent all during dessert. Supper, too, for that matter. Lydia had hesitated to speak too pointedly to her sister since Mamma's passing. The girl could turn on the shyness at will, it seemed. 'Specially so in the past seven days.

"Emma Flaud is makin' some suey stew and bringing it over for supper tomorrow night," Lydia said.

"Ach, now, I like the sound of that," Caleb replied.

"Jah, I 'spect you do."

Anna Mae didn't so much as raise her eyes.

"I'm thinkin' Fannie's the nicest friend you've got, Lyddie," Josiah said, nodding his head. "Her sisters and brothers are awful nice, too."

Lydia agreed. "The whole Flaud and Lapp family are nice."

"Doesn't make 'em kin," said Anna Mae, speaking up for the first time.

"No, but that doesn't seem to matter to God, now, does it?" She hoped that might squelch her sister's negative attitude for once. "*Does* it?" she said again.

Anna Mae lowered her head, looking mighty repentant.

Lydia's heart went out to her. "It's all right, Anna Mae. Honest, 'tis."

But Anna Mae kept her peace, sayin' nary another word.

Josiah plopped himself down on the rag rug made by Lydia, Mamma, and Anna Mae last winter. Soon the towheaded youngster was surrounded by smiling Hannah and sour-faced Anna Mae. A slight distance behind them, Caleb sat cross-legged, waiting with expectation.

"Time for a Tellin'," Lydia said, recalling a humorous but supposedly true tale she'd heard years ago at a quiltin' bee. Back when the Cottrells had first come here to "God's country," as Dat always liked to call Lancaster County.

"What's it gonna be tonight?" Hannah asked, but she was quickly shushed by Anna Mae, whose expression wasn't all so un-happy-lookin' as it was rankled.

"Anna Mae?" Lydia said softly. "You all right?"

Shaking her head slowly, Anna Mae folded her arms across her round chest. "Nothin's wrong." But she was pouting, makin' her answer less convincing.

Lydia put on a smile for her sister. "Aw, somethin's ailing you." She could see the problem a-frettin' on Anna Mae's freckled face. Yet she wouldn't push too hard with *this* sister. She would show more kindness than insistence.

Just then Josiah stood up and cupped his hands over his mouth, like he wanted to share a secret. "Bend down to me, Lyddie," he said, eyes still a-blinkin'.

"S'not nice to whisper in front of others," she chided.

But Josiah's eyes pleaded, and she gave in to the request. Before she could lean over and hear what Josiah wanted, Hannah blurted, "Anna Mae threw up before supper."

With that revelation, Anna Mae's face turned ashen. "I ain't sick," she declared. "I don't need no cod-liver oil, honest I don't!"

Lydia motioned for Josiah to sit back down. "I s'pose we've all felt sick this week, in one way or other."

Hannah and Josiah were nodding their

heads. Caleb had his eyes fixed on her, in one accord with what she was sayin'. Anna Mae was the only one peerin' down into her lap.

"It's all right to feel sad," Lydia continued. "Our bodies hafta give way to our feelings . . . lotsa times they do." She remembered feeling sick to her stomach after hearing 'bout Dat's farm accident. The details were awful bad, but it was thinkin' how he must've suffered — him lying on the ground, his blood oozing into the soil — that made her feel even worse.

"Lyddie's right," Caleb spoke up. "It's gonna take a long time for any of us to feel all right after losin' Mamma."

She was shocked to hear her brother go on. A young man of few words, Caleb's approach to things was similar to the way Anna Mae thought and acted. It was a good thing, too, for Anna Mae's sake, 'cause Lydia sure didn't have much in common with her sullen younger sister. Caleb's occasional coolness she could easily tolerate because he also had a hearty laugh and a jovial spirit. Anna Mae was something else altogether.

Lydia straightened her apron and sat on an oak bench, facing her family. "Are we ready for a story now?" she asked again.

Anna Mae's head came up at last, and she gave a rare nod — the go-ahead. The others sat with upturned faces, eager for the evening's entertainment.

"A long, long time ago, an old man lived deep in the woods," she began. It had been quite some time since she had first heard this story. Mamma's friend Susie had told it to the women one day as they gathered over at the Lapps' farmhouse to put the cotton backing on an old quilt.

Lydia had been sitting all quietlike under the giant quilt frame with two other little girls, listening in. . . .

"Jacob was an Amish widower with nary a hope of snaggin' a bride for himself — mostly to do his washing and whatnot 'round the house. The reason he wasn't such a good catch for a mate was 'cause he was known to be downright deceitful on occasion.

"Oh, he was hard workin' enough, got up at the crack of dawn to do the laundry chores all by himself. But he was never so happy 'bout it, wishin' he had a wife to do the womanly chores.

"Well, it got so there was a whole bunch of Plain women up and down the same road as the old man, and the full lot of them started up havin' a bit of competition. They made a game of it, seein' who was first to hang out Monday mornin' wash and get it dry.

"So they each started gettin' up early — very early — in the morning. Each week, nigh unto another whole hour earlier than the last, till the lot of 'em was gettin' up in the dark to hang out their laundry, hopin' to be the winner for the week.

"Now, all the elderly folk in the community testify up and down that this next part of the story about Washday Competition is one hundred percent accurate and true. They declare that the old man outsmarted those neighborly women friends of his at their own game.

"He devised an unbeatable system, proving that he'd gotten up the earliest in the morning. And he didn't have to say a single word 'bout it, neither, to prove that it was so. He simply went to his closet and took and hung a whole string of clean and dry trousers and shirts on his clothesline.

"When the womenfolk noticed his laundry a-flappin' on the clothesline 'bout the time theirs was just gettin' hung out, well, they *knew* he was the winner."

Lydia grinned at the children as she folded her hands in her lap. "Now, what do you think of that?"

The children clapped their hands, begging for more.

"Surely that story isn't true," Caleb said, still grinning.

"Well, I know what you're thinking, 'cause I hardly believed it when first I heard it myself," she replied. "But that just goes to show what some folk'll do to win, jah?"

Josiah kept a-lookin' up at her. "Mamma would say that's lyin'," he said. "Plain and simple."

"Jah, right deceitful it is," Caleb concluded.

Lydia waited for Anna Mae to say something, but she looked as if she were in a daze. And Hannah was gettin' mighty sleepy.

"I think we best turn in for the night." She motioned for Caleb to get the Bible down.

Anna Mae surprised everyone by saying, "Let's have the English Bible tonight for evenin' prayers."

"Jah," Hannah said with a smile.

"S'pose it's a gut idea," Lydia said. "We oughta get used to it, maybe."

'Specially if — and when — Aunt Sarah ever comes, she thought.

"Why's that such a gut idea, Lyddie?" Josiah asked.

She didn't want to end the evening on a sour note. Her dear little brother didn't need to be hearing 'bout her fears or her frustration over their aunt's obvious reluctance to accept her rightful place in the family.

"Well, now," she said at last, "Dat always wanted us to read from both the German *and* the English."

Just then she felt every bit as deceitful as old Jacob in the clothes-washin' story she'd just told.

"Please get Bill on the line," Sarah called to Heidi as she rushed into the front entrance to Alexander's Realty. "I need a last-minute favor from the boss."

"Uh-oh," Heidi muttered, her eyebrows rising.

"Yeah, isn't *that* the truth," Sarah whispered, marching down the hallway to her office.

Bill Alexander would have every reason to be irritated when she told him what she wanted to do. But she had given her word to a Mennonite attorney. She *had* to fly to Pennsylvania, if only for a few days. There was no alternative.

Choices, it seemed, had suddenly become a thing of the past.

Chapter Six

Sarah did not take time to mull over her day *this* morning while sitting in bed. Her trip took precedence, and she was literally too busy to meet Bryan for their casual breakfast date.

Picking up the cell phone, she scanned the data for his number. She located it quickly, then hesitated. Could she spare the extra half hour, or whatever it took, to meet with him?

She recalled their excruciating final date as college sweethearts. Stubbornly, they had argued their individual positions long into the night. To think that she and Bryan could have moved from that one tumultuous moment and reemerged as friends still boggled her mind.

Putting down the cell phone, she decided against calling. She had hurt him too much already to cancel their casual brunch date. Besides, Bryan might not forgive her if she didn't follow through on their spontaneous rendezvous. She couldn't afford to lose his friendship, even if he was a bit overbearing, this much she knew. So she scurried about the room, preparing to shower and dress.

It took her precisely forty-five minutes. She knew what she would wear, had thought it through the night before, prior to falling asleep. She wouldn't spend an inordinate amount of time on her hair or makeup, though. She let her hair hang free and easy, less of the buttoned-up look. Of course, she would do her best to look nice but would lean more toward her usual classy, but professional, style. After all, it wasn't her goal to impress Bryan. She must have accomplished that years ago.

"It's only breakfast," she whispered mockingly at the mirror. She brushed her honey blond locks away from her oval face, flipping her head forward and leaning over to shake her hair to encourage extra bounce. One of her many morning rituals.

Head erect, she sprayed her hair lightly, recalling the time Mother had observed Ivy combing Sarah's hair. Ivy had been a teenager, around fifteen or so. Sarah, only nine . . .

"You've got natural curls," Sarah had said to Ivy, watching her play with her own strawberry blond mane.

"Don't ever say that!" Ivy shot back.

"You should be happy about it," Sarah replied, determined to stand her ground.

Ivy stopped brushing, a stubborn look on her face. "You don't know what you're talking about," she seethed.

"Now, girls," Mother said in the doorway of the girls' bedroom. "Let's try to be kinder to each other."

Ivy waved her brush in Sarah's little face. "Tell *her* that!"

Mother shook her head, a hand on her nearly nonexistent hip. "Might be a good idea if the two of you separate for a while." She wagged her finger at Sarah. "Come along now. No need to stir up your sister's wrath."

"I was only telling the truth." Sarah turned when Mother wasn't looking and stuck out her tongue at her sister. "Ivy's hair is *so* naturally curly," she said defiantly.

Mother, wiser than either of them, put in not a word of defense of her older daughter. She took Sarah by the hand and led her out of the room and down the stairs. "It's time you stop poking fun at your big sister," Mother said, making her sit in the corner of the living room. "You must learn to show respect to your elders."

But in Sarah's mind, "elders" were much older folk. People in their twenties or more. Not rotten teenage sisters who were half-blind when it came to hair. *Her* hair, after all, was stick straight. And she wished it was anything *but.*

Thinking back, Sarah wondered if that had been the initial reason for their lifelong dissension? Did Ivy really and truly despise her own curls? Did she secretly wish for different hair?

Sarah checked her makeup once again, though she'd promised herself not to obsess over her appearance. Quickly, she sprayed her favorite perfume, the most expensive fragrance she owned — *Eternal* — wondering if Bryan would remember the scent. Then, standing before the floor mirror, she scrutinized herself from head to toe, especially noting the heather gray pant outfit and soft pink scarf at her neck.

Fabulous, she thought, hoping she'd made the right decision by agreeing to see him again.

Lydia was perty sure Mamma would've joined the Old Order Amish if Dat had wanted to years ago. But her parents had chosen the assurance of salvation with the New Order Amish Church over the rigid, tradition-based community of the Old Order.

Truth be told, she was glad they'd favored

76

the way of redemption through God's grace. 'Specially since with it came the belief that modern electricity and telephones were not as wicked as some brethren had originally thought. *This* doctrine she wholeheartedly embraced, along with the modern conveniences. Yet, she was content to be submissive to the bishop and the rulings of the People of their own church district.

Lydia honestly enjoyed being Plain. For her, it was the only way to be. Maybe 'cause she'd had some experience with the modern world to compare to the Amish life-style — the first five years of her life.

Sarah stood in the alcove of the anteroom. She scanned the specialty café and looked for Bryan, spotting him at the same moment he recognized her, his eyes softening instantly.

He still cares too much, she thought as she made her way to his table.

Bryan stood tall and lean as she approached, and she let him kiss her cheek. She caught a hint of his subtle cologne as he stepped back, smiling. "You look wonderful, Sarah." He pulled out a chair for her and she sat.

"How are you?" she asked, her head spinning with a dozen different topics, namely her upcoming trip.

"The question is how's everything going for *you?*" He had an uncanny way of turning questions back to her. On occasion, this had frustrated her. Today she would overlook it.

"I've been horribly busy," she replied. "The real estate market amazes even me . . . especially this time of year." Not wanting to dissect her career — not today — she reached for the menu, a slim, leather-bound green folder. "What looks good to you?"

"You do." He grinned.

She might have known he'd bait her with such a response. "I'm *not* on the menu, in case you hadn't noticed."

He reached for her hand, and she didn't have the heart to pull away. "I've missed you. Okay with you?"

She felt the passion in his palm, his long warm fingers wrapped around hers. Stiffening, she knew she shouldn't have agreed to see him after all and avoided his gaze.

"You seem jittery. Something bothering you?"

Confusion reigned as she looked deep within her soul. Should she confide in him, tell of Ivy's death? What would he say if he knew the implications facing her?

"Sarah . . . ?" he persisted, his eyes searching hers.

She held her breath, not knowing . . . not

wanting to answer. But Bryan Ford was as direct and tenacious a man as any she'd known. Truly, she must offer him a crumb of information.

"There's a family crisis," she managed.

"Oh, honey . . . what *is* it?"

Her throat closed up at his endearing word. Slowly, yet firmly, she withdrew her hand.

"I think we'd better order now." Abruptly, she set her gaze on the menu, knowing if she allowed her eyes to find his again, she might cave in and tell all. The knowledge of her orphaned nieces and nephews could only serve to create additional tension between them.

Bryan gave in to her request, it seemed, and they read their menus without speaking.

When the waitress came, Sarah noticed that her friend's demeanor had changed. He was mechanical. Too polite. She'd wounded him . . . again. She had attempted to shut him out, hoping he might clam up and choose another topic of conversation. She had been unnecessarily rude. Yet she could not help herself.

Soon the waitress was gone, and they were alone once again. Nervously, she played with her pinky ring.

"New?" He eyed her finger.

"Santa brought it . . . this year." She stared fondly at the ring, then hid her hands in her lap.

"How many diamonds does a girl need?" he quipped.

She laughed, welcoming the relief. "Oh, you know me. I like pretty things — and lots of them. What can I say?"

His eyes penetrated hers. "It's just stuff, Sarah. You can't take it with you."

He's talking death now. That's Ivy's department, she thought, wishing their discourse were off on better footing. Oh, to chat about something insignificant. Anything but her insatiable need for possessions.

"My material girl," he said more softly.

She couldn't avoid his dark eyes, the intense expression on his handsome face. "You know I'm not that, what you said . . . *your girl.*" She felt terribly flustered.

"But you could be. Just say the word."

She paused, thinking of ways to change the subject. At last she blurted, "My sister's dead, passed away last week."

"Ivy?"

She nodded, unexpected tears welling up.

He frowned, not understanding her sudden grief. No doubt he recalled her ongoing detachment from Ivy. Maybe that's what he was thinking, looking so concerned.

But she wouldn't second-guess him. "She named me guardian for her five children," Sarah told him. "Can you believe it?"

Bryan looked puzzled. "I'm stunned," he said.

"I'm leaving today for Lancaster, Pennsylvania."

His eyes were kind, thoughtful. "How long will you be there?"

She shook her head, feeling the hostility anew. "I hope this mess can be straightened out in a few days. Only God knows what sort of mother I'd be. And I doubt I'd take too kindly to the simple life. I prefer a cluttered, complicated, extravagant life style, thank you."

Bryan chuckled a bit. "A few days in Amish country might do you good. You might be surprised."

"So . . . we're back to the *stuff* issue?"

His irresistible smile drew her in. "Ivy's kids are related to you by blood, Sarah. I think you might enjoy them if you give yourself half a chance."

Half a chance . . .

Where had she heard that before? Ivy was forever inviting her to "come visit us in the country," implying some of the same things Bryan had just now.

Was there no one on the planet who understood her? She would absolutely not think of giving up a lucrative career to raise someone else's family. She loved her things, her life, her money too much to let it all go. And for what? Amish children . . . *Ivy's* offspring?

"I think we'd better skip this conversation." She studied his face, his brow, his eyes.

He winked at her. "If you can't talk it over with me, then who?"

A legitimate point. No one in her life had discerned the Ivy-Sarah issue over the years as well as Bryan Ford. No one else had ever taken time to decipher the frustration in her voice on the phone; the numerous times she'd felt guilt ridden after receiving yet another letter from her narrow-minded sister.

"May I at least keep in touch while you're there?"

"Believe it or not, there *is* a phone in the house. But I'll have my cell phone, too," she replied, patting her purse.

"And your laptop computer, I suppose?" He was grinning.

"Can't leave my email behind."

Their breakfast was coming — eggs and waffles for Bryan, a fruit plate and cottage cheese for her. She realized then, as the food was placed before them, she hadn't asked a single question about *his* life, how things were going back in Boston.

Suddenly she felt embarrassed, ridiculously self-centered. "Forgive me, Bryan. How's everything with you?"

"Thought you'd never ask." He leaned forward, studying her across the table. "As a matter of fact, my work is going along better than ever. It's very possible I might be able to get away again for a few days, visit you in . . . Lancaster, is it?"

"Oh, you mustn't come. Ivy's children aren't your problem."

He smiled knowingly. "But . . . we're friends, aren't we?"

"Thanks." Then she added quickly, "I mean, for your friendship."

He was nodding. "But you meant 'no thanks' to my coming to Amish country?"

She felt completely ashamed. "Yes," she said so softly she wondered if he heard. Bryan knew her far too well, yet loved her still. Seemingly, there was nothing she could say or do to make him change his mind about her.

Nothing at all.

Sunday afternoon, January 23

Ach, what a day of days.

83

Levi King asked if Caleb could drive me in the family buggy over to Singing tonight. Glory be! But I told him I'd best stay at home with my sisters and brothers. 'Course, I thanked him for asking.

"Maybe somebody could put a bug in Fannie Flaud's ear . . . just for tonight." He winked at me after he said that!

'Course, I knew what he was getting at. He wanted one of my other girlfriends to contact Fannie, see if she couldn't take over for me here at the house while I went to the Singing at the Eshes' big barn.

But then I thought of poor Fannie missing out on her own fun, and I knew it wouldn't be fair to cheat her out of a good time. No, I'd stay put . . . where I belong for now. I just have to give up this one chance to spend some time with Levi.

Jah, I could tell by the look on his face, he was more than just a little disappointed. But not enough to go looking for another girlfriend. He reached for my hands and squeezed them gently. "I'll miss ya, Lyddie, but there'll be other times for us. I know there will."

I'll never forget the sound of those words. Now I'm thinking — more convinced than ever — he really and truly loves me. Yet I daresn't let on a thing to Caleb or the others.

This courting business must be kept quiet. It's the way things have been done amongst the People for nearly three hundred years. Makes right good sense to me, too.

In spite of everything I've thought and worried about Aunt Sarah, still a part of me hopes there might be a way to get Sarah Cain to come right soon and maybe even stay. More than anything, 'cept for the promise I made Mamma, I want to be Levi's wife someday.

Chapter Seven

Sarah folded her lingerie, placing each item in the soft pockets of her wardrobe Pullman. Methodically, she checked off the categories of clothing she intended to pack for her trip — sufficient for a full week. Undergarments, hosiery, silk pajamas and robe, slippers, two suits, three skirts and blouses, pants ensemble to mix and match, two Angora wool sweaters, dress shoes, two pairs of casual shoes, jewelry, and necessary toiletries, including makeup and hair needs.

Of one thing she was convinced: She would remain in Lancaster County no longer than necessary. She fully intended to wrap things up on behalf of Ivy's children in a single week's time. Psychologically, she could better handle the stressful, complicated situation if she mentally limited the amount of time spent on Ivy Cottrell's Amish turf.

Fondly, she surveyed her suite of rooms, taking in the canopied rice bed done in a delicate but somewhat sophisticated floral-patterned duvet and solid ivory coverlet. A white wood fireplace with recessed bookcases over the mantel graced one entire corner of the room, surrounded by matching pale rose-hued overstuffed armchairs.

She would miss this opulent chamber. How could she not? She had closely involved herself in the impassioned process, working with an exclusive decorator, intent on creating the ultimate in fine design. This house — the three-thousand-square-foot town home — represented everything she had ever worked for. It was her Shangri-La, her haven in the storms of life.

Had she overlooked anything? Deliberately, Sarah combed the suite with her gaze, as one who dreads abandoning a shrine.

Then, nearly gasping, she spied the tiny gold frame on the bedside table — the picture of her deceased student, sweet and mildly handicapped Megan Holmes. Nicknamed "Meggie" by her friends, the youngster had been in Sarah's second-grade class in Stonington, Connecticut.

Lovingly, she wrapped the picture in several layers of tissue and placed it in the suitcase next to her silk pajamas. *Safe there,* she decided, rejecting the impulse to study the image again.

Satisfied that her packing was complete, she went to her writing desk and pulled open the deep middle drawer where she stored Ivy's recent letters.

Opening the first envelope her fingers touched, she noted the postmark. December 1997. She unfolded the off-white stationery, taking note of the greeting — Ivy's customary salutation. *Greetings, my dear sister, in the name of our precious Lord and Savior, Jesus Christ.*

Often, Sarah had wondered if Ivy's reference to *our Lord* was a subconscious approach to "preaching," or if her sister purposely wished to set an ultraspiritual tone for the body of the letter. Rereading this particular note, Sarah noticed that there was not a single trace of rebuke to be found.

We're having our share of cold weather here lately. Snow is falling and the wind is blowing just now as I write. Some of the womenfolk, including myself, will take turns going from one house to another during the next week, repairing old quilts and making new ones from scratch. It'll be fun, mixed in with the work, too. How we do enjoy the Tellings that come out of such gatherings. I must say, too, that I believe my Lydia is coming up in the ranks as a fine storyteller herself.

Susie Lapp and her daughter Emma and granddaughter Fannie soon will come to help cook up some cabbage chowder. We'll make plenty, as I know how much her family and mine do enjoy such a meal on a blustering day like today.

Two Tuesdays from this coming, a group of us plan to make up a batch of homemade doughnuts, the Lord willing. Oh, I wish you could smell the aroma as it fills the house. Sarah, I wonder if you recall how we helped Mother make her once-a-year doughnuts back in Connecticut. Do you remember the year we got snowed in? In late February, I believe it was — well after Valentine's Day. Dad wanted to put chains on the car and drive around in the parking lot near the little shopping center, making his own kind of doughnuts in the snow, I s'pose. But in the end Mother put her foot down, remember? You and I fell asleep to the delicious smells of yeast and dough, our stomachs full of sweet, warm pastry. I'm not sure, but those dough-nut-making sessions with Mother might just be where my yearning for baking got started.

Sarah readily recalled that winter day. The wind had howled in the trees beyond the fence as snow piled in drifts against the front door and covered every tree and shrub like fluffy white frosting on a cake. The family cat snoozed beside the hearth, and the fragrant warmth from the kitchen was deceiving, giving the illusion that all was well. As usual, though, Sarah felt the strong undercurrent of conflict, stemming from Ivy's need to be "in charge" — either of assigning aprons or measuring ingredients.

But for Sarah, frequent summer visits to the shore with her father were the memories *she* most cherished. Daddy had always been intrigued by seashells washed up on the sand. So the two of them went barefoot together in the spring, summer, and fall, their pants legs rolled up to midcalf, gathering dozens of shells; caressing each one — channeled whelk or moon shell alike. Daddy spoke as if each had an important life lesson to impart, and for him the shells *did* have something beautifully enlightening to share. Every aspect of nature seemed to communicate — reveal itself intimately — to Alfred Cain. Never had there been any doubt that her father was in tune with the Creator of all things. Thankfully, he had not pushed his theology off on her the way Ivy had attempted to do in recent years.

Refolding Ivy's letter, Sarah slipped it back into the envelope. She rose, carrying a handful of letters, and placed them into her suitcase before closing it.

Thoughts of Megan Holmes swept over her unexpectedly. Perhaps it was the reminiscing of sea creatures; moon shells especially, with their glossy-smooth surface and flawless spiral. *"The heart-core in the center is like an island,"* Daddy would say, pointing to the "dark eye."

Perhaps it was the subconscious connection to an island that brought Meggie to mind. At any rate, she found herself longing for the darling girl, overwhelmed by guilt once again.

Breathlessly, Sarah began to unzip the section where several pairs of pajamas were nestled, removing Meggie's picture. She chose to tuck it away inside her briefcase instead. At least it would be safe there, in the event her luggage became misplaced or lost.

Simply put, she could not allow herself to risk losing the one and only tangible memento of a precious life. A young life lost to Sarah's poor judgment.

Time spent collecting shells on the sand at Watch Hill had taught young Lydia fascinating things. Things a person didn't learn at school, 'specially not public schools. Jah, in Amish schools, for sure and for certain. But, thanks to Grandpa Cain, she'd learned the art of shedding unnecessary things early on.

"Watch closely the hermit crab," he would say, picking up a castaway shell house. *"See how* little *he seems to get by with?"*

91

She'd observed hundreds of seashells, too many to count — perty, simple shelters abandoned by former snail owners. No wonder Dat had taken up the refrain about casting off vanity. He'd heard it enough times, too, from Grandpa, long before they'd ever thought of becoming one with the People.

These things she pondered to the muted *clip-clop-clip* of the horse's hooves against the snow-packed road, ever thankful for Caleb's strong arms today as he reined in Dobbin, one of their two most reliable driving horses. Grateful, too, for Josiah's and Hannah's calm repose behind her in the second seat of the carriage. Anna Mae was again the quietest of all, sitting between her younger brother and sister. But now and then Lydia could hear Anna Mae muttering, like she was talkin' to somebody but nobody was listening.

Josiah spoke up from the back. "Preacher Esh was mighty long-winded today."

"Best not say such a thing 'bout God's anointed," she chided.

"Well, he *was,*" Anna Mae said. "I don't see no reason for not sayin' so."

"*Any* reason," Lydia corrected her sister out of habit, though she knew there was more to admonish Anna Mae about than her poor grammar. Her sister was becoming mighty headstrong — and all just since

Mamma's passing. She wondered if she ought to speak to one of the older women about what to do.

But, no, Sarah Cain was on her way, so she'd prob'ly just wait and leave it up to their aunt to apply the right discipline.

"When didja say Mamma's sister is comin'?" Caleb broke the silence.

She'd told them a dozen times, if she'd told them once, just since this morning when Mr. Eberley had called before breakfast, of all things. On a Sunday morning yet. It was as if her brothers and sisters had to hear the same thing over and again in order to believe it.

She couldn't blame them, really, for it seemed like a solitary dream to her, too, that Mamma's fancy younger sister was actually comin' to be their guardian. "Her plane's landin' at Harrisburg, and Mr. Eberley says it'll take her a gut forty minutes to get here."

"Ach, I wonder what it's like to fly in a plane high up in the sky," Josiah said, making buzzing sounds behind her head.

"The Lord never meant a person to go so awful fast," she said, offering words that Dat used to say about the pace of things. "Life goes by so terrible swift without forcin' it along faster." She felt she had to say the latter, just to put Josiah in his place.

It worked. He stopped making the whirring sounds right quick and began chattering with Hannah. All the while, Anna Mae carried on her private conversation with no one at all.

"How will we know it's Aunt Sarah when she comes?" Caleb asked softly, his left hand resting on his leg. His right hand held both reins loosely.

"Oh, *I* think we'll know."

Anna Mae whispered, "For sure?"

"Well, she must be an awful rich lady now, from what Mamma always said. Aunt Sarah drives fast cars and likes to dress up a whole lot. So I 'spect she looks perty fancy most all the time."

"She wears for-gut clothes *everywhere?*" Hannah said, revealing her astonishment.

"Jah, but I'm thinkin' it'd be best if we don't gawk or say anything 'bout how she looks. Promise me that?" She turned in her seat, eyeing Josiah and Hannah sternly. As for Anna Mae, Lydia reached around and patted her sister's chubby knees through her long woolen coat. "I'm almost positive we'll recognize her. She must look something like Mamma, after all."

"No . . . *you* look like Mamma," Anna Mae pointed out.

Lydia knew it was true. Everyone, from the time she was born till Mamma's funeral,

had always said she was the spittin' image of
her mother. Truth was, she was right proud
of it, in a humble sort of way. She had
Mamma's features and golden brown eyes
and hair, just not the same strawberry hues
as Mamma had in her flaxen hair. No, her
own was more like wheat after a hard rainstorm, blanched nut brown with no hope of
red. Still, she had the persistent waves that
sometimes worked their way into ringlets
around her hairline on a hot summer day.

"Where's Aunt Sarah gonna sleep?"
Hannah asked.

"Mamma's old room."

The enclosed carriage fell silent. Only the
soft snort of Dobbin the horse could be
heard.

Sighing, she thought maybe she shouldn't
have been so quick to volunteer their
mamma's former abode. Maybe it bothered
the children to think of Aunt Sarah coming
into their home that-a-way.

Sometimes, here lately, instead of having
to make so many decisions for the family,
she almost wished she were small enough to
fit inside the weathered channeled whelks
Grandpa used to pick up and talk about so
cheerfully. Up . . . up the tiny spiraling staircase, safe from harm, secure in his strong,
wrinkled hand.

Chapter Eight

In Chicago, Sarah made her connecting flight with little hassle. On board the plane, she found her aisle seat and settled into row ten. Immediately, she was greeted by the passenger in the seat next to hers. "Hello, there."

"Hello," she replied, not so interested in engaging in conversation.

"Where are *you* headed?" asked the woman, not much older than mid-thirties.

"Harrisburg."

"I'm going back to Lancaster," the brunette woman volunteered. "I'm a Bible school student there."

She nodded, saying no more, eager to get back to her novel.

"Are you from Harrisburg?" inquired the woman.

Sarah chose to remain elusive. "New England's my home."

The passenger's eyes lit up with recognition. "You know, I *thought* you might be from somewhere up there. I have relatives in New Hampshire . . . they sound just like you." She paused all too briefly, then continued. "What part of New England?"

Sarah didn't want to appear rude, but she did want to discourage a long discourse with a stranger and get on with her reading. "Not far from Mystic, Connecticut."

"That's beautiful country up there."

"Yes."

"I spent several summers in Stonington when I was in my teens," the young woman volunteered. "A long time ago, it seems."

She refused to admit to having been born and reared there. The wounds were still too fresh.

"I love Lancaster County. Ever been there?"

"This happens to be my first trip."

"Oh, then by all means, let me encourage you to take a bus tour of Amish country while you're there. It's like nothing you've ever experienced."

"Really?"

The woman was nodding, wide-eyed. "You'll feel like you've stepped back in time . . . at least to the nineteenth century and then some. It's so amazing how they can ride around with their horses and buggies, right on the main streets, no less. And the women and girls wear the cutest bonnets, like you'd expect to see on a storybook character in a play."

Storybook character . . .

The thought had never crossed her mind about Amish attire. Her own nieces and nephews were most likely as Plain as any of the other Amish sects in the Lancaster area. "Do they all dress the same?" she asked.

"The Amish, you mean?"

Sarah nodded, feeling brazen, as if she were inquiring behind someone's back. Her deceased sister's . . .

"It's hard to tell the Old Order from the New Order or the Beachy Amish and some of the other conservative circles. Surely you know there are many varieties. You'd almost have to delve into individual Ordnungs for each church district — if that were even possible — to know for sure what is allowed and what isn't. Most Amish adhere strictly to the Old Testament, but only certain passages of Scripture are taught in their Preaching services."

She was surprised at the knowledge the woman seemed to have of Ivy's People. "How do you know so much about the Amish?" she asked hesitantly.

"I've made a good many friends with Mennonite young people over the years. Some of them are related to Amish. One of the girls has even dated Old Order boys.

Can you imagine that?"

Sarah certainly could not. She was somewhat relieved to hear the pilot's voice over the intercom. Time for the plane to taxi out to the runway for takeoff.

"Nice meeting you," she mumbled.

"Oh, I guess I didn't introduce myself properly. My name's Theresa Barrows. What's yours?"

Sarah forced a smile. "Sarah Cain."

"Sounds Plain, you know? It really does. I think you'll fit right in over in Lancaster County."

Sarah made a slight head gesture, an unintelligible sound, reached down for her briefcase, and found her novel. A person engrossed in a book during a flight was usually able to avoid conversation. She was anxious to find out if that were true.

The historical novel — *Black Hawk* — was a riveting tale set in the northwest panhandle of Idaho, near a well-known 1910 mansion on Lake Hayden, now a refurbished estate. A Native American saga and love story wrapped up in one.

As she read, she soon found herself going back over the same sentence or paragraph three or more times. The young woman's comments had intrigued her more than she cared to admit.

"You'll feel like you've stepped back in time. . . ."

Just what she *didn't* need or want — an escape from reality. She was quite happy with her little self-made "kingdom" in Portland, thank you. A "world" that had been a long time coming. She was much smarter than to let herself get caught up or lost in the nineteenth century.

Exasperated, she closed her eyes but kept the book open, letting her thoughts slip away. . . .

When Mother had been ill — unable to tend to Sarah — it was Ivy who frequently volunteered, and all too eagerly. Her suffocating approach, even as a teenager, caused Sarah to lash out. She could scarcely tolerate Ivy's obnoxious behavior, under the guise of "helping Mother." Sarah had so despaired of the worn-out expression that she often clamped her hands over her ears. She'd much rather have Mother looking out for her, though their mother was sickly and sometimes too frail to keep up with Sarah's inquisitive mind, not to mention her mischievous fingers.

So it was Ivy — hovering sister that she was — who attempted to take up the slack for Mother's ongoing lassitude. *"You ought to be glad I'm here to look after you,"* Ivy would say, her hands on her shapely hips as she stood in the kitchen doorway, wearing one of Mother's handmade ruffled aprons, insisting that Sarah *"come inside and get out of the dirt this instant!"*

Thinking back to those days, Sarah realized anew that the ridiculous aprons Ivy wore in her late teens were a mere foreshadowing of the unfashionable clothes she would wear as a Plain wife and mother of five. Laughable, to say the least. Though with Ivy's life cut short unexpectedly, Sarah wondered now if she had missed something important along the way. Something that might have given her a clue — something tangible to go on — regarding Ivy's decision to abandon her modern heritage and join the ranks of the Plain community. What in her and Ivy's mutual childhood upbringing had supplied her sister with the fuel to fire such a change? Was it truly a yearning for the "Old Ways" as Ivy so often wrote, her hand steady on the simple, unadorned page, her letters and loops perfectly formed? Had Sarah failed to read between the lines?

What *had* she overlooked?

Second Officer Mitchell's voice intruded on her thoughts, pointing out their location over Cleveland, Ohio, and giving the current temperature in Harrisburg.

Sarah straightened in the seat, closing her book, eager for the flight attendants to serve up something cold to drink. Glancing out of the corner of her eye, she was thankful to see the Bible college woman engrossed in what appeared to be an Amish cookbook.

Terrific, she thought, eyeing the male flight attendant and toying with the idea of ordering a stiff drink or two. On second thought, perhaps she should tough it out soberly for whatever might lie ahead for her in the "back-in-time" land of Grasshopper Level.

Chapter Nine

"Jah, you must wear your warmest coat this-after," Lydia reminded Josiah and Hannah as they made ready to go outside and play following the Sunday noon meal.

"But, Lyddie, it ain't so awful cold now, is it?" Josiah insisted, his forehead knitting into a big frown.

"It was right chilly on the ride home from church, I'd say." She patted the top of his thick blond hair, cut straight under his ears — the common Plain blunt-cut.

"But I just *know* it's gonna get warmer!" the child insisted. "It's got to!"

Lydia bent low, eye level with her adorable brother. "And why is that?"

His round face broke into an angelic smile. " 'Cause me and Caleb are gonna build tall snow forts out near the barn, that's why!"

Chuckling, Lydia stood up. "Now, is that so?" She resisted the urge to correct his grammar. "Well, why didn't you say so in the first place?"

Josiah's blue eyes widened and his brow

wrinkled with wonder. "I been tryin' to tell ya things, Lyddie, honest I have. Seems you don't hear me half the time."

Her brother's words jabbed at her heart. Silence drifted through the kitchen, and Lydia folded her hands, not knowing what to do to dispel the awkward hush.

It was a relief, to be sure, when Hannah rushed across the kitchen and reached for Lydia's hand. "Don'tcha see, Josiah, our Lyddie's grievin' over Mamma," Hannah tried to explain.

Without another word, the sisters fell into a fond embrace. It wasn't long before Lydia felt Josiah wiggling through between them. "I miss Mamma, too," he cried. "Somethin' awful."

Lydia released her sister and gave her full attention to her youngest brother. "We *all* miss her," she said with all the strength she could gather up. "But Mamma wants us to live our lives to the fullest, even without her." She breathed deeply, willing away the painful spasms in her throat.

"How do ya know that?" Josiah asked, his eyes blinking.

"I just do."

Hannah spoke up. "Did Mamma tell you that . . . before she died, I mean?"

"Well, I s'pose she did, in her own way."

"Did she write it down somewheres?" Josiah persisted.

Lydia thought about that. There was a very good possibility that their mother *had* written encouraging words for them to read at a later date, perhaps. But for now, Lydia knew she simply couldn't begin to answer her little brother's questions satisfactorily. It wasn't that she couldn't try her best to do so. She just honestly didn't know what to say just yet. And she wasn't going to rummage through her mother's writings to find out. Not just now. Maybe never.

She gazed on the boy standing before her. Young Josiah had always been one to ask difficult questions. He was his father's son, and Lydia knew it sure as day. "All I know is the way Mamma lived *her* life," she began again. "Full up to the brim with the delights of each and every season. Mamma was joyful in the Lord God, too, just as she and Dat taught us all to be."

Josiah's lips puckered a bit, his pudgy hands reaching up to stroke her face. "I wish I could be joyful just now . . . like Mamma was."

"Ach, me too," Hannah piped up.

Lydia pulled out a chair and gathered both her younger siblings close. "Listen carefully," she said softly. "Mamma followed hard after our elder brother and Savior, the Lord Jesus. That's why she was so gut and kind. Mamma was clean from the *inside* out."

Young Hannah pulled away. "Let's *all* try 'n be like Jesus, jah?"

That set the mood for more hugging, then voices callin' upstairs to Caleb and Anna Mae. "Who's goin' outside to play in the snow? If you are, come and get your things on," Lydia said, straightening her long gray apron.

"I'm comin'!" the confident voice of Caleb wafted down the stairs.

Anna Mae emerged, shy and restrained from the wide hallway. "I'm here, Lyddie," she said, her pale green eyes glistening.

Taking one look at Anna Mae, Lydia was perty sure the girl must've overheard the conversation with the younger children. "What's-a-matter?" she asked.

Turning away, her sister cowered near the kitchen doorway, and Lydia suspected Anne Mae was hiding her tears. Quickly, she went to her sister's side. "Tell me all about it," she whispered, wrapping her arms around the girl's shoulders.

"B-best not to say," Anne Mae sputtered into Lydia's chest.

She held the sobbing girl, aware that Caleb,

Hannah, and Josiah were inching closer, observing the tender moment. On any other day, she would've shooed them off.

"She's awful sad," Josiah whispered. "Talks to herself all the time."

"Hush now," she said ever so softly. "The place Mamma went to is heaven." This she said for Anna Mae's benefit — for all the children's. "From what the Bible says, it surely must feel like goin' home, after bein' in a strange land for the longest time."

The children looked at her with wide, thoughtful eyes. Then Anna Mae wiped her tear-stained face and asked, "Home? You mean, like here in Grasshopper Level?"

"Jah, but even better" was all Lydia could say. Her own eyes were beginning to blur, and she thought better of tryin' to conceal the tears. It might do the others good, knowing that she, too, was struggling. But she wouldn't think of sharin' her thoughts out loud. Best to keep quiet over her fears about their future. Besides, Mamma's attorney had assured her that Aunt Sarah was on her way here.

Tonight things just might start to change, Lydia thought as she dried Anna Mae's tears with her own apron.

Soon she was waving out the back door to Hannah, Josiah, Anna Mae, and Caleb as

they scurried through the snow to the barnyard. "Don't stay out too long now. You'll
freeze off your noses if you do."

She heard their gay laughter as she leaned
against the door. The cold air seeped through
onto her legs, but she stayed to watch the
cloud of enormous black crows flyin' overhead. She wondered if the crow-control folks
had decided what on earth to do about thousands of 'em roostin' on top of the Park City
Mall roof. Last she'd heard, it was goin' to be
an awful expensive problem. She was glad it
wasn't *her* problem. She had enough to cope
with right here at home.

Turning from the window, she thought
about warming up an ample pot of potato
soup for supper. If she heated up a double
batch, there'd be more than enough for
Aunt Sarah tonight. She was mighty glad
she'd made so many "cooked-ahead" meals,
with Susie Lapp's help, what with company
coming and all.

Puh! Aunt Sarah wasn't exactly company,
but one thing was sure: Mamma's sister
prob'ly didn't know the first thing about
cookin' from scratch. 'Course, Lydia couldn't
blame her for that.

Tired from the long day, Lydia walked the
length of the house to the front room and sat
down, thinkin' there was a mighty good

reason why the Good Lord rested on the seventh day. Come Sunday, a body was altogether wore out.

She gazed hard through the picture window at ice-encrusted branches, arbors, and wire fencing. A deserted birdhouse caught her eye down by the spring house, just past the front lawn, covered with a good six inches or more of snow. A line of oak trees stood sentry along the north side of the land, their strong trunks unyielding, yet unfettered from a recent dusting of snow. All in all, the snowscape was a winter garden, offering a sort of poetry of its own making.

The way Mamma viewed life, she thought. *Through rose-colored glasses.* After all, it had been Mamma's idea, every single autumn since they'd come to Lancaster County, to choose certain garden elements — a cast-iron bench here, an urn or old wagon wheel there — placing them about the yard in advance of winter's shortened days, knowing full well that icicles in all the right places can and do reflect sunlight. Lift one's mood. *"Snow has a way of gathering ever so gracefully on pine boughs and old trellises. The more silhouettes you can make in your winter garden, the better,"* Mamma had told her last October, Lydia recalled.

She fought the urge to cry again, remembering instead two days before Mamma went to heaven, when Lydia had tucked sprigs of crimson holly into the railing along the front porch. She'd hoped to break up the monotony of a frozen sea of ivory all around them.

"For you, Mamma," she'd whispered, taken aback by her own breath as it crystallized quickly, drifting up, away from the snow-whitened earth to a low and lifeless sky.

Upstairs, Lydia was tempted to rest a bit while the children played outside. Sunday afternoons were made for snoozin', she'd always heard Mamma say. Even Grandpa Cain, who was never Amish and wouldn't have considered bein' so, used to enjoy his daily twenty-minute catnap. Afterward, if the summer day was clear and sunny, he'd get up and go out to stroll along the shoreline, searchin' for his beloved seashells, talkin' to the Lord all the while. *"Abandoned crab houses,"* he'd say, showing her one or two of them.

Crab houses, she thought, stopping just a few yards from her mother's bedroom, her eyes feelin' heavier by the second. What mental acrobatics might Aunt Sarah be doing to get from *her* home . . . to them? Was she shedding her worldly life like a hermit crab? And how long would she stay once she got here? Or would Sarah take them all away, back to her world of fine and fancy things?

So many hard questions.

How very strange it had always seemed to hear that Mamma's sister was so different from them. Two sisters, born to the same parents . . . well, you'd think they'd be something alike. 'Least, some tiny part of their personalities. But Mamma had always said Sarah was her "complete opposite."

She moved down the hall, stopping at the doorway to her mother's old bedroom. *Dare I go in?* she wondered. *And if I do, what then?* She knew this might be her last chance before Aunt Sarah came and occupied the room, before they started sorting through — and disposing of — Mamma's clothing and personal items.

Oh, what she wouldn't give to breathe in the smell of dear Mamma, wherever the lovely scent might be hiding. In that moment of longing, her prior resolve was shattered. She touched the door already ajar, pushing it open gently, and stepped inside the large room, this bedroom — the private world — of her deceased mother.

She sank back on her heels, staring at the

white ceiling and light gray walls — tiny cracks noticeable near one corner — the dark green shades at each of the four curtainless windows and the tall walnut chest of drawers. The double bed with its simple patchwork of reds, blues, and greens caught her eye, and without thinking, she pulled the covers back and crawled under.

Pulling up Mamma's handmade quilt, she felt the weight and warmth of it on the length of her slender body. She wiggled beneath its heaviness, more than anxious to have some of the burden of her present life lifted. Thank goodness, Aunt Sarah would soon be here. *Here,* in Mamma's house. Different or not, it would be real nice to have a grown-up under the roof again, twenty-four hours a day.

Then and there, she decided she'd do her part to make Mamma's sister feel welcome. No tellin' what would happen when Sarah came, though. One thing was sure, the coldness in her aunt's voice seemed somewhat less nippy. Lydia noticed it first thing when Aunt Sarah called after supper last night. Something was altogether curious about the way she spoke to Lydia. "I can easily book a room at a hotel if you'd rather."

"No, no, stay . . . with us," she had insisted, puzzled at Aunt Sarah's comment, but knowin' for sure what Mamma would've wanted. "We have more than enough room for you here."

Josiah and Hannah had crept into the kitchen, prob'ly wondering who on earth she was talkin' to. "It's Aunt Sarah," she'd whispered, covering the receiver end of the phone.

Josiah had shrugged his shoulders and turned back to the Carom board, where he and Caleb were playing in the front room. Hannah showed no particular interest regarding Aunt Sarah, either, and scurried back to the kitchen table, scooting in next to Anna Mae, where they colored pictures of the landscape near Blackhorse Pond.

"Do you have the address where we live?" Lydia asked into the telephone. Of course, Sarah did. She and Mamma had written letters through the mail all these years.

"I'll do my best to locate you" came the polite reply.

Lydia thought, at the time, Sarah's answer seemed a bit weak, like she wasn't sure if she was truly comin' or not. But Lydia was wise and recited their house address just for so.

"I do have the street address," Sarah answered.

"But the house isn't really *on* a street . . . it's set back a ways from the main road."

"And what road would that be?"

Lydia tried to explain, giving various landmarks, as was their custom in giving directions. But Sarah wanted specifics — highway numbers and street markings.

"The Lord will guide you here," she said at last.

There was a pause. Then, "What did you say?"

"Just let God lead you to us." Lydia echoed the words, more softly this time, because she felt less sure of herself now. Not uncertain of her faith in God's divine direction, but whether she wanted Sarah Cain disrupting their lives further. She didn't honestly know how she felt anymore about Sarah's coming . . . or Mamma's strange choice. Neither one.

If Mamma were still alive, Lydia would like to question her. "Why'd you ask for an outsider to look after us?" she would be pleading. "Oh, Mamma, what *were* you thinkin'?"

Lydia awoke with a start and looked across the room at the row of pegs on a narrow wooden board attached to the far wall. There, Mamma had last hung her brown choring dresses, two blue cape dresses for good, and one black woolen shawl, along with several clean white *Kapps*.

Staring at the hand-sewn garments, Lydia rose and moved slowly, reverently toward them. She stood, regarding the dresses with a sigh, then reached up and removed the more faded of the two blue ones. Ach, Aunt Sarah might just dispose of them anyways — not give them a second thought. She wondered who in their church might like to wear, or just have on a hanger, one or all of the dresses her mother had worn.

Susie Lapp and several others came to mind, but Lydia knew Susie could never fit into Mamma's clothes. Not even her aprons! But, as close a friend as Susie had been, there was a good chance she just might like to have one hanging in her bedroom. For the memory's sake.

Nary a promise for the morrow. . . .

Lydia, too, wanted to keep one of Mamma's dresses. And she removed the hanger from the peg, carrying the older of the two better ones to her own room.

Standing next to her own strip of wooden pegs, she lifted Mamma's dress to her face and breathed deeply, wishing for the slightest scent. Knowing full well that these clothes had been thoroughly washed and dried, she was able to detect only the fresh smell of detergent and sunshine.

Touching the dress, she hung it on the wall under her own things, fondly recalling the last Sunday Mamma was well enough to attend Preachin' services at the Old Meetinghouse. . . .

It had been an exceedingly warm October day. Oak trees sang the colors of gold and bronze. Sugar maples wore flaming crimson, their portly arms extended out over the lane as Caleb drove Dobbin to church, east on Route 896 to Rohrer's Mill Road, then south onto Iva Road.

During the sermon, Lydia had to try to squelch a coughin' fit, till she knew if she didn't slip out and blow her nose somewhere, she would cause too much commotion in the meeting.

Turned out the only bathroom was in use, so she tiptoed outside where she happened on Emma Flaud and two other mothers discreetly nursing their infants. Without sayin' a word to any of them, she fished for a handkerchief and walked the length of the sidewalk, far enough away from the Meetinghouse to give her sinuses a more than gentle blow.

While she waited to see if another tickle might creep into her throat, Mamma came outside, too. She sat on the steps, next to Emma Flaud. Lydia remembered standin' there behind a tree, observing her best girlfriend's mamma and her own sickly mother sitting side by side, not speakin' a word to each other, surrounded by gentle women . . . sisters in the Lord, suckling their wee babes. Just content to be sittin' there.

She watched as Mamma fanned herself with her long white apron, her face much too flushed to lay blame on the warmth of a mild Indian summer Sunday. Mamma stopped fanning long enough to reach over and touch the soft, round head of Emma's new little one.

Lydia had to swallow the lump in her throat, realizing that Mamma's heart was slowly giving out on her, that she might not live long enough to see her own grandbabies born into the world.

Live ev'ry day as if it's your last. . . .

Returning to Mamma's bedroom, her gaze fell on the tall bureau on the opposite wall. She wandered over to the chest of drawers Dat had made for Mamma years ago. For a moment she stood and stared at the bottom drawer, as if just lookin' at it would make any difference. Deep in the drawer, she knew there must be plenty of scrapbooks with birthday and Christmas cards she and her brothers and sisters had handcrafted at school, poems clipped from *The Budget* and *Ideals* magazines, newspaper articles, and obituaries. Lovely things such as hand-tatted bookmarks and colorful handkerchiefs with crocheted edges or embroidered flowers any Amishwoman might want to cherish. But it was her mother's diaries and the letters she'd saved over the years that piqued Lydia's curiosity most.

A girl perty near goes through her life tryin' ever so hard to walk the straight and narrow — doin' a right fine job of it, too — till somewhere along the line, the things of the world jump out and allure her. As they were temptin' her now.

Slowly, heart pounding, Lydia leaned down and opened the drawer, her hands on either side, steadying the heavy drawer as it slid out. A shoe box marked "Seashells" lay off to one side. On the opposite side were dozens of letters, all of them tied in plain white ribbons, prettily, like nothin' she'd ever seen.

She pulled out a small packet, hoping against hope that God himself might ultimately have mercy on her for what she was about to do. Spying the name on the return address — Miss Sarah Cain — and the date November 7, 1996, she trembled. What would Mamma think of her this minute if she knew?

Quickly, she put the letters back. But her eye caught the bright floral color of a diary, bound like a real book.

Can it be? she wondered.

Was this the journal where Mamma had recorded her most private thoughts, her sadness and loss over Dat, a possible explanation for her choice of Sarah as her children's guardian?

Without another thought, Lydia opened to the first page: *New Year's Day, 1998.* Sighing, she held in her hands the last year's writings of her dead mother. "Ach, what'll I do?" she whispered.

She scanned the first page, then the next, her heart wanting desperately to read — to savor — every single word, but her eyes flew over the lines irreverently, searching for a clue, anything referring to Sarah Cain.

And then she spied something. *It's been ever so long since I've had a letter from my sister. I pray she is well, but more than that I pray that she will come to know the Savior soon.*

So . . . it was just as she thought. Aunt Sarah was not a believer as they were. And not only that, Sarah was also an unheeding, neglectful sister!

Lydia read on.

I don't know just what it will take for the Good Lord to get Sarah's attention. I just have no idea how He's going to bring her into the fold. But I trust the loving heavenly Father to do that.

Suddenly she heard, "Lyddie, come quick!" Anna Mae was shouting from downstairs.

She leaped up and nearly dropped the notebook. Pushing in the drawer till it was secure again, she called back, "What is it?" She rushed pell-mell out of the room and scurried toward the top of the stairs.

"The snow fort caved in on Hannah!" Anna Mae hollered.

Lydia stumbled down the steps, her heart in her throat. Whatever had happened to her baby sister was prob'ly the judgment of God on her. Ach, how swiftly it had come.

Dear Lord, please . . . please let Hannah be all right!

She grabbed her long black coat off the wooden peg in the utility room, tripping momentarily on her skirt tail as she followed Anna Mae out the kitchen door into the frigid air.

Chapter Ten

"Let God lead you to us. . . ."

Her niece's words resonated in Sarah's mind while she stood in line at the Budget rental car desk at the Harrisburg airport. She turned her attention to the various travelers awaiting their luggage on the carousel across the wide corridor.

Sarah lamented anew her predicament. Last evening's phone call had turned into a dismal affair. Lydia had not adequately described — in specific terms — the whereabouts of the Cottrell farmhouse. It sounded so rural, quite remote. What had Ivy done to her children, taking them to live among Amish folk?

Waiting her turn at the rental car counter, Sarah recalled years-old arguments, how Ivy and her husband had made one eccentric choice after another for themselves and their children. They'd deprived their offspring of a normal American life, isolating them from the real world.

"It's how we want to live," Ivy maintained. *"And it's no one's business but ours."*

Now it's my business, thought Sarah. *If there's a God, He'll have to lead me. No question.*

Lydia clutched her throat as she spied Caleb running across the barnyard, carrying Hannah's limp body.

"Call the Amish doctor," Caleb was shouting. "Hurry!"

"Ach, no!" She knew better than to do such a thing. Dat and Mamma had never wanted anything to do with the powwow doctors in the area. Preacher Esh had even spoken out from the pulpit against occult practices such as that. She had no idea what Caleb was thinking, askin' her to do such a thing. Still, someone should be called. She could see it sure as day.

"We might be needin' help from the *Brauchdokder,*" he said again, his eyes more serious now as he approached the sidewalk leading to the house. "She seems to have the wind knocked out of her."

"Let me have a look at her," Lydia insisted. She followed Caleb through the screened-in back porch, utility room, and kitchen to the front room, where he bent low, placing Hannah gently on the flat cushions of the straight-backed sofa.

Josiah and Anna Mae hovered near. "Looks

like she's breathin' all right now," Josiah was first to say.

Little Hannah was trying to sit up, moaning all the while. "W-what happened to me?" she asked, rubbing her head.

"The snow fort fell in . . ." Caleb's voice trailed away.

"I nearly got suff'cated," Hannah cried.

Lydia knelt beside the couch to attend to her sister. "Can you breathe all right?"

Hannah drew in her breath and held it a second, then out. "Jah, I think so."

Lydia felt her sister's head. "Do you have any bumps anywhere?"

"Back here." Hannah pointed.

Lydia felt where her sister's hand rested, under a warm winter bonnet. "Let's take this off you."

"Am I gonna be all right, Lyddie?"

Nodding, Lydia truly hoped so, because without Aunt Sarah here, they — all of them — might find themselves in hot water with the local authorities. Though her parents never put their hope or trust in anyone but God himself, still, if Hannah needed medical attention . . . Well, Lydia just hoped and prayed she wouldn't have to risk puttin' her family in jeopardy, not that-a-way.

Mamma's lawyer had said the five of them *had* to have an adult guardian, couldn't just live on their own the way they knew how to. "Your aunt Sarah is in charge of you children." Mr. Eberley's strong words annoyed her. "We're required by due process to abide by Sarah Cain's wishes."

"Whether we take much to the idea or not," Lydia had muttered offhand.

But now, feelin' the hard knot on the back of little Hannah's head, Lydia wished Aunt Sarah would arrive this minute!

"If you won't call the *Brauchdokder*, then I *will!*" Caleb declared, removing his coat and black felt hat.

"Now, just wait a minute," she replied, putting the slightest pressure on Hannah's head. "I think all we need is some ice."

Caleb was gone in a jiffy, which was just what she'd hoped for. She could think more clearly without stress-filled remarks spoutin' out of her worrywart brother's mouth.

She stroked her sister's forehead. "You're goin' to be all right, Hannah," she whispered. "I believe you are."

"My head ain't broke, is it?" Hannah asked, trying to move it and wincing a bit as she did.

"Prob'ly just a bump."

"You won't let the powwow doctor come, will ya?"

She shook her head. "Mamma always said we should pray to God for our needs. So that's what we're goin' to do."

Hannah's head moved up and down slowly, and her eyes seemed to be getting brighter as she did. "Mamma knew things 'bout God, didn't she?"

"Jah, she did."

"So why don'tcha pray for my head the way Mamma used to?" Hannah's hand reached out to grasp Lydia's own.

"I . . . I don't know for sure what to pray." And she didn't, not really, but when she thought of the possibility of policemen coming and snatchin' them away, separating them far from each other, she knew there was *something* — surely, there was — that she could be prayin' in front of her hurt sister and the others.

Just then Caleb marched back into the room, carrying a plastic bag of ice cubes. "Will this do?"

"*Denki.*" She took the ice and turned Hannah gently on her side, holding the ice bag against her wee head. "This'll help the pain and make the bump go down right quick, I'm thinkin'."

Hannah smiled up at her, long lashes brushing her cheek. "You know, you could be a nurse, too, Lyddie . . . and a teacher both."

She felt gladdened, seein' the color begin to creep back into Hannah's cheeks. Relieved, really. Maybe everything was goin' to be all right after all.

"Don't forget the prayer," Hannah reminded her.

Lydia caught Caleb's eyes. "She wants someone to pray for her the way Mamma always did when we were sick or hurt." She truly hoped her brother might offer to do just that.

"Well, what're you waitin' for?" He sounded timid just now and a bit put out, all mixed up.

"Gather 'round, children," Lydia said, trustin' that she might find the right words, 'specially because she was still feeling guilty, knowin' she oughta be confessing her sins before almighty God instead of askin' for favors.

Sarah paused on the front porch of the old farmhouse before knocking. What she saw through the window kept her hand poised in midair. Inside, two girls and two boys knelt with bowed heads, hovering over a small girl who was stretched out on a tan sofa, wearing snow boots and a long black coat. The oldest of the group — most likely Lydia — also wore a dark woolen coat, her high-topped black shoes showing under the hem of her purple dress.

Sarah marveled at their clothing — the one thing she'd failed to consider until the passenger next to her on the plane had mentioned the distinctive Amish apparel. The younger boy, the one with golden hair, wore a wide-brimmed black felt hat, a gray coat, and snow boots. But it was the back of Lydia's head and the cap of white netting perched over a thick hair bun at the back of her neck that captured Sarah's attention. Observing the cap, she had a feeling it represented something devout, perhaps prayerful.

Not wanting to interrupt, she waited behind the beveled glass. If the family scene had not been so tender, she might've knocked. What they were doing, assembled that way around the youngster, she was not entirely certain. But the serene moment reminded her of another winter day, not so long ago, when children and teachers had gathered, bowed low around the body of a lifeless child on the playground's cold surface. The present scene became somewhat eerie in its scope due to the scalding memory, and she had to look away for a moment to compose herself.

After a time, the tallest boy rose from his kneeling position and left the room. His gait was measured, though his facial expression seemed to indicate that he was irritated.

She took advantage of the lull and, inhaling sharply, knocked on the door.

Instantly a teenage girl came, followed by a younger boy and girl. "Hullo?" said the girl in the dark purple dress and black pinafore-style apron. "Are you . . . Aunt Sarah?"

Stunned, Sarah looked into the face of the beautiful Amish girl, nearly identical to Ivy's — a youthful rendering of Sarah's own sister. "Yes, and you must be . . . are you Lydia Cottrell?"

A robust smile spread across the rosy-cheeked face. "Jah, I'm Lyddie."

The other children, except the youngest, pushed in for a closer look. "Ask her in out of the cold," whispered the tow-headed boy. "She'll catch her death . . ."

"Oh, I'm awfully sorry," Lydia said, opening the door wider. "Please, come in and get warm. *Willkomm*, Aunt Sarah."

Rather astonished at the children's reaction to her, Sarah forced herself to remain composed. One child asked to take her coat; another, her knit scarf; yet another, her gloves. "Thank you," she replied, noticing the girl on the sofa.

"We'd best introduce ourselves so you know who's who," Lydia said, seemingly in charge of the brood. "But first, will you excuse me for just a minute?" She turned toward the kitchen, calling, "Caleb, come now and meet Aunt Sarah. She has just arrived."

Sarah was surprised at the speed with which Lydia's brother responded. Ivy's oldest son was before her in an instant.

"Hullo." He extended his hand. "My name is Caleb."

"Very nice to meet you, Caleb." She shook his hand briefly.

Lydia tapped the top of her sister Anna Mae's head, then Josiah, saying each of their names and ages. Quickly, then, she went to the sofa, glancing over her shoulder as if expecting Sarah and the others to follow. "And this is our little sister, Hannah."

"I thought you'd *never* come," the diminutive girl said, struggling to prop herself on one elbow to have a look at her.

Gazing into the radiant face of this exquisite child, Sarah felt tense, yet transfixed. "I'm here now," she managed to say. Then, "Have you been ill?"

"Hannah fell in the snow . . . had the wind knocked clean out of her," Lydia explained. "She's got a knot on the back of her head." She lifted a bag of ice off Hannah's head. "We were praying for her just as you came." She shot an ardent glance at Caleb. "So I don't think we'll be needin' a doctor . . . 'specially now that Aunt Sarah's here."

Sarah was confused by Lydia's comment

but leaned down to inspect Hannah's head, aware of the thick braids that wound about the little girl's head. Her fingers located the bump. "Does that hurt, dear?"

Hannah winced.

"Can you sit up at all?" Sarah asked.

Hannah strained to do so with Lydia's help. Caleb promptly stuffed a sofa pillow behind his sister. "I think I'm better now, since Lydia prayed," Hannah said. Without skipping a beat, she added, "Mamma always prayed for us, ya know."

Sarah didn't know firsthand, but she *had* read various accounts of Ivy's daily religious routine via the many letters her sister was so fond of writing. It seemed Ivy's spiritual bent had indeed rubbed off on her children.

Lydia suggested that Caleb and Josiah bring Aunt Sarah's suitcases and things into the house. She peered out the window, mighty surprised to see a shiny red sports car parked in their lane. Disguising her gasp by coughing a little, she hoped her aunt wouldn't notice just how surprised she *was*.

Hastily, Caleb and Josiah came huffing and puffing up the snowy walkway to the front porch, pulling a large suitcase on wheels and two squarelike bags. "Guess we shoulda had her park her fancy car 'round back," Josiah whispered, lugging the two smaller suitcases.

"Never mind that now," Lydia said, holding the door open wide.

"I daresay she's brought enough clothes for a year," Caleb said softly with a wistful smile.

Lydia thought differently, remembering the stories her mamma had told 'bout Aunt Sarah's fondness for clothes and shoes. Truth be told, she wondered where her aunt's trunk was or when it might be arrivin'. Or if Aunt Sarah had *other* plans — that she had come only to take them away to Oregon. She took a deep breath and stifled the troubling thought. They would find out soon enough.

She followed the boys as they hoisted the luggage up the steep flight of stairs. "My brothers are mighty strong," she remarked to Aunt Sarah, who'd stepped out to lock her car. "Don't worry 'bout them droppin' your suitcases."

Her aunt only nodded, as if the mindful part of her was hundreds of miles away.

Then Caleb and Josiah came running downstairs, all smiles. Lydia led the way for Aunt Sarah up the steps to Mamma's bedroom. "This is where you'll be most comfortable, I'm thinkin'," she said, standing in the doorway.

Aunt Sarah's face turned nearly pale as the moon as she paused at the entrance to the large room. "Was this Ivy's . . . I mean your *mother's* room?" the slender woman asked softly.

"Mamma and Dat's both, when they were alive."

Her aunt made a little motion with her head that Lydia could not quite grasp, then moved past her, going into the room where just less than an hour ago Lydia had committed the sin of meddling. "I best go and check on Hannah," she said, excusing herself.

Hurrying downstairs, she thought it was just as well that Aunt Sarah was settling into Mamma's old room. It was the respectful thing to do.

Downstairs, she found Hannah propped up with even more pillows as she sat on the sofa. Only now Caleb was telling her a story, and Josiah and Anna Mae listened, too. The children seemed positively engrossed, and Lydia wondered what in the world he was saying.

"A huge billy goat just a-chased me all the way home from school that day," Caleb said, his voice lowered, making it sound ever so eerie.

"What happened after that, when you got

home?" Josiah asked.

"Jah," asked Hannah. "Were ya safe and sound, or did the billy goat come chargin' after ya, right up the porch steps and into the house?"

Caleb chuckled good-naturedly, but Lydia didn't wait for her brother's reply. Glad that the older children were entertaining their suffering little sister, she headed for the kitchen. Mamma had taught her young ones well.

She washed her hands thoroughly before taking the frozen soup out of the freezer. Then she lit the front burner on the old gas stove, humming softly to herself. She could hardly wait to heat up and serve the honest-to-goodness best potato soup Sarah Cain had prob'ly ever tasted. She hoped it might be taken as a thoughtful gesture to lay out a nice hot supper for their aunt, who'd come such an awful long ways.

With all her heart, Lydia hoped the evening would go off without a hitch. At least as well as things had gone thus far, 'cept for one thing that bothered her. Mamma's sister hadn't uttered a single word about stayin' here or takin' the whole bunch to Oregon. Neither one.

Chapter Eleven

Without question, Ivy must have gotten a certain vengeful pleasure out of joining the ranks of the Plain years back. Of this, Sarah was absolutely certain as she placed her portable computer on the wooden chest at the foot of the bed. Skeptically, she surveyed the sparsely furnished room, pacing the plank floor as she did.

The nondescript bed was smaller than any double bed she had ever seen. It stood against barren gray walls, unrelieved by not so much as a single painting, although a picturesque calendar hung near the radiator across from a walnut highboy.

It was a large room, spacious enough for a small brown sofa, a three-drawer dresser, the tall bureau, and a wooden blanket chest at the foot of the bed. The only chair in the entire room was a straight-backed cane. As for a rug, there was a single oval rag rug positioned near the bed, but only on one side. The bed was festooned with an old quilt, whose colors did not coordinate in the least.

Pondering her situation anew, Sarah attempted to freshen up for supper in this poor excuse for a room. In her moment of displeasure, she supposed she ought to offer to assist young Lydia with whatever supper plans the girl had in mind. But the mirror over Ivy's dresser drooped so low on the wall, she had to bend her knees and hunch down to see the sum total of her head. She brushed her hair, peering forward and noting that the mirror was chipped on one side.

No wonder Ivy had had such trouble in life, she thought, staring at the crack.

Yet, there was no arguing one fact: Her sister had raised some remarkable kids. Courteous, even thoughtful. But she wouldn't let their good manners influence her. Sarah envisioned the plan she had conceived in her mind, and with less than a week to go, she didn't have any time to waste.

"Pass the crackers and cheese," Caleb said after the silent suppertime prayer.

Please, thought Sarah, who made the interesting observation that Ivy's children were far less polite at the table. Not a single "please" or "thank-you" was sprinkled into the conversation at any juncture. She thought this quite odd as she dipped her spoon into the plastic soup bowl.

"This soup's from scratch," Lydia offered, glancing up, her lovely eyes gleaming. "Hope you like it."

Scratch . . .

"Oh yes," Sarah replied. "Thank you, it's delicious."

Caleb and Josiah, across the table, were busy crushing a wad of crackers into their bowls, sprinkling crumbs about.

Lydia must've caught her staring. "My brothers take after our father, I'm afraid."

"Dat liked a little soup with his crackers," Josiah explained.

The boy's comment brought sidesplitting laughter from Hannah, who, now that Sarah looked at her, appeared to be completely recovered from her head bump.

Hesitant to interject, she wished the children would eat more quietly — *all* of them — including Lydia. The smacking of lips and even occasional belching was nearly more than she could endure. But being a guest in this house, and this the first night of such venture, no less, made her reluctant to speak up. There *was*, however, something she was determined to discuss over the rather insubstantial meal, but it might be better if she postponed the topic until dessert.

"Preacher Esh said he might be droppin'

in on us sometime this week," Caleb spoke up.

"Is that right?" replied Lydia, looking somewhat surprised.

"He's worried, prob'ly," Josiah added.

"About *us?*" asked Lydia.

Anna Mae was nodding her head up and down, as if she might not stop unless asked to. Then she said, "Susie Lapp's just as fretful, I'm thinkin'."

Susie Lapp . . .

Sarah's ears perked up. She clearly recognized the name of Ivy's close friend.

"Now, why on earth wouldja say such a thing — that Susie's frettin' over us?" Caleb said, making strange twitching movements with his eyes.

Lydia intervened, and not too soon, it seemed. "Well, nobody need be worryin' any longer." Her voice was confident and strong as Ivy's ever was. "Look here who's sittin' at our table tonight." Lydia didn't wait for the younger children to acknowledge what she meant. She continued. "Seems to me we've got right here exactly what Mamma was wantin' for us."

"Are ya sayin' if Preacher Esh stops by, we'll just hafta set his mind at ease?" Josiah asked, trying to avoid Sarah's gaze.

"You heard me right," Lydia answered.

"Everything's just fine now. Aunt Sarah is here. And besides, Susie's most likely comin' to sort through Mamma's clothes and things."

"Ain't that Aunt Sarah's job?" Hannah asked, eyes bright.

"Jah, but I'm sure she could use some help," Lydia replied, glancing at Sarah, then lowering her eyes to look down at her soup bowl.

Sighing inconspicuously, Sarah thought now was as good a time as any to express herself. "Children . . . I would like to say something, if I may."

As if connected — in unison — all five heads turned to focus on her.

"I realize this is not the most ideal situation," she began. "It must be quite puzzling to you why your mother should have wanted me, a non-Amish woman, for your guardian."

Anna Mae was the only child whose head was bobbing in affirmation. The others wore the most serious facial expressions, as if they questioned their deceased mother's judgment.

The silence was as thick as black strap molasses.

Lydia was first to speak. "Whatever Mamma chose is the best thing for us. We know that."

Little Hannah joined Anna Mae in nodding her head, brown eyes trusting and wide. "But we hope 'n pray that we won't hafta leave here and go way out to Oregon to live."

"Hannah, please . . . not now," Lydia scolded. "That's Aunt Sarah's choice to make for us."

Sarah regarded the children's responses, the hopeful expressions on each face. It occurred to her that they had no idea she had not come to stay permanently. Tonight wasn't the time to reveal her plan. "One of you mentioned that Mrs. Lapp might visit this week," she said. "Tell me more about that."

"Jah, Susie *said* she would come sort through Mamma's clothes," Anna Mae insisted, looking wholly sincere. So much so that Sarah felt a twinge of regret for having disregarded Lydia.

But before Sarah could backtrack, Caleb defended his sister. "If Susie Lapp says she's coming, you can count on her showin' up."

Sarah saw her opportunity again. "And what day might that be?"

"Prob'ly Tuesday or Wednesday," Lydia said.

"Where does she live?" Sarah asked.

"Not far from here, over on Rohrer's Mill Road."

"I'd like to see her as soon as possible. If

139

you could give her a call, Lydia, ask if it would suit for me to visit her tomorrow."

"Tomorrow?" Lydia looked fairly bewildered.

"If it's convenient."

"It won't suit Monday. I'm sure of it."

"Why is that?"

"Susie's busy with washing and ironing just like all the rest of us. Mondays aren't a gut visitin' day 'round here."

"I see." Sarah wouldn't query further. On either Tuesday or Wednesday, she would definitely be on hand to explore her idea with the illustrious Mrs. Lapp.

"Susie Lapp is known to have a biting tongue sometimes," Caleb said, his eyes earnest.

"But she's awful nice, too," little Hannah put in.

"None of us are perfect," Lydia offered. "The main thing is, Susie was Mamma's dearest friend."

The words jabbed her soul. "I've heard many good things about the woman."

Caleb frowned. "How's that?"

She breathed deeply, attempting to remain calm. "Your mother mentioned Mrs. Lapp often in her letters."

"Then you prob'ly know that Susie is the grandmother of *my* best friend," Lydia said.

"Maybe Fannie Flaud will come along, too, when Susie visits. That would be awful nice."

Ivy had never made mention of Fannie Flaud in her letters. Sarah only knew that Susie Lapp had numerous children and grandchildren. Ivy had never given specific information about the woman who had been her confidante through the years.

"I'll look forward to meeting both Susie *and* Fannie," Sarah said. In all actuality, she thought it might be ideal that she make their acquaintance sooner rather than later.

Lydia hurried to the refrigerator and took out two desserts — a large bowl of soda cracker pudding and a coconut custard pie. Cutting the pie into equal parts, she considered the peculiar way Aunt Sarah had of stating things. 'Specially the way she said *your mother* this and *your mother* that. Why didn't she just come right out and say "my sister"? It made for a taut feeling in Lydia's stomach.

Mamma would've wanted her to keep her peace and not cause strife amongst family members. Sarah Cain certainly was family. No gettin' around it. The tall woman was every whit Mamma's sister. Lydia could see it in the way Sarah's eyebrows sometimes arched unexpectedly, the way she had first

141

walked into the house — how she'd held herself upright, like she had not a speck of worry 'bout coming into a strange household, meetin' relatives she'd never laid eyes on before. Little things like that brought Mamma's image flyin' right back.

The lump in her throat seemed to block the air, but Lydia carried the dessert dishes to the table without speaking, setting them down nearest her aunt's plate. How on earth could she suffer through the rest of her *Maedel* days with this constant living reminder of dear, dear Mamma before her?

All she could think of was the next chance she might be alone in her room, pouring out her thoughts onto her journal pages. Later tonight she would do just that, for she feared if she did not somehow release the mounting pressure inside, she might say or do something she would long regret.

As a child, Sarah had learned through one life experience after another that she was not an adaptable person. *"Why do you get so upset over the slightest change in plans?"* Ivy would often sneer when Sarah was young.

Once again, she was merely tolerating an unwelcome alteration in her life. Seven days was positively all she could manage — the limit to which her disposition could endure,

142

considering the peculiar situation.

Standing at the bureau that had once been Ivy's, Sarah looked over every inch of the room again, completely amazed that anyone could live this way. There was nothing lovely here. Nothing of consequence about the arrangement of furniture or the choice thereof. As far as she was concerned, the room was hardly an extension of someone's personality. For she knew — *had known* — Ivy to be an outgoing person, even fun-loving. How was any of that reflected in her selection of woods or bed coverings? And those hideous green shades — where had Ivy found such things?

Uneasy about sleeping here at all, Sarah entertained the notion of slipping out of the house, escaping to a more refined environment during the night.

"Everything's just fine now. Aunt Sarah is here. . . ."

Lydia's comment at supper still rang in her memory. Why the girl was so resolute, she did not know. Though Lydia was the very likeness of her mother, she possessed nothing of Ivy's temperament. Strangely enough, in many ways, Ivy's eldest reminded Sarah of herself. Painfully so.

Delaying the inevitable moment when she must slip into Ivy's bed, pull the handmade spread over her own body, and force herself to drift off to sleep in this drafty old farmhouse of her sister's choosing, she intentionally turned away from the bed, toward one of four unadorned dormer windows, and peered out.

The half-moon was a white cradle in the sky, shimmering against a black-ink firmament. Silvery stars scattered out across the vastness of space, winking earnestly down at her.

It was then she remembered the way the sky had *felt* dusky — weighty, in space and time — the horrendous moments following the disaster at Stonington Elementary. She recalled with surprise that she had actually looked up at the eerie gray expanse of space, when she might better have hung her head and stared down at the snow-buried earth.

Unable to ponder sleep just now, Sarah trudged back to the small chair near the bed and sat stiffly until she felt her bones push hard against the cane. Then, turning out the light, she headed back to stand in the window, delighting in the darkness.

Sunday night, January 23

On nights like this, I can't help but think about Grandpa Cain, wishing he and I could go walking together along the beach. Like when I was a little girl. I'd like to know what he would say about things. Would he have agreed with Mamma — entrusting us children to the care of an unbeliever? Really makes me wonder how Aunt Sarah turned out the way she did, having such a thoughtful, loving father like Grandpa was. Seems to me a lot of him somehow got missed getting passed along to her.

I need to be talking things over with Fannie. If it wasn't for her and the rest of the People, I s'pose I'd be floundering like some fish struggling to live on the Rhode Island shoreline.

I can't help thinking that Aunt Sarah seemed to perk up her ears, maybe too much, over Susie Lapp stopping in sometime this week. She can't pull the wool over my eyes. I'm perty sure she has something up her sleeve about that.

Lord, please lead me beside your still waters . . . calm my troubled soul.

Chapter Twelve

Sarah stood at the side of Ivy's pitiful bed, staring down. Mentally, she compared it to her own magnificent bedstead, nearly three thousand miles away. A startling thought seized her: On which side of the bed had her sister breathed her last? She had no way of knowing and wouldn't inquire of Lydia. Her niece — *all* the children — were struggling with their great loss, she knew.

She would literally grit her teeth and hope the bed linens were indeed fresh.

As a youngster, she was often glad she had never had to share a room with her teenage sister. Ivy's idea of orderliness was a far cry from her own.

There had been one occasion, when the house seemed to overflow with company, that their mother had planned for the two of them to sleep in the same bed in Ivy's room . . .

"Do we *have* to?" Ivy whined.

"I don't have cooties," Sarah had spoken up.

"I'll draw a line down the middle, and you

better not cross it — not even with your bony knees," Ivy insisted *after* Mother left the room to entertain the visitors. "I hate this as much as you do."

"Couldn't possibly," Sarah retaliated. She felt quite rejected. "Am I such a horrid little sister?"

"When it comes to certain things, you are."

Unwilling to hear a recital of her faults, she did not risk the question. "So . . . I'm not perfect, and we both know it. Let's drop it there."

"Being blunt doesn't become you, Sarah Cain."

She recoiled at the sound of her own name. "I hate the way you say that."

"I hate the way you *look* at me!"

Sarah fought back tears. "Why can't you be more like . . . like —"

"Like who?"

"Never mind." She bit her tongue. Their peace-loving father would be altogether displeased if he had any notion what she was thinking — bringing him into their spat.

"I'm telling Mother," Ivy said. "She'll have to make a pallet for you on the floor, because you're not getting anywhere *near* my bed."

Sarah glared at the bed with built-in bookshelf at the head. Sleeping all night long in the same space with Ivy was the last thing *she* wanted, too!

Poking her head into the hallway, she checked to see that her sister was out of sight. Then she went to the bed and knelt down as if to pray but clenched her tiny fists and pounded the spread. "Please, God, can't you make Ivy nicer to me?"

No more fighting over territorial matters. Ivy was dead. And, surprisingly, she had handed her own flesh and blood over to Sarah, for goodness' sake! No lines drawn in the sand here. All decision-making had been delegated to Ivy's "horrid little sister." And to think, now Sarah would have preferred otherwise.

She sat on the bed, testing its firmness. Perhaps God had answered her prayer, after all, making Ivy *nicer*. What lyricist wrote, "Only the good die young"?

A ridiculous commentary, she decided. Yet the memory of Ivy's numerous letters — penned in rather amiable tones on occasion — came back to taunt her. Something *had* changed Ivy's perspective on life. Something . . . Yet Sarah knew not what it could have been.

The patter of feet on stairs awakened

Sarah. She sat up in bed, disoriented for a moment, squinting at the murky room. Glancing at her clock radio, Sarah saw that it was only four-thirty. The middle of the night.

What was happening in the house this early?

She donned her robe, then opened the door leading to the hallway, cocked her head, and listened. More whispering and scurrying, followed by a rumbling sound.

Unmistakably, the sound of an old washing machine drumbeat its way up the stairs to her ears. Recalling that the day was Monday, she wondered why neither Lydia nor Anna Mae had mentioned anything to her last night prior to their interminable evening prayers, through which she had suffered, remaining seated on the sofa while the children knelt.

The clunking and thumping continued, and she wished now that she had allowed herself more time to wind down last evening, gone to sleep sooner. Due to frustration and her overactive mind, she'd had little more than four hours' rest, if that.

"I'm sorry, Aunt Sarah. We forgot to tell you we wash our clothes and hang them out *every* Monday morning long before dawn," Lydia informed her when Sarah had located the origin of the laundry noise and activity — in the dank cellar. "It's our way."

Lydia, who seemed overly zealous about explaining, went on to say that after the clothes were hung out to dry, they still had many chores to do in the barn, "and we milk three cows twice a day." The girl stopped to catch her breath. "Prob'ly doesn't sound like much work to you, but we do it all by hand. Saves on machinery expense, and Dat always said it was gut for his children to keep their hands and minds busy."

"Why must you get up so early to do laundry?" she asked, regarding her energetic niece through a haze of fatigue.

Anna Mae flashed her green eyes. "It would never do for us to wait till the sun comes up to hang the clothes on the line."

Sarah nodded, wondering. Since the family had indulged themselves with electricity, unlike other Plain sects, why in the world didn't they own a clothes dryer? She attempted to remain tactful, however, and did not probe the reasoning behind whatever mandate this action represented. "Well, since I'm up, I might as well help."

"Many hands make light work," Lydia said softly, handing her a large homespun bag of clothespins. "Just make sure you hang similar things together on the line."

Elisha D. Smith Public
Library
440 First Street
920-967-3680

Item ID: 0030302380115
Title: The redemption of
Sarah Cain
Author: Lewis, Beverly,
1949-
Date due: 10/8/2018,23:59

Item ID: 0030302816498
Title: 4th of July : a novel
Author: Patterson, James,
1947-
Date due: 10/8/2018,23:59

Item ID: 0030303537861
Title: Loitering with intent
Author: Woods, Stuart.
Date due: 10/8/2018,23:59

Item ID: 0030300717045
Title: The last ranger
Author: Grey, Zane, 1872-
1939.
Date due: 10/8/2018,23:59

Check us out on the web:
www.MenashaLibrary.org

The girl motioned for Anna Mae to demonstrate. "It's much more orderly to hang all the boys' trousers in a row, and all the girls' aprons, and so on."

Sarah was dumbfounded. "You're required to do this a specific way?"

"Ach, no! Nobody says we *have* to." Lydia tossed the damp laundry into a heavy-duty wicker basket. "It's just the way the People have been doin' it for over three hundred years."

"Does anyone ever think to change . . . or do things differently?" she ventured.

Anna Mae piped up, "The folks who do usually end up leavin' the community." The younger girl pursed her lips as if sorry she'd spoken at all.

"Old Order Amish shun those who're itchin' to change too much," Lydia explained on the way outside.

Sarah had only heard of shunning by way of Ivy's letters. Her sister hadn't explained much regarding the practice, but Sarah did remember — a couple of years back — that Ivy had mentioned several folks who were "under the ban" in another area of Lancaster County, as she recalled.

More than anything, Lydia wanted to tell Aunt Sarah the story of the old Amishman

151

who lived in the woods. But now wasn't the time. There was much work to do, 'specially out here in the cold with her fingers turnin' ever so numb. She wished she'd thought to wear Mamma's old fur-lined gloves. Even though there was a rip between the thumb and pointer finger, they'd be much better than this bone-chilling cold.

She looked over her shoulder, shocked, really, to see Aunt Sarah workin' alongside Anne Mae in the sub-zero-degree weather. Seemed to her their fancy Oregon relative would've wanted to stay indoors and keep warm.

"You really don't have to stay and help," she said again, feeling a little sorry for Aunt Sarah, who prob'ly wasn't used to workin' outside much. "Anna Mae and I do this every Monday mornin' — cold or not. I'm sure we could almost do it blindfolded."

"Jah, that's the truth," Anna Mae shot back.

"Well, if you don't mind, I'll skip the blindfold," Sarah added.

Lydia was downright befuddled by this unexpected glimpse of humor but said nothing. Her mother's sister was a hard one to figure.

When will I meet Susie Lapp? Sarah wondered while Lydia and the other children milked the cows, doing whatever they did in that big barn. The sooner the better, she decided, determined to make a connection with a possible replacement for her services as guardian.

She ran her bath water upstairs, sprinkling soothing salts into the rather small tub, telling herself she could put up with such inconveniences for a mere week. This being the only upstairs bathroom in the farmhouse, she was grateful that her sister and brother-in-law had purchased a home with *indoor* plumbing. It was one positive note in the otherwise primitive surroundings.

Her bath was warm and pleasant, and the sweet fragrance of her own soap, which she had brought from home, offered a few moments of luxury.

What inexplicable circumstances had brought her to this place? She cared not to relive the initial phone call from Lydia, the summons that had kicked off this extraordinary chain of events, nor her procrastination that followed.

While brushing her damp hair later, Sarah enjoyed the feel of her thick and sumptuous terry cloth robe as never before. She plugged in her hair dryer and longed for the rest of the modern conveniences back home.

Her cell phone rang, and she saw that it was Bryan Ford. *He's up early,* she thought, smiling as she clicked the Talk button. "You must have meetings this morning," she said into the small mouthpiece.

"Well, hello to you, too," he mocked. "I thought I'd try to catch you before you rushed out to milk the cows."

She chuckled, actually glad to hear his voice. "The cows are being milked today without my assistance."

"I understand."

"I doubt it."

"So . . . how's life in Amish country?"

She wouldn't go there, wouldn't give him the blow-by-blow he was probably eager to hear. "You're into computers, not journalism. Shall we keep it that way?"

"Okay, I'll rephrase. How are *you* holding up, Sarah?"

"I'm fine."

"And I'm Mahatma Gandhi."

She sighed. "There's running water in the house and electricity. What else do you want to know?"

"How're you handling . . . everything?"

What he really wanted to know was how she was dealing with the children. She knew him too well. "My nieces and nephews are

154

busy little bees. You'd like them, Bryan. They're model children, straight out of the nineteenth century — no piercings or tattoos, no serious attitude problems, either." Then she recalled Anna Mae's momentary outburst, mild as it was. "Well, there may be *one* child who needs a shrink."

"Tell me more."

"Another time." She heard commotion below. "I think I'd better get downstairs and help with breakfast."

"When can I see you again?"

"Must you always ask?"

He laughed, obviously misunderstanding her comment. "So I can just show up . . . don't need to make a date of it?"

"You know better than that."

"I have an idea," he said, his voice growing softer. "Why don't *you* call *me* when you want to chat?"

"Deal."

"Have fun on the farm."

"Right." She couldn't help herself. She grinned at the cell phone, switching it off with a flair.

Chapter Thirteen

Fretting over the lateness of the hour, Lydia tried to get Josiah to stop dawdling over his hot cocoa. Hannah was out in the utility room fussin' about not being able to find her snow boots. Caleb had disappeared upstairs again for the third time — for something he said he needed for school. Anna Mae was the only calm sibling, sitting near the back door, arms crossed over her chest, like she was awful close to surrenderin' her patience.

"Ach, it's just never like this, of a mornin'." Lydia glanced at Aunt Sarah, who was busying herself with washing dishes.

"With so many children to get ready, I'd expect it would be this way *every* morning."

Lydia forced a smile. "They're goin' to be late if they don't hurry, that's for sure."

Aunt Sarah stopped what she was doing, turned, and dried her hands on the towel hanging over the counter. "How can I help expedite things?"

Expedite?

Lydia made sure she didn't laugh at this peculiar English word. But she knew if her brothers and sisters didn't leave in the next minute or two, they most certainly would be tardy. And tardiness was not tolerated at Amish schools. Lydia herself knew better than to foster or excuse any such slowpoke behavior in her siblings. Especially if she was to help oversee the household till Aunt Sarah caught on to what was needed.

Truth was, if you were consistently late to school, you might also fall into the bad habit of bein' tardy for most anything in life. Bishop Joseph and the elders knew it to be true. And often Preacher Esh's sermons tolled the folly of such neglectful deportment.

So it behooved them to heed the Scriptural warnings. Besides that, Dat used to quote Benjamin Franklin while sweeping out the barn or pitchin' hay to the horses: " *'He that riseth late must trot all day, and shall scarce overtake his business at night.'* "

Lydia knew the passage well, for she often took great pleasure in memorizing most everything her father said by way of special phrases and recitations. 'Specially from the time she finished up the eighth grade and began to stay at home with Mamma, helpin' clean, cook, sew and mend, and raise a vegetable garden, among other things.

"How can I help you get the children off

to school?" Aunt Sarah said again.

"You could see if Caleb's comin' down. Just call up the steps to him, why don'tcha? I'll put a bee in Hannah's bonnet and rouse Josiah away from the table." She was surprised to see Aunt Sarah drop the towel and scurry off to the bottom of the stairs.

"Look, Lyddie. My boots were right where I left 'em," little Hannah was sayin'.

"I'm not surprised at that." She pulled Hannah's warmest coat and scarf off the wooden pegs and handed them to her. *"Kumm mit!"* she called.

And the children came. Anna Mae led the way out the door, but not before the younger girl hugged Lydia good-bye. "Maybe Aunt Sarah will help ya bring in the clean wash later."

"Don't you worry none."

Anna Mae's eyes twinkled. "Aunt Sarah could use another lesson on hanging out the clothes, jah?"

Lydia shooed her off, grinning as she did.

Hannah asked her to feel if the bump was "all gone." Lydia found the spot on her little sister's head. "Ach, it's so much better. Now go!"

Soon all the children had hugged her and marched off into the white wonderland outside.

"Do they ever cancel school for snow?" Aunt Sarah asked, peering out the window with Lydia.

"Not that I remember. We don't miss school for nasty weather. You just watch. Somebody'll come along with a horse and sleigh an' pick up my brothers and sisters and take them off to school. That's perty much the way it goes 'round Grasshopper Level."

Aunt Sarah said nothing in reply.

Lydia would've liked to know what her aunt was thinking. Just now, she would've given her far more than a penny for her thoughts.

Arms loaded down with freshly ironed Sunday shirts and trousers for the boys, dresses and aprons for the girls, Lydia went depositin' the clothes in the correct bedrooms upstairs.

"Looks to me like you could use a breather," Aunt Sarah said when Lydia came back downstairs. She was sitting in the kitchen, near the window, sipping her third cup of coffee.

"Mamma always said, '*A man works from sun to sun, a woman's work is never done.*' It's just the way things are." She lifted her shoulders, spreading her hands. "The men work outside this time of year, removin' the big stones out in the fields, and they go off to farm auctions and whatnot all, too. The women have the responsibility of the indoor chores — cooking, cleaning, washing clothes, and mending *all* year long — but just now it's the season for quiltin'."

Aunt Sarah's eyes opened wide. "You mean you don't quilt the entire year?"

"In the winter the farm families quilt, while the soil is restin', ya know, waiting to be worked over, plowed, and planted again. Some of our womenfolk do run quiltin' businesses in Strasburg or other places, so they must sew off and on all year."

"I see."

"More and more, though, the women are going out and settin' up craft stores and whatnot. Some rent or lease a small space along the streets of Intercourse or Bird-in-Hand. Other folks just set up shop in a shed behind their houses." She would've liked to, but she dared not sit down and sip tea or cocoa with Aunt Sarah. If she did she might not get up and get goin' again. And there was work to be done.

Aunt Sarah seemed a bit restless this morning. Not that she hadn't seemed fidgety last evening, too. But there was something unsettled about her, and Lydia thought she

160

might know what it was.

"Are you thinkin' of finding a home for us?" she said, biting her lip once she'd asked.

Sarah's eyelids fluttered suddenly, and she looked downright disappointed, like Lydia might've guessed her secret. When she spoke, her words were guarded, and Lydia saw a mirrored reaction of her own mamma yet again.

"I wouldn't lie to you. So, yes, finding a good Amish family to take you in is the best choice I can make on your behalf, Lydia — yours and your siblings."

She hadn't heard her given name said like *that* for a long, long time. She was Lyddie, through and through. Not since before Dat died had someone called her *Lydia*. But she felt comforted by Aunt Sarah's respectful approach, and she listened.

"I do believe your mother felt she could rely on me to make family decisions for all of you," the fancy woman said.

Lydia tried not to frown, but she felt her muscles tensing up. "What if you can't do that — find a home for us, I mean? Will you take us back with you to Oregon?"

"We'll have to cross that bridge when we come to it. Your mother wanted her children raised Plain, I'm fairly certain. She didn't have to spell things out for me to know that.

I'm only here to help expedite her last wishes."

Lydia flinched. *Expedite* — there was that word again! She was beginning to think that Aunt Sarah was here on a business transaction. She saw no compassion in her aunt's eyes, not even during this morning's Bible reading and prayers when Hannah shined up to her English auntie, sliding over next to Sarah on the sofa. No, there wasn't a speck of tenderness in those eyes. Not in her English heart, neither.

"I'm going to Lancaster to meet with Mr. Eberley, your mother's attorney, this afternoon. On the way back from town, I hope to do some shopping at one of the outlet malls."

Lydia said nothing.

"Are *you* allowed to shop, uh, outside the Amish community?" Aunt Sarah asked unexpectedly.

"I may shop wherever I choose."

"Well, then, how would you like to ride along with me?"

Lydia shook her head. "I really can't think of one thing I need just now."

"You could get out of the house for a few hours," Aunt Sarah persisted.

Lydia wondered if her aunt just assumed she was house-bound most of the time. "Oh, I get out plenty."

Aunt Sarah was thumbing through the *Official Map and Visitors' Guide of Lancaster County and Pennsylvania Dutch Country*, not payin' much mind to what Lydia had said. "What do you know about Rockvale Square Outlets?" she asked.

"I've heard there are over a hundred and twenty stores. Are you lookin' for something special?"

"I just thought it might be fun to do some shopping. I *love* outlet shops." Sarah's eyes were shining just now. "I can't come all this way and not cash in on some brand-name bargains."

"Jah, and I s'pose if I weren't Plain, I might go hog wild in a place like Rockvale Square," she replied.

Her mamma's sister opened the map in the center of the visitors' guide, studying it further. "How far is it to the intersection of Routes 30 and 896?"

"Well, I have to say that we don't normally take our team that far north of Strasburg. Reason bein' it gets awful busy with cars on most of the main roads. Isn't safe anymore, really."

"By 'team,' do you mean your horse and buggy?"

"That's right."

Sarah's eyes seemed to bore a hole through

Lydia. "I don't mean to sound rude, but are you even allowed to ride in a car?"

"We can ride, just can't own." The words jumped off her tongue. She'd heard the expression many times growin' up.

"Are you sure you won't come with me?" Aunt Sarah asked, almost as if she hoped to purchase a new wardrobe for Lydia. A kind of make-over.

"That's all right, really. I have more bread to make and cleaning to do, but you go and have yourself a gut time."

For Lydia, makin' so many choices at a store for Englischers would make her head all but spin anyways. For sure and for certain. Besides, she was ever so grateful to have some time to herself, gettin' caught up on chores and whatnot.

"*Watch closely the hermit crab*," Grandpa Cain's words whispered in her memory. "*See how little he gets by with?*"

Truth be told, she was mighty glad Aunt Sarah was goin' away for the afternoon.

Chapter Fourteen

"Thank you for coming, Ms. Cain." Charles Eberley motioned for her to sit across from his wide desk.

She noted the many framed documents heralding Mr. Eberley a state-certified attorney. Along with certificates there were family portraits as well, smiling and rather plain-looking children and grandchildren.

Opening the Estate Document Portfolio, the attorney thumbed through several papers. "As I relayed to you during our last phone conversation, your sister has selected you for the guardianship of her minor children."

Sarah nodded.

"First, allow me to read Ivy's will to you, as required by the state of Pennsylvania." Eberley pushed his reading glasses up toward the bridge of his nose and began. " 'I, Ivy Cain Cottrell of Lancaster County, Pennsylvania, mindful of the brevity of this life, having placed my faith and hope in Jesus Christ, my Savior and Lord, who redeemed my soul through His shed blood and death upon Calvary's Cross for my sins and who thus promises me Eternal Life, do make, publish, and declare this to be my Last Will and Testament, hereby revoking any and all other Wills and Codicils by me at any time heretofore made. . . .' "

After the attorney finished reading Ivy's will, he set the papers down and removed his reading glasses. "Before we proceed, do you have any questions, Ms. Cain?"

Sarah shifted in the chair, crossing her legs at the ankles. She had one question. "How do we legally transfer my guardianship to someone in the Amish community?"

Charles Eberley sighed. "If you must, I can handle the arrangements. Once you've become legal guardian, we'll have to petition the court, but I don't foresee any problems."

That was good news for Sarah. She signed the necessary documents, and they rose to shake hands.

"I understand the awkwardness of this situation, Ms. Cain. Surely anyone would have expected Mrs. Cottrell to select an Amish family to care for her children. But there must be a very good reason behind Ivy's decision."

"That remains to be seen, Mr. Eberley." She turned toward the door, then remembered her manners. "Thank you for your time."

"Very well," he replied.

The nip in the air refreshed her as she crossed the parking lot to her rental car. Now on to her shopping spree.

What's keepin' Aunt Sarah?

Lydia glanced at the day clock high on the kitchen wall. Her aunt had left for Lancaster hours ago. Here it was comin' up on time for the children to return home from school, and still their aunt had not made it back.

Deciding not to fret but to make wise use of her time, 'specially with all her chores done, Lydia wrote in her journal.

Monday, January 24

I think Aunt Sarah must surely be caught in the grip of the world and its pleasures. When she began talking about her shopping trip, this became clear to me. Well, her eyes lit up near like Wal-Mart come nighttime. I've never seen someone so eager to accumulate things as Mamma's sister is.

Her life — even the clothes she wears — seems so complicated. And all that jewelry and makeup. Why, it must take her hours to dress of a morning. Does she ever think to

167

wonder that she's missing out on a whole lot of peace, running to and fro? Could it be she ever yearns for a simple life the way Mamma and Dat did before moving here to Lancaster?

How on earth could two sisters be so awful different? It wonders me. . . .

Closing the diary, Lydia slipped out of her bedroom and hurried to the room Aunt Sarah had claimed as her own, for the time being. Once inside her mother's former bedroom, she made a beeline for the walnut highboy. Knowin' now what she thought she knew 'bout Sarah Cain, she decided the sin she'd committed yesterday was somewhat justifiable.

She wasted no time diggin' through the wide drawer at the very bottom of the dresser. Scooping up some letters and several journals, she repeated the action till the drawer was completely empty, including Mamma's cherished box of seashells.

Back in her bedroom, she ordered the letters according to postmark dates and made room for them in the pine chest at the foot of her own bed. Dat had made the hope chest for her thirteenth birthday, and it was full of dozens of handmade things — crocheted doilies and pillow slips. Beautiful things she had made over the years with Mamma's help. One day, these perty things would grace her own home. Her and Levi's home — together — Lord willing.

But she dared not think of Levi just now. He might question her deed if he was privy to it. For now, though, her secret was safe. Truly, she hoped God would forgive her in spite of her willfulness.

Closing the heavy lid on the pine chest, she sighed momentarily, then scurried back downstairs. With the letters from Aunt Sarah hidden, along with Mamma's journals, she could take her time reading through the whole lot of them, late at night when no one was up to disturb her or discover what she had done.

And Aunt Sarah would be none the wiser.

The drive back to Grasshopper Level from the Rockvale Square Outlets encompassed snowscapes Sarah did not recall having seen yesterday upon first arriving in Lancaster County. Random drifts of snow bunched up the landscape, and ice clung to trees and barn roofs. A covey of crows flew en masse over a nearby silo, heading west. The panorama offered her a respite from the bustling atmosphere of discount shopping.

Reaching for the CDs she had taken time

to pack, she chose the Chopin waltzes, eager for a reminder of home. Yet as she drove over freshly plowed Route 896, she noticed the Amish village, Ed's Buggy Rides, and a classy-looking craft shop — Country Creations — where Plain folk, no doubt, capitalized on their homespun lifestyle.

Perhaps it was the confusion caused by snow-shrouded route signs as she arrived in the village of Strasburg, but somehow she got off track and made a wrong turn. More than likely, it was the fact that she was still preoccupied with the lengthy paragraph at the beginning of Ivy's last will and testament — a declaration of faith, or so it seemed — that caused Sarah to lose her way.

Having placed my faith and hope in Jesus Christ, my Savior and Lord . . .

She found herself on the outskirts of town, heading south on Esbenshade Road. The countryside was curiously dotted with occasional multisided birdhouses, which protruded out of the frozen ground, thrust high into a pristine sky.

As she drove in the general direction of Grasshopper Level, she passed one farmhouse after another, most with two or three additions built onto one side. *Amish dwellings,* she thought, recalling several letters Ivy had written over the years with reference to the *Grossdawdi Haus* — Grandfather House — concept. She was well aware that such extensions to a dwelling meant several generations of families resided there.

Just ahead, off to the right, a one-room schoolhouse came into view, its white picket fence providing a stark, yet protective barrier against the world. A dozen or more snow sleds were lined up in a row alongside the school.

Checking her watch, she was surprised that it was already nearly three o'clock. Schoolchildren would soon come pouring out the door, was her guess — by the presence of so many waiting carriages.

Slowing the rental car, she pulled off the road and onto the shoulder and braked, staring in wonderment.

In a moment, children came by twos and threes, Plain students emerging from the tiny school. She was a magnet to the scene. Was this the school her nieces and nephews attended? And if so, would she be able to spot them amidst the crowd of Amish youngsters? Old and young children alike — girls in long dark dresses and woolen capes, black candle-snuffer bonnets, and black high-topped shoes or boots; boys wearing black felt hats and what looked like heavy winter coats over wide-legged black pants and snow boots — swarmed out of the building, all smiles.

She flinched in the comfort of her car. The sight was unbearable, and not because the scene was so wonderfully quaint. No. She was unnerved by this glimpse of so many merry children.

Megan Holmes, darling girl, was no more. Gone forever. Her little body buried in a Connecticut cemetery plot. Sarah's young student could no longer laugh and sing or do any of the things the girl had once loved.

Sarah simply could not bear to watch these Plain children, carefree and seemingly happy. What sort of teacher instructed them daily? Was she kind and patient, always vigilant for possible danger? Was she eager to succeed as a teacher, preoccupied with her achievement?

Leaning her arms across the top of the steering wheel, Sarah buried her face in the folds of her jacket. "Oh, Meggie . . . Meggie, how can I ever forgive myself?" she whispered.

Time stood still, at least for a few moments, before she gathered her wits and dried her eyes. Sitting up, she flicked on the car blinker and pulled away from the edge of the road. How very different, surreal most things were here. Even the color of the sky over Strasburg was a distinct cerulean.

But young children — her nieces and nephews included — had similar needs, no matter where they lived or attended school. She had gleaned this from college studies and the numerous in-service classes taken as a teacher, as well as the few years of actual teaching. Every child required, even craved, love and security in order to thrive.

Hard as she tried, Sarah could not dispel the vision of joyful young students issuing forth from the little white-washed school building.

Chapter Fifteen

"Fannie, it's awful nice to see you!" Lydia hugged her slender brunette friend, then set about taking Fannie's coat, scarf, and mittens and hanging them up back in the utility room. "You must be freezin'-cold. Here, let me make you some hot cocoa."

Fannie Flaud rubbed her hands together, standing near the stove where a large pot of stew was simmering. She laughed at herself, looking down at the black pot. "I daresay, I forget you don't have a woodstove like my Mamma Susie does in her kitchen."

Lydia hugged her dear friend again. "I'll get you warmed up in no time." And she scurried about, fixing a mug of hot chocolate.

"Aw, don't go to any bother," Fannie insisted, blowing her breath into her hands.

"It's no trouble." She stirred the cocoa thoroughly before giving the mug to Fannie. "I'm so glad you stopped by, 'specially *this* day." Glancing outside, she checked to see if Aunt Sarah was back yet.

"What do ya mean?"

"You prob'ly heard by now that our English relative is stayin' here under our roof."

"Jah, we heard." Fannie's hazel eyes squinted a little, like she might be sensing the quandary Lydia was in.

"Aunt Sarah's nice enough, don't get me wrong."

"Will she be takin' you and your brothers and sisters away from the People?"

Lydia couldn't help but notice the worry lines on her friend's face. "Things are up in the air just now. That's all I best say." She didn't tell Fannie that Aunt Sarah was caught up with worldly things, shoppin' and spending her money on clothes and suchlike. 'Twasn't her place to condemn, though she thought it *en Sin un e Schand* — a sin and a shame. Sighing, she bowed her head.

"You can tell *me* what you're afraid of, Lyddie." Setting the hot cocoa on the table, Fannie rose and came over, reaching out to take Lydia's hands in both of hers. "Whatever I can do, I'll do it."

"You're a gut friend, but I wouldn't want you to be worryin' over us, truly not."

" 'Two heads are better'n one,' Mamma always says." Fannie put her forehead to Lydia's.

"Your mamma and mine, both." She was moved by her friend's compassion and concern, and the two girls went and sat on the wooden bench. She filled Fannie in on what Aunt Sarah had said earlier today — 'bout hoping to find a family to take them in.

"But, Lyddie, *I* thought —"

"Jah, I know . . . I did, too," Lydia interjected. "But we shouldn't be casting blame on Mamma's sister, really. Aunt Sarah's behavin' the way any fancy woman would, mind you."

Fannie was still for a bit. Then, hemmin' and hawin' like she wasn't sure if she oughta be askin' such a question, Fannie said, "Um . . . what *does* your mamma's will say anyways . . . do you even know?"

Lydia shook her head. "Never saw it. But, honestly, I do think we can trust Mr. Eberley, Mamma's lawyer. He's a nice Christian man. Mamma told me so before she died. She said, *'That Mr. Eberley's a prayerful Mennonite man, so you don't hafta worry one bit.'*"

Fannie looked mighty skeptical all of a sudden. "Well, he may be God-fearin' and all, but I just don't know. . . ." She scratched the back of her head under the veiling. "Seems to me we oughta think up something right quick to make sure all of you get to stay together . . . and right here around Grasshopper Level, too!"

Lydia was secretly glad her friend had come to this conclusion on her own. "I'm all ears. What're you thinkin'?"

Fannie reached for her cup of hot cocoa. Then she tilted her head, like she was ponderin' real hard. "You know, there's always Preacher Esh's unmarried cousin down the way. Miriam Esh just might be someone who could come and live here with you."

Lydia had never even thought of *en alt Maed* like Miriam. "That's a wonderful-gut idea, uh . . . except that Miriam, well, you know, she . . ." She paused, hesitating to say.

"I know just what you're gonna say. Sometimes I can hardly say 'hullo' to her at the meetinghouse, she smells so awful bad." Fannie started to giggle. "Maybe you could *educate* her on takin' a bath once in a while."

"Well, now, aren't you *kalwerich* — silly." Lydia was glad for a gut laugh. It had been too long since she'd wrapped up her troubles in a smile. "I'm glad you brought up Miriam, though. Truly, I am."

"I have no doubt she'll clean up right nice . . . 'least for a day or so."

"Long enough for me to take Aunt Sarah over for a visit, 'cause I know — for sure and for certain — your Mammi or anyone else 'round here couldn't begin to think of takin' in all five of us."

Fannie was frowning again. "What's this about my grandmother?"

"Oh," Lydia said, waving her hand nonchalantly, "Aunt Sarah's got it in her mind that Susie might be a gut choice to be our second mother."

"Well, how on earth does she even know her?"

"It's 'cause Mamma and Aunt Sarah wrote letters for many years, that's how."

"Does your aunt have any idea how old Mammi Susie is?" Fannie said, leaning forward.

"S'pose not, though it's possible she does."

"Well, my mammi has her hands full with her *own* grown children and grandchildren, and her little craft shop, besides. So I think you're right about Miriam Esh bein' the best bet."

Lydia didn't know how to tell her best friend what she was thinking. Wasn't sure *if* she should say anything at all. Slowly, she breathed in before speaking in a near whisper. "Nobody knows this, Fannie, but I made a promise to Mamma before she died."

"Aw, Lyddie." Fannie reached over and touched her hand. "You don't hafta say, honest ya don't."

"No . . . no, I *want* to tell you." She

178

paused, covering Fannie's hand with her own. "I gave Mamma my word. I promised her, while she lay dyin', that I'd keep the family together. And I will!"

Fannie's eyes glistened. "I would do the same for my own mamma if . . ." Her voice trailed away, and the girls fell into each other's arms. "Oh, Lyddie, I'm awful sorry 'bout your terrible loss. I do love you so!"

Lydia's throat went dry, too dry to voice the same words of affection back to her friend, but she clung to Fannie all the same.

When they'd dried their tears, Fannie said, "You know, I heard my brother talkin' in the barn this morning. Seems there's goin' to be a need for a schoolteacher real soon here at the schoolhouse over on Peach Lane."

"You don't say!" Lydia's heart did a little flip-flop.

"And . . . there's talk that you'd be a gut choice, since you got nearly straight A's in school, and you're still single and all."

Lydia felt her face blushing to beat the band.

"Wouldja be interested?"

"I'd be more than happy to teach if the People want me. But I s'pose I oughtn't to say I will, not till we know what's goin' to happen to us." Lydia got up and went to stir the thick beef stew, noticing that the baby onions and carrots were cookin' up gut and tender. "You know, I've often wondered if the Good Lord might not open the door for me to teach school someday. But why just now, when things are so unsettled 'bout my own future?"

Fannie's eyes grew serious. "You're thinking 'bout Levi, ain't so?"

No need to share fanciful secrets just yet. "I'm more worried 'bout Aunt Sarah and where we'll end up."

"You must hurry 'n take her to meet Miriam."

Lydia could only hope and pray that things worked out with Preacher's cousin. It was their best chance.

"Well, I'll be prayin' for you, that's for sure." Fannie's smile spread wide across her delicate face. She seemed to have warmed up at last, 'bout the time she wanted to be headin' on home.

"God be with you," they said, kissing each other's cheeks, before Fannie hurried out the back door.

Standing in the doorway, Lydia watched her dearest friend pick her way over the ice and snow to the waiting carriage. She was ever so glad Aunt Sarah must've decided to dawdle comin' back from the outlet stores.

Overjoyed, as well, that Fannie had come to visit by herself, with neither her mamma or Grandmammi along.

Jah, Fannie's visit was surely providential. In more than one way, it was just what Lydia needed to fill the afternoon with hope. She could hardly wait to hear what Preacher Esh had to say 'bout her future as a teacher!

Secretly, she wished she might run into Levi King soon. Levi would be mighty pleased to hear the news. That is, if he didn't know 'bout it already.

Chapter Sixteen

"There is no dispute over either this house or the land — everything will remain in your immediate family," Sarah explained, eager to put away her many purchases, including a pair of brand-new leather boots. "You and your brothers and sisters will inherit all assets, including farm animals, indoor furnishings, and personal effects."

Lydia caught up with her at the top of the stairs, and Sarah hurried to the row of wooden wall pegs, impatient to hang up the smart new teal suit, two woolen skirts and vests to match, a chic sienna pantsuit, and several silk blouses, noting that Lydia had not followed her into the room. Like a shadow, the girl stood humbly in the doorway.

"Mr. Eberley and I are working together now. You have nothing to worry about." Sarah proceeded to put away her new purchases, then turned to the highboy, opening the bottom drawer. Noticing it was completely empty, she said, "Well, it appears there's some extra room here."

"Jah, Mamma stored her journals there," Lydia said softly, on the verge of tears.

"My sister kept a diary?" She found it amazing, though true, recalling how Ivy as a teenager often had her nose in a spiral-bound notebook, writing feverishly.

"I don't know just how many," Lydia mumbled.

"But . . . you saw her writing?"

"Now and again." The girl's answers seemed painfully vague. No longer did Lydia stand erect but leaned against the wide doorjamb as if her legs might not hold her up.

"Your mother always tried to encourage *me* to keep a diary," Sarah said, hoping to brighten things. "She was never successful."

"Oh?" Lydia seemed interested.

"I wasn't one for scribbling down my feelings."

"Twice a day, *I* keep a journal, or at least try to."

Lydia had been influenced by her mother, no doubt. "Journal-keeping is a good discipline, for those who are so inclined."

"Jah," Lydia agreed. "Sometimes I wonder what people will think when I pass on . . . like Mamma, you know. What will my loved ones say 'bout me if they read my most secret thoughts and dreams?"

"Risky, to be sure" was all Sarah could think to say.

"But the writing does help some folk get through life, I guess."

"Certain temperaments find solace in journal-keeping, but I'm certainly not that type of person."

Smiling faintly, Lydia replied, "But you *did* write letters to Mamma."

"Oh," — Sarah dismissed the observation with an airy wave of her hand — "mine were always at least one-third shorter than hers."

"Was that because Mamma turned Amish on you?" Lydia spoke too quietly.

Sarah wasn't sure if she had heard correctly. "I beg your pardon?"

"Oh . . . nothin'." Lydia's half-whispered comments ceased abruptly. She left without Sarah knowing the precise moment when she had.

Glad for the solitude, Sarah unzipped one of several garment bags, removing her designer pant ensemble. She fingered its wide V-neck collar, imagining Heidi Norton's reaction — Bill Alexander's, as well.

Any number of her dazzling shoes, at home in Portland, would accessorize splendidly. She would waltz into the real estate office next Monday morning, wearing one of her terrific Lancaster outlet purchases.

Monday afternoon, January 24

My sister. . . .

That's how Aunt Sarah spoke of Mamma today, far different than before. Even the tone of her voice, when talking of Mamma has softened some — more the way I would expect her to be.

I don't know for sure, can't tell really, if Aunt Sarah's grieving much at all. English folk must have their own way of sorrow. It just seems awful strange that she would go out and shop, of all things, when she's here to look after her family's needs. I tend to think Mamma's sister is altogether ferhoodled. *Prob'ly needs some tending to herself.*

"There's someone I'm hopin' I can take you to meet soon," Lydia said with uncertainty after supper. "An Amishwoman you might want to consider for a foster mother . . . for us."

Her aunt looked somewhat wary, all of a sudden. She draped her damp tea towel over the dish rack.

Lydia forged ahead. "Miriam Esh is well respected in our Plain community. She's a kind, Christian lady — never married — but she has a tender place in her heart for children."

"What about Susie Lapp?"

"She's out of the question, I'm sure."

Aunt Sarah stiffened. "How old is this other woman — uh, Miriam?"

"Mid-thirties or so."

"Single, you say?"

Lydia nodded her head. "Not that she didn't have the chance to wed. She just never did."

Aunt Sarah folded her arms and moved to the bench near the table and sat. "Are you fond of her?"

It wasn't fair for Lydia to speak up and say that *she* prob'ly wasn't the one to be askin', 'specially if she ended up marrying Levi King and makin' a home with him in the near future. "Miriam's wonderful-gut, really she is."

"But do you *like* her?"

Sometimes you just do what you have to, whether you like it or not, Lydia thought. She nearly smiled to herself, for Aunt Sarah reminded her of her own persistent streak. "I s'pose I'd have to say I don't know Miriam all too well. We attend the same quiltin' bees and work frolics sometimes, but that's mostly all . . . and Preachin' at the meetinghouse, too."

"What about the other children? How would they feel about Miriam as a mother figure?"

186

Lydia had to think on that. "Caleb prob'ly wouldn't have much of an opinion, but Anna Mae might. Josiah and Hannah perty much go along with what the older ones say or do."

Aunt Sarah's eyebrows lifted, then lowered slowly. "So you don't know the woman well enough to live with her?"

"She could come here . . . live with *us*," Lydia responded quickly. "Miriam doesn't have much of anything, seein' as how her parents live in northern New York now — moved up there with some of Miriam's married brothers, hopin' for more land than is available 'round here. Her cousin, our preacher, and several other distant relatives look after her and keep her farm goin'."

"I believe you've thought about this a great deal."

"Well, it would *expedite* things." Her use of Sarah's word must've triggered the momentary furrow on her aunt's brow.

"Please don't misunderstand, Lydia."

"But . . . well, isn't that why you wanted to talk to Susie Lapp?"

Aunt Sarah leaned forward slightly, her painted lips parting momentarily, as if she were truly surprised at Lydia's blunt remark. "Please give Miss Esh a call whenever you can. I'll meet with her at her convenience."

No longer smiling, Aunt Sarah went and poured herself another cup of coffee.

For all the world, Lydia wanted to tell her aunt that no one in the Amish community referred to the women as "Mrs." or "Miss." Truth be known, it was prob'ly a very good thing Aunt Sarah would be headin' home in a few days.

Normally, Lydia wouldn't have thought of using the telephone to chat with Fannie at such a late hour. Bishop Joseph wanted the People to limit phone conversation and visiting — save it for the face-to-face meetings. Yet she felt she must talk things over, at least briefly, with someone. Fannie's was the best ear to bend.

"When you get around women like Miriam, you hear things — *learn* things. Know what I mean?" she said, relaying her conversation with Aunt Sarah on to Fannie.

Fannie seemed to understand. "Miriam sees and hears a-plenty, and lots of folk think she's makin' up half of what she tells. In spite of all that, she's ever so kind-hearted."

"Jah, and I think my aunt prob'ly needs a ladle full of expert storytellin' . . . from the mouth of a prudent woman."

"But what 'bout *you*, Lyddie? You could

tell your aunt a story or two."

Her back against the kitchen wall, she glanced around in the darkness as she held the phone against her ear. "Between you, me, and the fence post, I think Miriam's the one prospect to hold this family together — in one piece."

"I think you might be right."

That clinched things for Lydia. She said her good-byes and hung up, returning the receiver to its phone cradle. Then she tip-toed back upstairs to her room.

Come tomorrow — if all went well — she and Aunt Sarah would have themselves a visit to the best storyteller 'round Strasburg and Paradise both. And if Miriam consented to be their substitute Mamma, then Sarah Cain could be on her way back to modern city life, with an inspiring story churnin' inside her fancy soul.

Sarah relaxed more comfortably in Ivy's bed tonight. Neither did it distress her that she might be stretched out on her sister's side of the mattress or that Ivy's spirit might have, indeed, left her body in this very spot.

Something else was more pressing. She wished now that she had had the presence of mind to broach the subject of Ivy's journal-keeping with Lydia. Having brought a

189

number of Ivy's letters with her, Sarah was eager to peruse them once again, refresh her memory as to the things pertaining to her sister's Plain life. But it was the mention of Ivy's journals that stirred up increased curiosity. Surely Lydia knew of their location in the house.

If Lydia ever brought up the subject again — perhaps later in the week — she would plunge right in and ask. Possibly Lydia would find it in her heart to oblige Sarah and offer one.

She felt herself drifting toward that predream state of neither here nor there. How odd that she should care one way or the other about Ivy's writings.

It was Lydia who was too restless to sleep. So much so that she got up and opened the wooden chest at the foot of her bed. Quickly, she located the shoe box where Mamma's seashell collection was stored. Though she had not looked inside since she was a young child, she recalled the rainy afternoon, years before, when Mamma had taken time to sit Caleb and herself down, showing off the colorful shells.

"When I was a girl, I was a collector," Mamma told them. "I cared only to gather seashells — the more I took from the sand, the happier I was. But, soon, my backpack became too heavy with dozens and dozens of shells, and at home my windowsills were too cluttered to dust. My father — your grandpa Cain — taught me to discard the ordinary ones, to be more particular. He used to say, *'Choose only the perfect ones, and your collection will become more important. Remember, there is only one sun and moon in the sky. Think how trivial a harvest moon would be if there were three.'* "

Enjoying her recollection, Lydia opened the lid on the box and peered inside. Mamma had chosen wisely, for certain. And now that Lydia was old enough to appreciate what had gone into the gathering — the choosing — she touched each of ten perfect shells. They were cool to the touch and smooth as could be.

Returning the prized collection to its shoe-box home, Lydia located her mother's journals. She had promised herself that each night she would read a good many pages, startin' with the most recent writings and working backward in time.

So she curled up in her bed with the first of several diaries, attempting to nudge her aunt's words from her mind.

"My sister kept a diary?" Aunt Sarah had said, lookin' a bit stunned.

Now that Lydia thought on it, she wondered, *What if she asks to read Mamma's journals?*

Clutching the precious books to her bosom, she felt just now that she fully understood Grandpa Cain's shell lesson. Mamma had not left behind hundreds, not even dozens, of bound diaries. There were only seven, and they were as important to Lydia as the sun is to God's green earth.

She began to read.

December 9, 1998

It's a cold, blustery day today. The dampness is strong in my bones, and my chest is heavy with pressure like never before. My doctor thinks I should be admitted to the hospital, but I will trust the Great Physician for my healing, if it is His will. If I am to die, it should be here at home.

Lydia and the younger children are so good to play quietly downstairs when their morning chores are finished. They must be told soon about my failing heart. I think my oldest girl suspects how weak I am. I can see it reflected in her sad eyes. She is so attentive to my needs — tries so hard to be patient with her siblings, in spite of the tension she surely feels. Lydia really does see through me, clear to my soul. In many ways, she reminds me of my sister when Sarah was young, before the accident that claimed her spirit.

O heavenly Father, help my children continue to love and serve you even if it is your will for me to be absent from this life. May they know your peace, joy, and great love.

Reading what Mamma thought of her made Lydia feel like weeping. All too clearly, she recalled the heavy weight of concern she'd carried during the weeks and months of her mother's grave illness.

Instead of giving in to tears, though, she read the prayer Mamma had written once again. So, most likely, Mamma had known well before Christmas that she was going to die. The realization did not bother Lydia as much as something else. She had never heard of any mention made of an accident involving Aunt Sarah. What exactly had Mamma meant: *the accident that claimed her spirit?*

Lydia slid Mamma's journal onto the bedside table but thought she heard someone up. Quietly, she went down the hall to check on her brothers and sisters.

Caleb and Josiah were sound asleep in their room, but the light was on in the girls' room.

"Five-thirty comes awful soon," she reminded Anna Mae gently but firmly. The same tone of voice Mamma often used when one of them was lax.

Anna Mae looked mighty sheepish, perched there in her bed. She glanced meekly at the single bed next to hers, where little Hannah lay curled up, fast asleep. "I'm bein' quiet as a mouse."

"Mice can be downright noisy sometimes," Lydia reminded.

"Sorry, Lyddie." Anna Mae's lips started moving again, silently.

Lydia sat on the edge of the bed. "Are you still talkin' to yourself?"

Anna Mae shrugged.

"I *know* you are." She placed a hand on the long lumps under the quilts that were Anna Mae's legs. "Forever mumblin' won't make things better."

"Ya mean it won't make Mamma come back alive?"

"I didn't say that," she whispered.

"But it's what you meant, ain't so?"

Lydia was still. Then — "I just don't want you to get the wrong idea . . . that I'm reprimandin' you. I'm just —"

"Worried that I'm *ab im Kopp* — off in the head?"

"Well . . . honestly, I wonder that some-

194

times 'bout myself. 'Specially here lately."

"*You,* Lyddie?" Anna Mae frowned. "That's awful hard to believe."

"I'm not sayin' you shouldn't grieve for Mamma. Just be careful how you do it, jah?"

Anna Mae smiled a fainthearted smile, her red braids dangling over her pudgy shoulders. "I won't let Aunt Sarah catch me talkin' to myself, if that's what you're worried 'bout."

It wasn't. Not really. Anna Mae had misunderstood a bit. Still, Lydia was glad they'd had this nighttime chat. "You're a gut girl. Now, sweet dreams." She got up and turned out the light.

Before she tiptoed to the door, Anna Mae whispered into the dark. "Is Miriam gonna be our mamma?"

Lydia froze. "Miriam Esh will *never* be our mamma. No one will ever be that to us," she insisted.

"But I overheard you and Aunt Sarah talkin'. Sounded like Miriam might be comin' here to live with us instead of Aunt Sarah."

"That's yet to be decided. But livin' here won't make Miriam our mother. You know that." She had said all she wanted to on the subject. She closed the door without chiding Anna Mae on her eavesdropping.

Dat always liked to say a Pennsylvania Dutch proverb 'bout folks who listened in on another's conversation. She had memorized the old adage straight from her father's lips. *Wer lauert an die Wand, heert sei eegni Schand* — "He who eavesdrops by the wall will hear that which shames himself."

Lydia crept back to her bedroom, wondering 'bout reading through Mamma's journals and a handful of Aunt Sarah's letters. Was *that* "eavesdropping," too?

She was ashamed, deeply so, but knew not what to do 'bout it.

Chapter Seventeen

It was past midnight when Lydia awoke to the sound of a team driving in the lane. Quickly, she rose and threw on her long white bed robe, peering out the window. By the light of a partial moon, she made out the dark figure of a young man tying a horse, black and glistening, to the snowy fence post out in the barnyard, the open carriage parked nearby.

Levi?

She ran her fingers down one of her thick, waist-length braids, waiting for his flashlight to shine through her window, to cast its expectant glow onto her bedroom wall. Going to the bureau, she removed a tiny mirror and studied her face. Jah, she looked awake enough for a visit just now.

A flickering light appeared on the wall opposite her bed, and she knew Levi had come — during the veil of night, in secret — to see her. She dared not hope, nay, not even wish, that this could be the night of nights.

Again, she went to the window and looked out. Her heart leaped at the sight of him on the ground below, his thick bangs peekin' out from under his black felt hat. His were such sturdy, squared shoulders for a tall and lean fella. Lanky he was, really, but she didn't mind. His face was upturned, gazing at her in the window high above, and she signaled for him to meet her downstairs.

As quietly as possible, Lydia tiptoed down the steps, hopin' she wouldn't disturb the sleeping household. The encounter with Levi must be kept private, between just the two of them. The People's way.

She scurried silently to the back door, through the utility room and screened-in porch. There stood Levi on the stoop, hands hooked into both his pockets, grinning from ear to ear.

"Hullo, Lyddie."

She felt both abundant joy and awkwardness, all mixed together. Then, noticing that Levi seemed to be shivering, she remembered her manners. "Do come inside and get warm." She opened the door wider.

When he was inside, she closed the door silently and led him past a maze of work boots and overshoes, lined up in order from Caleb's big galoshes down to tiny Hannah's rubber overshoes. In the kitchen she turned on the small light over the sink, and when she turned around, she saw that he'd removed his wide-brimmed hat already.

Without speaking, they sat side by side on the wooden bench near the table. They stayed that way for a bit, Lydia fully aware of his closeness, his coat sleeve brushing against her arm. She was ever so glad she'd finished sewing the new bathrobe she wore tonight.

When Levi spoke at last, his voice was confident, yet soft enough not to waken the upstairs sleepers. "I missed ya at Singing last night."

"I just couldn't get away. *Es dutt mir leed* — I am sorry."

Silence again.

Then Lydia spoke up, eager to share her news. "Fannie was over for a visit today. She says Preacher Esh might be comin' to ask if I'd be the teacher at the school down the hill."

"Peach Lane School?"

"Jah, and I'm hopin' it'll work out."

"Sounds like it just might."

Her heart pounded, having shared her happy news and wonderin' what Levi had on his mind just now. "I didn't mean to speak out of turn," she said softly.

"No . . . no, that's nice to know." He reached for her hand and held it for a moment before speaking again. "I came here to say somethin' important, Lyddie."

She suspected why he'd come but waited quietly, submissively, waiting for this wonderful-gut young man to speak his mind. Or his heart. One of the two.

"I've been thinkin' on this ever so long now."

She held her breath. Could this be the moment Levi had chosen to reveal his intentions? Would he say that he loved her? That he wanted to marry her, spend all his days together with her and her alone?

Levi turned and looked deep into her eyes. "I hope you won't be leavin' here," he said, gaze strong and true. "We could run away an' get married . . . right quick, if that would help."

She listened with all eagerness.

"We could sneak away some weekend, maybe run over to Hickory Hollow, see if Bishop John Beiler might not tie the knot for us." Both his hands had found hers now. "That way you could stay with me, for always."

"Oh, Levi . . ." She thought of the endless possibilities for love and living — *here* — as Levi's bride and the mother of his children.

His hands stroked hers tenderly, eyes searching hers, pleading for her sweet answer. "Lyddie? Will you be my wife?"

Oh, to belong to Levi! She wanted to sing for joy, wanted to whisper back, "Jah, ever so much, I do."

Yet the promise she'd made to her dying mamma held her fast. Truth be told, she didn't trust Aunt Sarah, couldn't hand over the guardianship of her brothers and sisters to an outsider. She pulled away a bit.

"What . . . what is it?" His brow was creased with more than worry.

"I love you, Levi. I surely do. But runnin' away might not be the best thing, really."

"What'll happen to us if your aunt takes you away?" Dread cloaked his solemn voice.

"I'd never want to hurt you, Levi. But maybe . . ." Her voice trailed off. "If things worked out for someone to live with us, then my siblings would be looked after, and you and I could be wed next fall, durin' wedding season. I've already said something to Aunt Sarah 'bout Miriam."

"Miriam Esh?"

"Jah."

"How on earth are you gonna talk Preacher's cousin into such a thing? She's mighty set in her ways, I hear."

Lydia hadn't given much thought to Miriam's disposition. Levi was right. 'Twould be an obstacle, all right.

"What 'bout your aunt?" he continued. "I

201

thought *she* was in charge of your family now."

"Such a long story it is. I know you prob'ly don't want to hear me goin' on and on."

"But I do!"

Because she knew his heart, she did her best to share with him — that Aunt Sarah had no intention of stayin' put, as Mamma had requested in her will. "Sarah Cain is English, for pity's sake. She doesn't know the first thing 'bout Amish ways."

"But she's your flesh-and-blood aunt, ain't so?"

Sure seemed like a good question, comin' from Levi. But just now she was beginning to feel mighty exhausted, worn out from thinkin', really. "Maybe we'd best not plan anything now," she heard herself say. "Not till something's decided, with or without Miriam Esh."

Levi was silent again, though he'd moved a bit closer to her. She almost expected him to put his arm 'round her shoulder and maybe even draw her near, same as he'd done last month in his open buggy on the way back from a Singing over in Summer-Hill.

Instead, he seemed to stiffen. "I'd do anything in the world, Lyddie, anything to make you mine."

"I'm awful sorry, truly I am" was all she could think to say.

"Please don't turn me away." His breath was warm on her cheek. "I love you so."

"I daresn't give you false hopes, Levi. It wouldn't be fair to you." She wouldn't let herself cry in front of him. Not here in the house Dat had chosen for them, where Mamma's dreams and hopes for the future were bein' shattered nearly every other day, it seemed. Where the only boy Lydia had ever loved had just proposed marriage. And what had she done? Put him off.

"My dear Lyddie," he said, gathering her close.

She hesitated, trembling in his arms, and he took her off guard. His lips found hers, and as much as she knew she prob'ly ought to resist, she let him kiss her. One little kiss wouldn't hurt nothin', but his lips were ever so fervent.

She pulled away and not anytime too soon.

The light overhead burst into their eyes. Lydia turned, and there was Aunt Sarah standing across the floor. "What's going on here?" she demanded.

Levi stood up. "I best be goin'," he said, nearly running out of the kitchen.

Lydia started after him, then heard the

back storm door slam shut. Her wonderful-gut night was over all too abruptly.

"Lydia?" came Aunt Sarah's stern voice.

Standing in the middle of the dimly lit kitchen, face-to-face with her mamma's sister, Lydia was speechless. How could she possibly make her aunt, so unfamiliar with Amish ways, understand that Levi had meant no ill?

She waited for her niece's response. The girl's bottom lip quivered uncontrollably, and by the wide-eyed expression on her face, it looked as if Lydia might burst into tears.

What *were* her niece and that Amish boy doing alone together in the kitchen in the middle of the night? It certainly seemed that Lydia had taken advantage of the quiet house; of Sarah's trust, as well.

"I . . . I . . ." stammered Lydia. "I don't know what to say."

Sarah wondered if her sister would have allowed such uncomely behavior by Lydia. Hardly. "Who was that young man?" Sarah asked, the tension building between herself and the young woman standing like a statue before her.

Lydia sniffled. "He's a . . . gut friend."

"Does the young man have a name?"

Lydia, head bowed, shook her head. "I can't . . . *shouldn't* say anything, really not. It's the People's way . . . we . . . this is the way Amish have been courtin' for over three hundred years."

Sarah pondered the incredulous reply. "You're expected to sneak around at night?"

"Most dating is done in secret, till the wedding is published at a Preachin' two weeks before" came the explanation.

"Published . . . as in the newspaper?"

Lydia shook her head. "No, it's the bishop who *announces* the wedding date at the end of a church gathering."

Aghast, Sarah asked, "Are you being courted? Engaged to be married?"

"I best not say more." Lydia was weeping.

"No, you *best* go upstairs . . . to bed." With that ultimatum, she flicked off the kitchen light overhead. "And don't forget to turn off the sink light," she said, hoping Lydia would follow her upstairs and not throw a fit about getting caught with a boy, the way Ivy once had at age seventeen.

She recalled the night when Mother had discovered Ivy and her boyfriend kissing in the living room. Ranting and raving, their mother had called for their father to "come down and talk to your daughter."

It had been one of the few times Mother

had lost her temper with her favored daughter. Ivy had been put on restriction for two long, unmerciful weeks, and what a miserable fourteen days they had been. For young Sarah, as well. With Ivy banned from phone privileges, along with her many other social engagements, life became nearly intolerable.

Once again, Sarah was very glad to have her own bedroom. Sharing space with Ivy during those weeks was the last thing she would have wanted. So she practiced the piano an extra hour each day, filling up the after-school and evening hours. All the while, Ivy sulked in her room, sometimes more loudly than other times. Ivy's idea of taking discipline with grace meant throwing shoes about the room at the most unexpected moments. At least, that was what Sarah came to envision whenever the clamorous bumps landed overhead as she sat at the piano soothing her soul with Bach or Chopin.

How very strange that Mother, who cherished peace and quiet above all else, seemed to disregard the fits of fury befalling the house those weeks.

Waiting for young Lydia to ascend the steps, to get her tail upstairs and back into bed, Sarah paused in the hallway and recalled again Ivy's teenage temper tantrums and other transgressions. Why would her sister, ill-tempered as she had been, want to abandon city life and come here to live in a peace-loving place — almost a foreign land — like Amish country?

Something monumental must have happened to change her. Over the years, Ivy had endeavored to convey to Sarah in her letters that such a transformation *had,* indeed, taken place, though Sarah had always rejected the notion. Yet this night she considered the possibility of a spiritual conversion, perhaps for the first time.

Lydia was coming up the steps now, her head low. Brown braids, long and thick, hung forward to her waist. Sarah started in bewilderment at the near specter of her sister — Lydia was, indeed, a younger version of Ivy.

"We'll talk more tomorrow," she said as the girl passed.

"Jah, good night, Aunt Sarah."

It was difficult for her to accept Lydia's description of the People's dating habits. Was her niece purposely hoping to trick her, trying to cover up for wrongful actions with her boyfriend? She hardly knew what to think.

Exhausted from the extremely long, grueling day — and the night, as well — Sarah literally could not wait to return to bed. But sleep did not come as readily as before. She considered appropriate discipline for Lydia's seemingly underhanded conduct. Restricting the girl from social activities hardly seemed an option. After all, what events could be going on in the middle of winter around here? Humdrum sleigh rides, boring quilting bees . . . what?

Settling in once again, Sarah realized anew how little she knew or understood of Ivy's family's Plain life-style — "the People's way," as Lydia liked to put it.

Tomorrow she would ask to read one of Ivy's journals. Maybe skimming through her sister's personal writings would give her some much-needed insight. The idea that such a conservative group of people actually condoned their young people's courting practices — the way Lydia had described — seemed hard to swallow. Exactly what would Ivy have done if *she* had discovered Lydia tonight in the arms of that wiry young fellow completely unsupervised?

Eager as Sarah was to return to modern civilization, she felt far less urgent about meeting either Mrs. Susie Lapp or Miss Miriam Esh. An irresistible emotion welled up inside her as she reached for Ivy's home-made quilts, covering up for the night. She had not encountered such an empathetic feeling, almost maternal, for a long time now, and she scarcely knew what to do about it.

Most of all, she felt compelled to get to the bottom of Lydia's late-night liaison, and as soon as possible. On behalf of her dead sister she would do this. For no other reason.

Monday night, January 24

I am horrified (heartbroken, too). Aunt Sarah burst into the kitchen tonight while Levi kissed me, right after he'd proposed marriage and I'd turned him down. Ach, I don't see how our courting relationship, if it's even to continue, can ever be kept secret now, as is our custom. I can only hope my aunt leaves before she spills the beans to anyone!

So awful mixed up, I am. I do want Aunt Sarah to help us find a family, if that's what Mamma intended. Somehow, I don't believe our dear mamma had that in mind at all. I think she wanted Aunt Sarah to raise us herself. But how can that be, when Sarah Cain doesn't know the first thing about bein' Amish . . . or a mother? Neither one.

My heart truly belongs to Levi King. Someday I hope to be his bride, but first some mighty important things must be worked out for my brothers and sisters. Then, thank goodness, Aunt Sarah will be on her way. I can only hope and pray Levi will wait for me!

Chapter Eighteen

The house began to stir somewhat later than it had the day before, Amish laundry day. Today, the scurry of feet on the stairs diminished rather quickly as the children hurried outside to tend to barn chores. Neither Lydia nor Caleb had ever hinted that she should assist with outdoor duties since her arrival, and even if the suggestion were to be made, she knew she would have to decline. Not a single item of clothing in her fine wardrobe could withstand the grime and mire associated with farm work.

Tired as she was, Sarah did not opt to lie in bed, nor did she take pleasure in the quietude. Instead, she got up and purposely ignored Megan's framed picture on the bedside table, going to the washstand.

Peering into the mirror, she noticed dark circles under her eyes. "I should have stayed in bed," she whispered to her reflection.

I should have stayed in Portland. . . .

Catching sight of a white towel where decorative brooches of flowers, birds, and a ladybug were pinned in a row, she felt the towel's smoothness and wondered if Ivy had ever worn this jewelry. She studied each pin, recalling a letter from Ivy written several years ago. Her sister had casually mentioned a brooch purchased at Wal-Mart on sale.

At the time, Sarah had been struck by the humor of Ivy's comment. For an Amish-woman to be shopping at a discount store, or *any* store for that matter, seemed peculiar to her. She had always assumed that ultra-conservative women either made or grew the items they needed. It never occurred to her, until this moment, that Ivy might have actually desired something pretty. Something like these little gold and silver pins, store-bought items.

What else did Ivy enjoy? she wondered.

Meandering to the highboy, she opened the top drawer and discovered a simple, black leather-bound Bible. She turned the first pages and was surprised to see that it was written in English, not the German she expected. There were also five handmade bookmarks near the front of the drawer, two with pressed wild flowers — sky-blue and russet-colored blossoms — she could not identify. And there were three dainty hand-kerchiefs with crocheted edging, one with intricate embroidery in the corner, creating a pink rose in full bloom.

She inspected Ivy's personal items briefly, then returned them to the drawer, noticing various undergarments and slips tucked away in the same compartment, obviously store purchased.

Abandoning the dresser, she went to her own suitcases, removing fresh clothing for the day. She had thought of unpacking but was determined not to settle in here, knowing that she planned to leave next weekend, one way or the other. She would not consider changing her mind.

During morning Bible reading and prayers, Hannah pulled on Sarah's hand when it came time to kneel. For the first time since coming here, Sarah knelt along with the rest of the children. She decided it wouldn't hurt for her to do as Hannah wished. At least once.

When the youngsters headed out the door for school, Sarah was still thinking through her plan of attack regarding Lydia's indiscreet conduct last night. How did one introduce such a delicate topic? Was it her place to initiate such talk?

She waited until all the children were well on their way down the lane before turning to Lydia. "I want to talk with you," she said, making an effort to sound more confident than she felt.

Lydia wiped her face with her long apron, silently leaning against the kitchen counter. Her eyes were wide — like a fawn caught in headlights.

"About last night, Lydia . . ." She stopped, groping for the right direction the conversation should take. "If your mother were alive, she would be appalled, no doubt."

Lydia sniffled, shaking her head. "Mamma would never have come downstairs. She trusted me completely."

"I see," Sarah said, but she did not. "Perhaps you should explain your courting customs, or whatever I encountered in your kitchen . . . since you are obviously quite taken with your young man."

Lydia sighed audibly, standing more erect, as if on trial. Her hair, parted down the middle without bangs or curls to frame her face, was pulled into a bun at the back of her neck, covered by the same white veiling she wore each day. She folded her hands in front of her.

Only one time had she not seen Lydia sporting the little cap. Late last night. Because of this, she presumed Amish women slept without their coverings, but she had no way of knowing for certain.

"What you witnessed last night is personal — to be kept a secret, really. I pray you

214

will act as if you never saw us, as though my friend had never come here. Can you promise me this?"

Who does she think she is? Sarah wondered. Her niece was treating *her* like a child, making unreasonable demands. Without question, she would have pushed the issue further, but tears welled up in Lydia's eyes. The girl looked positively panic-stricken.

"I don't understand," she said, yet something inside her struggled to reach out to her niece.

"S'pose if I thought you were truly interested in knowing, I would try hard to make you understand our ways. Forgive me for bein' blunt, but I don't think you care one bit what happens to any of us." Lydia covered her face with her hands and began to sob.

Sarah was at a loss to know what to say or do. So when Lydia ran past her, heading upstairs, she set about cleaning the kitchen, starting with breakfast dishes and ending with sweeping the floor.

That done, she trudged into the living room and sat down with an Amish newspaper — *The Budget*. Inside its pages, she discovered short anecdotal accounts of events and nonevents, written by Plain folk. Unusual, indeed.

The day had started out wrong — not much of a morning. She was not so interested in what Martha Yoder or Nancy Bontrager or any number of other Amish "scribes" had written in what seemed to be a column-type rendition of a backwoodsy paper.

Wishing she was anywhere else in the world but here, Sarah rose from the spot on the threadbare sofa and went to the window to look out. There was bread to be made and a soup stock to be boiled and turned into a stew for lunch, but since Lydia was upstairs sulking, having a pity party alone, Sarah decided to take a moment to reflect.

A cold mist stole across the meadow to the east, and the sky seemed to sink even lower as she watched. A northern thin strip of woodland was in tatters, and a heavy snow had fallen in the night. She saw the imprint of boots where Caleb, Anna Mae, Josiah, and Hannah had walked along the roadside.

"What *am* I doing here?" she whispered.

Lydia brushed away tears, sitting on the straight-backed chair near her bed. She fought hard the bitterness that came near to takin' her over. *I'll be ever so glad when Aunt Sarah goes home!* For sure and for certain, she and her sisters and brothers wouldn't be needin' their aunt if Lydia could get Miriam Esh to live with them.

But how?

Far as Lydia was concerned, 'twasn't necessary to hope and pray Sarah Cain would stay, after all. The Children and Youth Agency would *not* have to be called in — wouldn't need to split them up at all — if Sarah could appoint Miriam somehow. Simple as A-B-C. Still, she worried 'bout making her case for Preacher's cousin.

She washed her face and smoothed her apron, then headed downstairs to call Miriam Esh right quick.

"Hullo?" the woman answered on the second ring.

"It's Lydia Cottrell," she said, a bit weak in the knees. "I was wonderin' if we — *I* — could come visit you today." She didn't want to give Miriam time to say no right off. "I'd be beholden to you if —"

Miriam's answer came all too swiftly, interrupted her, really. "I'm awful sorry, Lyddie. Just won't suit today. A batch of dough is a-starin' me in the face, and the house needs cleanin' and whatnot all."

If Lydia hadn't known better, she might've thought Miriam was puttin' her off but good. She thanked her, said she hoped to see her at the quiltin' at Susie Lapp's later this week.

Miriam replied, "All right, then." And they hung up.

Downright disappointed, Lydia went to knead a great handful of dough for her own bread-making. Her brothers and sisters had eaten down the remaining loaf to less than half, so she knew she mustn't dally. Not one little bit.

Grateful that Aunt Sarah had washed the dishes and swept the floor, Lydia set about preparing three loaf pans for baking. She was also glad her aunt was nowhere 'round.

Best this way, 'least for the time bein', she thought, remembering how she'd fled from the room in tears earlier. Now that she thought on it, prob'ly was a good idea Aunt Sarah was upstairs doin' whatever she was doin'. Lydia needed to put some space between herself and the woman who called herself Mamma's sister but didn't seem to fit in anywhere at all. Not for the life of her, she didn't!

Lydia turned her attention to Miriam Esh. *What's ailin' her?* she wondered. Surely the word hadn't already gotten out that Aunt Sarah hoped to find a family for them. Even so, if Miriam *had* heard such a thing, why would she act like that on the phone?

Just wasn't becomin' to the usually gracious woman. Unless maybe Miriam simply wasn't interested in bein' asked to be a substitute Mamma. Was *that* the reason why Preacher's cousin had been in such a hurry to end their telephone chat?

Sliding the loaf pans into the hot oven, Lydia heard a buggy rattle into the barnyard. She went to the back window and saw Preacher Esh unhitching his horse from the carriage, then leading the sorrel mare to the barn for water, prob'ly.

Preacher must be plannin' to stay for a bit, she thought, glad her aunt had gone upstairs to ret up her room. She could only hope that Aunt Sarah might stay put, 'specially if Preacher's visit had anything to do with her bein' the one to fill the opening at the Amish school. She sure didn't want Sarah blurting out anything 'bout Levi coming over here last night!

About the time the man of God knocked on the door, she'd washed and dried her hands, ready to greet him. "Willkomm, *Breddicher* — Preacher!"

"And hullo to you, Lyddie." His hat was off almost before he was inside, and she smelled wood smoke on his heavy black *Wamus* — coat.

She waited for him to maneuver his long

219

arms out of the woolen winter outer garment. "I'll hang it up for you."

"Denki, 'tis kind of you."

How embarrassed she was not to have baked goods, warm from the oven, ready to offer at a minute's notice, as Mamma always had. Not wanting to confess to bein' lazy — and she wasn't — she just wished with all her might that she wasn't so awful distracted. Because of Aunt Sarah bein' here. 'Course, she wouldn't go tellin' Preacher Esh any of that. He was here to ask her 'bout teaching school. Sure as anything.

"If you had come after lunch, I would've had plenty of fresh bread on hand," she explained.

"Ach, that's just fine, Lyddie." He patted his round stomach. "I've got me a gut cook at home."

She laughed along with him. "A blessing, ain't?"

"A plump wife and a big barn never did a man any harm," he said with a wink. Then, settling down in a rocker nearby, he pulled it up close to the stove, as if forgettin' that this wasn't a woodstove. Just the way Fannie had yesterday. "I'm here to ask a favor of you." He leaned back, his gray head bumping the back of the hickory rocker.

She wouldn't think of jumpin' ahead of

him, even though she was perty sure what was on his mind.

"Wouldja be willin' to teach the schoolchildren . . . 'least till the end of May?"

He hadn't wasted any time gettin' right to the point. She was overjoyed. "I'd do it in a minute. There's only one thing that might keep me from teachin'." She went on to tell him but it turned out he already knew. "Then you've heard 'bout Aunt Sarah Cain comin'?"

He nodded his head a little jerkily, like he was thinkin' hard on something. "Word's going 'round fast here lately, I'd hafta say."

"Do you think it's a gut idea for me to start teachin', then?"

" 'Tis an honest question, Lyddie." He scratched his long beard. Then a sly smile spread across his face. "Maybe it would serve you well to start teachin' right away — next Monday."

Just what she'd been thinking. "Denki for askin' me."

"You'll do a right fine job for the People. And we'll just hope you can stay till school's end . . . at least."

This minute, with the homey smell of yeast and dough mingling together, she wished she had the nerve to ask if it was displeasin' to the Lord God heavenly Fa-

221

ther, her reading through Mamma's journals and all.

Instead, she said, "What would you think of your cousin comin' to live with us, 'least till little Hannah is grown?"

"Which cousin do ya mean?"

"Miriam, down the road a piece."

Something akin to opposition rippled over his brow and settled in his eyes, striking fear to Lydia's heart.

"Have you talked to her lately?" He scratched his head where his hat had been.

"Just this mornin', by telephone."

He nodded. "Best go on down to Susie Lapp's quiltin' frolic this Thursday. Far as I know, Miriam will be goin', too."

"I'd thought of that, but how do I get her off alone so I can talk to her?"

"Trust the Lord God for His timing in all things, Lyddie."

Mamma had said those words to her often enough. She shouldn't have been surprised that the preacher was reminding her now.

"And what'll I do with Aunt Sarah during the quiltin' bee? Wouldn't be right to leave her home alone," she said, lowering her voice.

"Take your mamma's sister along with you. Surely she can be taught to make stitches, ain't?"

Lydia hadn't thought of that. She had no idea, really, what her aunt could or couldn't do with a needle and thread. Guess she'd just have to find out.

"About Aunt Sarah . . . uh, she's busy upstairs," Lydia said, hoping the preacher wouldn't ask to meet her aunt today.

"Sorry, I can't stay too awful long," he replied. "Would be nice to meet your mamma's sister sometime soon, her bein' your temporary caretaker and all."

"Oh, you'll prob'ly meet her here 'fore too long."

"Jah." Preacher Esh got up out of the rocking chair and moseyed toward the back door. "Blessings on ya, Lyddie."

As she bade him good-bye, she could hardly stand still, thinkin' that come next Monday, she had herself a fine job as a schoolteacher. With all her heart — and with the help of God — she would do her very best.

Now if she could just get Miriam to be more agreeable.

Chapter Nineteen

Susie Lapp showed up in a hurry 'round noon, just in time for homemade noodle and beef soup, melted cheese sandwiches, chow-chow, and pickled beets. Their talk 'round the table flitted from the weather — which was s'posed to turn even colder, with "more snow and wind on its way," said Susie, eyeing Aunt Sarah — to the quiltin' bee come Thursday.

"You'll be comin', too, won't you?" Lydia said quickly, addressing her aunt.

"Jah, *do*," Susie insisted, her gray eyes lighting up. "You'll have a gut chance to look us over once."

Aunt Sarah blinked, appearing to be ever so shaken at Susie's off-the-cuff remark. "Excuse me?" she said.

"Ach, you Englischers are all the same," Susie said, shakin' her head and chuckling. "We know you're lookin' us over, so go ahead 'n get it over with."

In the worst way, Lydia wanted to change the subject. Susie seemed downright *gretzich* — cranky. Right outspoken, too. Just why, she didn't know.

"Was Ivy also curious when she and her husband first came here?" Aunt Sarah's offhand question made Lydia squirm.

"Well, forevermore," murmured Susie. "Whatever gave you that notion?"

"English are all alike," parroted Aunt Sarah.

Dismayed, Lydia could no longer sit by and witness the barbed exchange. "Anybody hankerin' for pie?" she asked, forcing a cheerful air.

Susie seemed a bit cool, like she hadn't heard. Aunt Sarah, on the other hand, was leaning forward, her elbows on the table. It looked as if they were goin' to go at it here and now!

"Jah, I'll have a piece," Susie said 'bout the time the silence was so thick you could've sliced it in two. "And while you're up, Lyddie, give your aunt some, too."

Lydia's face burned as she dipped her knife into the pumpkin pie. Both her mamma's sister and her mamma's best friend were actin' like children, of all things! What was the matter with them?

"It's beyond me why Ivy wanted an English woman to pick up the pieces for her family," Susie huffed.

Aunt Sarah said nothing, but her face went white as the snow on the front stoop.

225

Lydia cleared her throat and brought two dessert plates filled with generous portions of pie and ice cream. She set the plates in front of Aunt Sarah, then Susie Lapp. "We best talk 'bout other things," she said, fully aware that she was speakin' out of turn, 'specially in the presence of her elders. Still, she felt she *had* to put an end to this prattle.

"Lydia's right." Aunt Sarah caught her eye, then turned her attention toward the pie in front of her.

Several minutes passed before Susie spoke again, her gaze on her dessert. "I shouldn't have said what I did, Sarah. It was wrong of me."

She didn't go on to offer a clear apology, which Lydia thought was necessary. Still, the remark did seem to clear the air a bit. 'Least enough to get through their coffee-drinkin' and, later, sorting through Mamma's clothes and personal things.

Hours after Susie Lapp had hitched her horse to the carriage and carried off several armloads of Mamma's dresses, aprons, and prayer veilings, Lydia set more hot cocoa to simmerin' on the stove.

She was mighty glad the sad ordeal of goin' through her mother's belongings was behind them. Susie had settled down a bit, minded her manners, but still was adamant 'bout taking the upper hand with nearly every aspect of the sorting process, from what should be done with the Sunday dresses, capes, and aprons to who might want the nightgowns, Kapps, and shoes.

Going upstairs, Lydia brought down a pile of socks to darn at the kitchen table while she waited for her brothers and sisters to arrive home from school.

Aunt Sarah was foolin' with some kind of flat typewriter attached to a square with lit-up words. "Your mother's friend seems to thrive on conflict," she said from across the table.

"Oh, now and then, maybe. She and Mamma used to have their moments sometimes, too, but, oh my, how they loved each other; even more than they fought, guess you could say."

"So they argued often?"

Lydia, surprised at her aunt's inquiry, looked across the table. "So . . . I guess Susie's definitely out of the question?" She didn't wait for her aunt to answer. "I'm thinkin' Susie's not someone you'd pick to raise us."

Aunt Sarah's face broke into a grin. "I wouldn't wish her on my own worst enemy."

Lydia had no intention of fussin' with Aunt Sarah and changed the subject. "Well, then, how do you feel 'bout going to the quilting . . . at Susie's house?"

Turning pale again, Aunt Sarah mumbled something unrecognizable to Lydia. Maybe a cuss word. Maybe not, though she couldn't be sure.

When no further comment came from her aunt, Lydia forged ahead. "Miriam Esh will be there. Preacher Esh said so."

"Was it your minister who came earlier?" Lydia nodded.

"Sometime I want to speak with him," Aunt Sarah said unexpectedly.

"Not 'bout last night, I hope?" She felt ever so bold speakin' up.

Sarah got up at that moment and, without excusin' herself, left the room.

Fearin' the worst, Lydia darned much too fast and pricked her finger, spurting blood on Caleb's church sock.

Sarah was desperate to contact Bryan, but she didn't want to disturb him in the middle of an important meeting. She wrote a short email message, hoping he might read between the lines.

Bryan,

This place is closing in on me. What was it you said about Amish country doing me good? Well, think again! The truth is I'm going stark raving mad. I need to hang at a club somewhere. Care to join me on a binge?

Sarah

Almost as soon as she'd sent the hasty message, she regretted her spontaneity. Sure, Bryan would come to her rescue — he always did — but had she been too presumptuous to ask?

While Sarah chopped lettuce for a salad, she overheard Anna Mae mumbling to herself. Sarah was certain the girl had no idea she was being observed, yet the more she listened to the idle chatter, the more she felt she should approach Anna Mae.

Leaving the salad fixings behind, Sarah washed her hands and went to the doorway to the utility room. There stood Anna Mae, facing a row of winter coats, hats, and scarves, a glazed look in her green eyes.

"Anna Mae, are you all right?" Sarah asked.

Startled, the girl turned to face her, eyes too wide and the look of a polished plate on her face. "I . . . uh . . . Lyddie!" hollered Anna Mae.

Puzzled, Sarah stood her ground. "You don't have to call for your sister. You can

229

talk to *me,* if you like."

Anna Mae put her hands over her ears, lowering her head to her chest, still talking, but nonsensically. "Mamma's gone away . . . she's gone away from here. Ach, Mamma —"

"Anna Mae," Sarah interrupted, "look at me!"

The whispered chanting continued. "Mamma's gone home to heaven now . . . gone far away to heaven now."

Suddenly Sarah fought tears that threatened to blur her vision, though she could see only Meggie Holmes in her mind's eye, remembering her student's mildly autistic mannerisms — recalling the breakthrough that had come at long last, after months and months of reaching out to the pixiesh girl. All for naught, in the end. . . .

"Anna Mae?" she whispered, crouching down to the child's level. "Your mamma didn't want to go away. You must believe that."

Her young niece said nothing in response. No more muttering or covering her ears. But she was quivering hard.

"Please . . . let me help you." She reached out to the girl.

But Anna Mae backed away, stumbling backward, falling into the wall of coats and scarves. "No . . . no . . . no," she whimpered.

Just as she was about to touch the girl's shoulder, Lydia emerged in the doorway. "What's wrong with my sister?" she asked, a ring of accusation in her voice. "Aunt Sarah, what's happened to Anna Mae?"

The heartfelt moment — that glimmer of verity — had passed, burst like a bubble against a barbed wire.

Lydia's hands were on her hips, demanding an answer. "Anna Mae was yelling for me. I *heard* her."

"Your sister's upset," Sarah replied, turning toward the kitchen. "I couldn't seem to help her."

"I want Mamma back," Anna Mae was crying, still in the utility room. "Please make Mamma come back to me!"

Sarah returned to the kitchen and picked up the knife. She slashed through the head of lettuce, her mind replaying the insinuations, the vicious whispers that had turned to public furor after the accident in Stonington. Remembering caused her to feel nauseous.

Bryan, please hurry, she thought, chopping the lettuce into much finer pieces than necessary.

"What happened with Anna Mae earlier?" Lydia asked her while they washed and dried supper dishes.

231

"I think your sister may need to talk to a therapist. Do you know what I mean by that?"

"Head doctors are for English folk," Lydia said softly but firmly, wringing out the dishrag.

"You don't understand. I'm quite familiar with cases like Anna Mae."

Lydia spun around to face Sarah. Her eyes were fire. "My sister is *not* a case study!"

"I didn't mean —"

"But you're thinkin' it all the same. I can see it in your face."

Sarah was struck by the similarities between her deceased sister and Ivy's daughter. The slant of her lips in a display of anger, the tilt of her stubborn head.

"Anna Mae needs love and attention, that's all. She'll be fine, you'll see."

"I do hope so" was all Sarah said.

"Our mamma knew how to care for us," Lydia said, almost sadly, suffering her own loss anew. "She loved us through the Lord Jesus himself. She always said it was God's love pouring out through her to us. But more than that, Mamma was a kind and loving *person*, too."

Sarah listened, amazed. This was a side to Ivy she had not known. The things Lydia was saying about Ivy were difficult for Sarah to grasp, but she wouldn't admit her feelings to her niece. She did think, however, that this might be an opportune time to inquire of Ivy's journals, if such writings existed. "I'd like to know more about my sister's adult years," she said, tempering her words. "If you don't mind . . . if you feel comfortable . . ."

"What would you like to know?"

"I wonder . . . may I read your mother's journals?"

Lydia drew in her breath. It was obvious to Sarah that the girl struggled with the notion.

"I don't know . . . I —"

"You have every right to guard your mother's personal things, I understand."

"Mamma didn't keep many diaries, really," Lydia blurted. "She learned from Grandpa Cain about being particular, 'bout taking care to discard the ordinary. If you must know, Mamma kept only a few journals."

How strange to hear Lydia reiterate the words of Sarah's own father. *Grandpa Cain, indeed.* It seemed the man had affixed his imprint on his oldest grandchild quite effectively.

"One diary will do," she said.

Lydia frowned. "You'll return it, then, when you're through?"

"Of course." She folded the tea towel, noticing the embroidered words for the first time: *God's way is the best way.*

Not a single light flickered on the wall this night as Lydia snuggled down under the warm quilts Mamma and she had made together. Her thoughts were of Levi, a hopeful but somewhat troubling shift from her mental scuffle with Aunt Sarah.

She'd ended up handin' over one of Mamma's journals to Aunt Sarah before going off to bed, having chosen one of the earlier diaries because she wouldn't be ready to read it herself for several more nights.

Sick in spirit, she skipped writing in her own journal, finding that it was almost too much to bear, her giving an account of the past day, 'specially with the growing hostility between herself and Aunt Sarah.

And what was to become of her and Levi's love? Sadly, they weren't courtin' at all, and not seeing Levi broke her heart — puttin' her beloved off as she had. All because of them bein' orphans . . . and Aunt Sarah not willing to take her rightful place.

Turmoil had come a-callin' when Mamma's sister stepped foot in this house. And all in just a matter of forty-eight hours.

★ ★ ★

Sarah sat propped up in bed with a single pillow, wrapped in her warmest bathrobe. She opened randomly to Ivy's diary.

March 17, 1989

Our Lyddie is seven years old today. She is the apple of her father's eye, and mine, too.

Can it be that already we have lived in Lancaster for nearly two years? Susie Lapp has become the dearest friend a woman could ever want. I believe God planned our friendship, bringing the two of us together in a spiritual bond. In some ways, Susie has become somewhat of a sister to me, though we have much more in common than I ever did with Sarah. We are true sisters — Susie and I — in the Lord and otherwise.

Sighing, Sarah marked her spot in Ivy's journal. She might've thought, for a moment, that she was too tired to read further. The truth was she had no desire to go on. Ivy's observation about Susie Lapp being a "true sister" pierced Sarah's soul. And quite unexpectedly, she felt she understood the reason behind the friction she had experienced with Susie Lapp today. Clearly evident were the psychological goings-on between

Mrs. Lapp, one of Ivy's "spirit sisters," and herself, Ivy's one and only biological sister.

Bryan, psychology nut that he was, would have a field day with this if he came and *if* she decided to divulge any aspect of her discovery.

And there was Anna Mae, poor thing. Sarah felt helpless to interfere, but the child needed professional help, of this she was nearly certain.

She placed the diary written by her late sister under the pillow next to her and turned out the light.

Lydia had just begun to doze off when she was aware of someone in her room. She sat up, peering into the darkness.

"Lyddie, it's me . . . Anna Mae. I'm awful scared."

She lifted the covers till Anna Mae had slipped into bed with her. Wrapping her arms around the younger girl's round little body, she asked, "Why are you frightened, sister?"

"Aunt Sarah scares me."

Lydia probed no further. She was content to hold Anna Mae near, wondering if Mamma had ever done the same for her little sister when young Sarah was alarmed. Maybe, though, Mamma and Aunt Sarah had never been chummy enough to share their fears or worries. She suspected that was the case. Well, Lydia could *not* imagine growin' up like that.

She would cradle Anna Mae till she was fast asleep, maybe even longer. Maybe she'd let Anna Mae share a spot in her bed all night long.

Mamma would be pleased if she knew. Jah, ever so pleased.

Softly humming a hymn, Lydia thought of Levi again, wonderin' if he might consider taking in Anna Mae and the others once he and Lydia were married. *If* they ever wed, that is.

But, no . . . the more she thought on it, 'twasn't fair to expect such a thing. If their courtship ever *did* get back on track, she shouldn't be askin' Levi King to be her sisters' and brothers' stepfather. Besides, he might be entirely opposed to the notion. She didn't know for sure, really. This was a right touchy situation!

Looking over at Anna Mae next to her, she felt helpless to meet the youngster's emotional needs. Aunt Sarah was the one best suited, Lydia was nearly certain. Jah, for some reason, she felt Aunt Sarah knew better 'bout whatever it was Anna Mae was goin' through than most anyone.

Chapter Twenty

Five o'clock . . .

Sarah heard footsteps in the hallway and on the stairs. So soon? Rambunctious chirping of birds outside the window further irritated her. In the distance the steady *clip-clopping* of horses' hooves tramped down the snow-packed road.

Why was everyone up already? Then she remembered — in Pennsylvania Amish country, everyone rose before dawn.

Sarah groaned and turned over. How was it that each day should be precisely the same as the day before, varied solely by the work that occupied every minute, every hour of every day from the rising of the sun until after dark?

Plumping the feather pillow, she lay there a few moments longer and gazed at the picture of Megan Holmes in the dim light. Dreaded memories flooded her mind, and she leaned up and reached for the frame. She held it in both hands. "I won't let it happen again . . . ever," she whispered, promising herself. How many times had she said the same words to the smiling face? At least a thousand.

Returning the picture to the small table, she grasped for a ray of hope, something to carry through the day. She recalled the message she had sent to Bryan via email. Had he replied?

She bounded out of bed to check. Turning on her laptop computer, she found herself eager to hear something from the modern world. The *real* world, the world filled with sensible decision-making and logical-thinking people. None of these archaic notions and rituals.

It was while she waited for her computer to boot up that she settled on the best discipline for Lydia's impropriety, maybe the only beneficial restriction: not permitting her niece to attend the quilting bee tomorrow at Susie Lapp's home. Not only did she think it was a good idea to deprive Lydia of the social event, but staying home herself would make it possible for her to avoid another uncomfortable encounter with Ivy's "true" sister.

"You've got mail," stated the computerized voice.

Clicking on the appropriate spot, she read:

Sarah,

Impossible to get away. Sorry.

Later,
Bryan

She was taken aback by his brief note, so unlike his usual jocularity coupled with an eagerness to communicate. That was always Bryan's style when either sending electronic messages or phoning.

Shrugging her dubious thoughts aside, Sarah prepared to bathe and dress for the day. She had survived any number of stressful situations without him. Why should she care if Bryan was busy *this* time?

A boisterous rooster crowed as Sarah uncovered her sister's journal from one of the bed pillows. She turned to the beginning, to the first entry, and began to read Ivy's words.

New Year's Day, 1989

My lap was full of fabric nearly all day, what with it being the dead of winter and all. While Lyddie was at school, young Caleb was a good little helper, keeping one-year-old Anna Mae happy in her playpen nearby. I must've embroidered five or more pillow-

cases and worked on two different samplers.

In just a short time, I've learned that a wise woman is content with sewing, knitting, and embroidering. Crocheting is a bit tricky yet for me, but I'm doing my best to get the knack of it. When my hands are busy pushing a needle gently through folds of fabric, well, it brings such a deep kind of joy to me, a freedom from the cares of life. Sometimes I actually feel a part of the material I'm sewing, and it's a wonderful-gut feeling, to be sure.

Susie Lapp surprised me with a big pot of Chilly Day Stew near lunchtime. It hit the spot, and my children seemed to like it, too. All of us, Gil included, are still getting used to the enormous amount of vegetables used in cooking here in the Amish community, everything from potato rivvel soup to zucchini squash cake. I think we're already healthier, too.

I sent a letter to Sarah, put it out in the morning mail. It's been weeks since I've had a letter from her. Still, I won't give up sharing the things we're learning here. The People have taught Gil and me not to dwell on the visible things so much, but on the coming world — God's blessed kingdom. Oh, if only my sister could see the change in me!

Lydia watched in amazement as Aunt

Sarah trudged through the snow a few strides behind little Hannah, sporting the fanciest brass-colored boots she'd ever seen. The worldly getup didn't mix well with the farmland on either side of the road; not the Plain attire the children wore, either. Marching single file, they were stairsteps — Caleb in the lead, Aunt Sarah bringing up the tail end, the fancy caboose.

A chuckle escaped her lips, and she wondered what had prompted their English relative to follow the children to school, for goodness' sake!

Lydia stood in the window, observing the peculiar sight till she could see them no longer. 'Bout that time, she wondered how it would be goin' off to school herself next week. A teacher at last.

Tomorrow, for sure and for certain, she *must* talk to Miriam Esh. Honestly, she wondered if maybe by now Preacher Esh had already put a bug in the woman's ear. She could only hope and pray he might be able to soften Miriam up a bit. 'Cause without Preacher's cousin, all was lost. Not only would Lydia miss her chance to teach school, she might also lose out on bein' Levi's wife!

If asked, Sarah could not have logically

pinpointed the reason, but she found herself hiking through ankle-deep snow with four of her nieces and nephews on their way to school. Perhaps the perplexed expression on Anna Mae's freckled face at breakfast had prompted her somewhat impulsive decision. Part of her wanted to extend something of herself to the girl, yet she knew not how or what to say. Another side of her wanted to book a flight out of here tomorrow!

Yesterday she had tried to soothe Anna Mae, clearly wounded and unsteady of mind, but the girl had become terribly frightened. Sarah had seen the terror on the girl's face.

So it was that she walked in the midst of a bitter cold day, single file, along a snow-covered roadside that Caleb said led to the Amish schoolhouse. "Someone might come along and give us a sleigh ride," he said, a glint of hope in his eyes.

"Noah Lapp might," Josiah piped up. "He's the nicest man alive."

Sarah's ears perked up at that, and she wished Josiah might turn around and offer her his perpetual grin. Asked her opinion, she would have said it was the younger of the two Cottrell boys — Josiah — who most favored his deceased father. But this many years removed, she found it difficult to evaluate. The reality was that she had not seen either Gilbert or Ivy since their move from Bridgeport, Connecticut, to Lancaster County nearly twelve years ago.

Little Hannah seemed to purposely slow her pace, waiting for Sarah to match her stride. Together, they made their way through the snow, side by side, for quite a long way before Hannah said, "Mamma sometimes walked to school with us, too."

Anna Mae was quick to correct her little sister. "Mamma only walked with us on the warmest days."

"*Always* in the springtime," Caleb added. "Early May was Mamma's favorite time of the year."

Sarah's thoughts flew to the passage in Ivy's journal. *If only my sister could see the change in me.* So Ivy's life *had* changed radically. She must have delighted in her and Gilbert's existence here with the Plain people of the Lancaster area, loved it enough to give birth to five discerning children; children with whom Ivy enjoyed walking to school and soaking up warm breezes along the way.

"Mamma loved the locust trees," Josiah said.

Caleb nodded. "Remember, she used to say that Susie Lapp was never allowed to go barefoot back then — when she was little — not till the white flowers started a-danglin' from the locust trees. By then, everyone knew summer was here to stay."

"There aren't so many of them trees 'round here anymore," Anna Mae said.

"*Those* trees," Caleb said. "You best mind your grammar if Lyddie's goin' to be our teacher, come next week. You know what a stickler she is for correct speakin'."

"That's just 'cause she was raised English for five years, don'tcha think so?" Josiah asked.

"Could be," replied the older brother.

"Lyddie won't get to teach at our school if we have to move away," Anna Mae said, a resonant sting in her voice.

"And that's not all she won't get to do," Hannah piped up.

Absolutely curious, Sarah asked, "What do you mean by that, Hannah?"

"*Himmel!*" Hannah clapped her mittened hand over her mouth. "I daresn't be sayin'."

Josiah blurted, "Lydia'll hafta marry some English man, that's what. Ain't nobody Plain out in Oregon."

Grateful that the children were facing forward, away from her, she took in the nuance of meaning. From what she had just gathered, she understood that Lydia must have been asked to teach at the Amish school, possibly fill in as a substitute. And the children also seemed concerned about being removed from the area — their home — by Sarah's own hand. Worst of all, Lydia might have to forego marriage to the boy she loved.

The almost singsong rhythm of conversation among the children reminded her of playground duty. But she wouldn't allow lurking memories to mar her day.

There was little warmth in the sun, even though its intermittent beams cast extended shadows away from the snow fences on the right side of the road. Ahead, on the left, a steady stream of smoke rose like a pillar from a white clapboard farmhouse. Into the pale sky it billowed, then dissipated.

In a few seconds, Noah Lapp *did* show up with his horse and sleigh, and before she could say proper good-byes, the children had leaped aboard, calling their greetings to friends and classmates in Pennsylvania Dutch.

"Hullo there — Sarah Cain, is it?" the Amish driver called cheerfully from the front of the enormous sled filled with laughing, merry children.

Wondering how the man knew her name — her full name, at that — she decided that her first inclination was correct, the man

246

was Susie Lapp's husband. Contemplating yesterday's visit with his outspoken wife, she wondered what *else* Mrs. Lapp had told her jovial husband.

She waved to the entire group and was pleased when tiny Hannah waved back, most energetically. The gay twitter of the children mingled with the bitter cold, the hoarfrost, and the blustering smell of winter around them. Unknowingly, the Amishman with horse and sleigh had brought Sarah's trek to school to an abrupt end. Mr. Lapp's arrival had also dispelled the tension the children's revealing chatter had brought her way.

Before she turned to head back to the farmhouse, she noticed Anna Mae sitting in a heap all by herself, her lips moving silently as she kept her bonneted head bowed. How was she to coax Anna Mae out of her shell? What old methods should she reconstitute, if any?

This child, her sister's child, lacked encouragement, comfort from life's worst bum rap of all. Anna Mae — so lost and alone in her own little world. What could *she* do for the youngster without revisiting painful memories, without associating Anna Mae with her own personal misery, the tragedy of Meggie Holmes?

Pushing her hands down into her coat pockets, Sarah strode with perseverance back up the road toward the farmhouse, Gilbert and Ivy Cottrell's haven set apart from the world and its countless tentacles of sin and woe.

Literally, she would have scoffed last week if anyone had told her that at this moment she would be wearing her dead sister's mittens, even if they were quite holey, too worn to do much good.

Chapter Twenty-One

Lydia was tempted to cut corners and not sweep out the utility room completely. Forgetting the clutter of work boots and other items over in the corner wouldn't hurt nothin', would it?

Things done by halves are never done right. Mamma's oft-repeated saying flew 'round in Lydia's head, urging her on. Oh, how she missed Mamma, her friend and confidante. How long would it take for the pain in her heart to subside? How long before she could get through the day without thinking of her mother, gone to heaven?

She thought back to three years earlier, when they'd lost Dat to the farming accident. For months and months they'd mourned him, each in his own way. It was Mamma who missed him most. Still, the rest of the children felt the loss, the heaviness in their spirits.

They had even talked of selling the farmhouse, giving up on the idea of tryin' to keep things running without Dat 'round to help keep the cows fed and milked, the fields planted. All the things that a hardworkin' man could do. Jah, it had been mighty hard, till several of the men from their church started pitchin' in and working, without pay, on a regular basis. Lydia knew now, more than ever, if it wasn't for that kind of help durin' the growing season, come next summer, they'd be at a loss to know how to manage, 'specially now with Mamma gone, too.

Twice tempted to drop the broom and go finish her mending or cut more quilt squares for the frolic tomorrow, she instead went ahead and swept the floor as Mamma had taught her, followin' through with what she'd started. She made sure she did not miss a single corner of the long room backed up to the screened-in porch.

Lydia wondered what had prompted Aunt Sarah to walk the younger children to school, or at least part of the way, 'specially on such a frosty day. She was dumbfounded by Mamma's peculiar sister. No getting 'round it, Sarah Cain was as unpredictable as anyone she'd ever known.

It wondered her — when should she take courage and ask Aunt Sarah about Mamma's journal entry, the one about the "accident that claimed her spirit"?

The solo walk back to the house was far

less than gratifying. With cruelty, the wind had regathered its strength, sending stinging snow crystals against her face as she leaned into the gale. She shielded her eyes as best she could, trying not to breathe through her mouth in spite of the exertion she was putting forth to walk against the wind, hoping to keep the icy air out of her sensitive lungs. Her throat and upper respiratory system had been the weakest part of her since childhood, so she held the scarf in place around her nose and mouth, hoping she could avoid contracting bronchitis *this* winter.

Above all, she dreaded having to inform Lydia of the punishment she had discreetly chosen. She did not relish imposing her judgment, exerting her will against her sister's eldest daughter.

The propagation and management of children was one of the main reasons she and Bryan had argued so bitterly in college, the cause of their final breakup. . . .

Sarah had known for quite some time that Bryan was in love with her. They had even gone so far as to discuss whether or not to exchange wedding bands, Bryan having a yen for the "more simple side of things." As for large houses and expensive cars, he had often said, *"Who needs rooms when all you really need is a roof over your head?"*

Dutifully, she would laugh at his remarks, but deep down Bryan's philosophy irritated her beyond her ability to espouse it. Despite their incongruity, she found him nearly irresistible. In his arms, the earth ceased its orbiting, the resident birds trilled grand arias, and the twilight rose up around them, turning the ocean a resplendent fine pewter.

The night they parted ways, he had taken her to a lively delicatessen, complete with Tiffany lamps, full bar, and soft classical music — piped-in Chopin waltzes, as she recalled. Poor Richard's Bistro was off campus by only two blocks, one of the few upscale haunts they'd enjoyed as a couple.

For all her growing-up years, prior to meeting Bryan, she had supposed herself to be the result of some rueful miscalculation. She had convinced herself she was a byproduct borne of contention — both her mother's and sister's unified dissension invariably directed toward her. Even her overly religious father had offered her nothing of real substance, only nebulous discourses on the shores of Watch Hill while gathering his beloved shells — and there was his constant chatter regarding God and the universe, "the Creator's playground," as he put it. All that sort of nonsense.

Sarah had come to her relationship with Bryan a mere silhouette of a woman, hungry for acceptance, but too apprehensive to embrace it wholeheartedly.

As the evening drew to a close, Bryan brought up the topic of children. "I hope you want at least a half dozen."

Sarah, under the influence of fine wine, thought he was joking. "And *I* hope you're kidding," she replied, letting him caress her hand across the table.

"Actually, I'm nuts about kids, Sarah. Always have been."

"Well, I'm not breaking my back getting my teaching certificate for nothing," she taunted, hoping to bypass the topic. At this juncture in their association, she was not ready to offer her treatise on family, namely children. Why couldn't Bryan be satisfied with her, enjoy what *they* had together, without planning the future . . . marriage and offspring?

"Can we talk about it?" he asked gently, eyes bright with devotion.

"About what?" Sarah asked, tensing up.

"Your sudden resistance, for one."

"To what?"

"To me . . . I can feel it all the way over here."

She slipped her hand out of his. "Having children is the last thing on my mind."

"You mean you haven't *ever* thought about it?"

She wouldn't tell him she'd thought about nothing else, especially while growing up under the iron hand of her older sister and her unsympathetic mother. Sincerely, the best thing she could do for herself was to dodge the motherhood bullet, forget about having children. Bottom line: She couldn't bear the thought of precious babies growing up to suffer as she had — chafing under the alienation she had always felt.

So the great debate ensued.

"Are you telling me you don't want *any* kids?" he persisted, leaning forward now, his handsome face serious to the point of near trepidation.

"Not today." She didn't say *not ever*, but she firmly believed, by the unwavering response she was getting from Bryan, that it was best if they steered clear of the parental issue.

"Anyone can see you'll never be the mother hen type." Ivy's flippant teenage remark came back to plague her.

"We can work things out," Bryan said, coming around the table and sliding into the booth beside her.

"I don't think so."

"Shouldn't we at least try? This is important stuff."

She shook her head, because she had already said *no* in so many words. But her opinion had made no impression on him. Neither had it altered the course of their controversy.

He wrapped his arm around her shoulder. "You're everything to me, you know."

She could not cry nor think. Could scarcely speak, but she knew in her soul this was the end for them. He would never understand where she was coming from, the pain of her past intertwined with an unhealthy relationship with a domineering sister. And there was Bryan's nearly irrational insistence.

Even now, she recalled how they had walked together under a dark sky, their unresolved tension so thick she could still feel the blackness that had penetrated their love. By the time she arrived back at her dorm, the moon had risen, a hazy hoop of a thing, fading fast in a bank of clouds to the east.

Now, struggling against the cold, Sarah turned into the lane leading to the Cottrell farmhouse. *Life is so ironic,* she thought. Here she was, attempting to place her own flesh and blood — well, her sister's — into the hands of any Amish family who might agree to take them, exhibiting some of the seemingly nonmaternal attributes that had grieved Bryan Ford long ago. Yet last night she had contacted him, requesting his company in the midst of this mess.

What *was* she thinking?

Mulling over the children's morning chatter, she recalled her initial plan for Lydia's discipline: to keep her home from the Lapp quilting. Having heard what Lydia's sisters and brothers let slip — their worries and fears for their existence, as well as Lydia's marital future — she wondered if she shouldn't reconsider and make every effort to meet Miriam Esh at the quilting, after all. She resolved to go halfway with the Esh woman, do what she must to make the arrangement suitable for Ivy's children. Her career and modern life-style had been put on hold. She *must* get on with her own life, lest Ivy's world lay claim to her against her will.

Chapter Twenty-Two

"Preacher Esh asked me to teach at the Amish school where my sisters and brothers attend," Lydia said as she sat in the front seat of Aunt Sarah's rental car on the way to Susie Lapp's quilting frolic.

"Is that why he came to visit?"

She felt a bit sheepish to answer. "Jah, 'tis."

"How is it that someone your age is qualified to teach?"

Lydia understood a little of her aunt's wariness. English schools were run by highly educated folk. Amish schools, on the other hand, were operated by the community. The bishops and the People themselves had the final say. "Any girl who goes through all eight grades in an Amish school — usually the ones who had the best grades — teach in our schools. We're allowed to teach till we marry."

"Oh? And when would that be?"

Lydia thought she knew why her aunt was so interested. "Anywhere from age fifteen or sixteen, up to nineteen. Most girls are married by age twenty 'round here."

"Well, in my opinion, that's entirely too young to settle down and marry."

"Did *you* ever think of . . . marryin'?" Lydia ventured, eager to know.

Aunt Sarah responded more quickly than Lydia had intended. "I dated a couple of young men in college."

"Either of them propose?"

"Why do you ask?"

"It's just that Mamma told me you were more interested in music and other things in high school, but that you had one special beau in college."

"Your Mamma and I were writing letters during those days, so I guess she should know."

Lydia thought on that. "I'd like to hear about your life from *you*."

Aunt Sarah glanced at her, then turned back to face the road ahead, hands gripping the steering wheel. "What would you like to know?" She seemed a bit uneasy.

"You didn't marry, like Mamma did. How come?"

Aunt Sarah was still.

Lydia wondered if she'd pried too much. "Sorry, I s'pose it wasn't polite to ask," she said quickly.

The woman said nothing.

"You must've *liked* children, 'cause you

were a schoolteacher yourself once."

"As a matter of fact, I was. But only for a short time."

"Mamma told me 'bout it . . . before she died."

Aunt Sarah turned to look at her again. "What did she tell you?"

"That something awful sad happened to you. Something that *made* you quit teachin'."

Aunt Sarah did a surprising thing just then. She signaled and brought the car to a stop on the side of the deserted road. "What else did your mother tell you?"

"Well, uh . . . she didn't ever really *tell* me more than what I already said just now. But the other night, while I was readin' one of her diaries, I came across something." She was breathless, almost afraid to go on, 'cause Aunt Sarah was starin' hard at her.

"Go ahead, Lydia. I'm listening."

Lydia took a breath and wondered if she was doin' the right thing by Mamma. 'Course, then again, Aunt Sarah was readin' Mamma's writings, too. "I don't honestly know a thing 'bout this, but in Mamma's 1998 journal, for the month of December, she wrote that there'd been an accident of some kind."

"Yes."

"It . . . well, that accident must've been

259

awful bad. Mamma wrote that it claimed your spirit, or suchlike."

Instantly her aunt's face drooped, and she was shakin' her head back and forth, unable to speak.

"I'm so sorry," Lydia offered, genuinely contrite. "I shouldn't have brought up such a sad rememberin'."

Opening her leather pocketbook, Aunt Sarah fished 'round inside and pulled out a tissue. She leaned up to the rearview mirror, dabbing ever so carefully at her eyes, prob'ly so she wouldn't smudge the makeup, positioning the mirror once again when she was finished. Then, without another word, she looked back over her left shoulder and slowly steered the car onto the road again.

In all her days, Lydia had never seen a woman's face turn so completely ashen and drawn — like Lydia had somehow had the power to make her mamma's sister age awful fast in just five minutes!

The quilting at Susie Lapp's drew fifteen Plain women from their church district, a bigger turnout than Sarah ever expected for such a cold, wintry day. She was also surprised by the number of women *her* age present. She had presumed such get-togethers were predominantly attended by older women in the community. But on this particular day, the eldest woman sitting at the large quilt frame was Mammi Elizabeth.

"In all of Strasburg and Paradise, Mammi Elizabeth sews the tiniest stitches of anybody," Lydia whispered as they hung up their coats in the little mud room adjacent to the kitchen.

Observing Elizabeth, her face deeply wrinkled with the years, her white hair tucked neatly under a cap, Sarah wondered how the woman managed to quilt without glasses. That old adage about eating plenty of carrots — was it true? The Amish certainly consumed their share of vegetables. In fact, now that she thought of it, not a single woman gathered at the quilting frame was wearing glasses.

"There'll be thousands of stitches in this quilt when it's finished. We call it the Diamond in the Square, one of our most popular patterns," Lydia said, pulling a chair up for Sarah at the edge of the quilt. "We can use your help."

Sarah didn't wish to cause a scene nor reject the sincere offer on the part of her niece. She assumed Lydia was merely being polite, because looking over the wide girth of the enormous frame and the intricate work already underway, she was fairly certain she could not do what these women were doing. Furthermore, she didn't want to ruin the lovely quilt for its soon-to-be owner.

Lydia must have sensed her reticence and proceeded to show Sarah how to hold the needle, where to put her free hand. "It's all in the wrist," the girl said. "Here, watch me."

"Maybe I should *just* watch for a while," she said softly, hoping Lydia would back off a bit.

"Either that, or you can practice on a remnant. Lots of new quilters do just that."

What Sarah truly wanted was to blend into the woodwork, but being the only Englischer in the room made blending rather difficult. Looking around, she tried to pick out which woman was Miriam Esh.

Lydia said something about going in search of scraps and got up to look. She wasn't giving up anytime soon, reminding Sarah once again of the unyielding aspects of Ivy's personality. Lydia, indeed, had something of her mother's temperament. The fact was becoming more evident to Sarah as each day progressed.

"We oughta be sayin' who we are, for Lydia's aunt's sake," the eldest quilter, Elizabeth, spoke up.

"Jah, by all means," Susie Lapp agreed, glancing at Sarah and offering a pleasant grin. "I'm sure she remembers me."

"Yes, hello again," Sarah said quickly, offering a quick smile.

"Oh, by the way, my husband said he saw you out on the road with the Cottrell children yesterday mornin'." As quickly as Susie had spoken, she put her head down, careful to keep an eye on her own nimble fingers guiding the needle up and down through the fabric and batting.

Sarah listened as eleven women told her their names, noting several Marys and Beckys. Fannie Flaud and her mother, Emma, also introduced themselves. But there was only one quilter present by the name of Miriam Esh. Sarah had *not* been able to identify her before the introductions, although she stood out — unfortunately, because she needed a bath!

"I'm one of Preacher's first cousins," the black-haired woman said without cracking the slightest smile, though the others chuckled. She avoided making eye contact with either Sarah or Lydia, which puzzled Sarah greatly.

She also observed that Miriam appeared to be older than her midthirties, as Lydia had told her earlier. The Amishwoman wore a green cape dress, the same hue and styling as several other women at the quilting. Her black cape was attached to a long black apron, as well. By the smile lines around her full lips, Sarah guessed the soft-spoken woman was apparently fun-loving, at least on occasion. At the present, however, it was hard to determine just how happy a person Miriam Esh might be.

After several hours, the quilters had themselves a lunch break. Aunt Sarah seemed willing to sample most everything set before them, including the pickled eggs. And when they bowed their heads for the silent prayer, she did, too, which pleased Lydia to no end.

She's tryin' real hard, Lydia thought, glad things had worked out for her aunt to come along. Glad, too, that she was makin' an attempt to sew practice stitches on three or four small scraps of fabric. And Aunt Sarah was joinin' in the chatter every now and then, and asking questions, too.

Truth be told, Lydia had a sneakin' suspicion that Mamma's sister was actually enjoying herself, if only a little, for the first time since she'd come here last Sunday. 'Course, then, she wouldn't go so far as to get her hopes up 'bout that.

It was Miriam's almost curt response that

264

set Lydia back a bit, left her unsure of herself. No, it actually spoilt the rest of the afternoon for her altogether.

"I was hopin' you and I could have a talk," she said, seekin' Miriam out at the long table and sitting down next to her.

"Oh?"

Lydia held her breath, trying for the life of her not to breathe in Miriam's offensive body odor. "Jah, there's something I think you might be interested in doin' — for Mamma."

"And what would that be?"

Lydia's heart sank. Dare she go on? "Can you stop by our house this-after, maybe?"

"Well, I'd planned to stay 'n help till the work's done on the quilt, ya know."

From past experience, Lydia knew the expert quilters would finish off things with the final stitches in a rapid show of energized motivation to "get the quilt out" before nightfall. That's how it was done. So she couldn't blame Miriam for wantin' to stay. After all, the woman had an empty house to greet her — no husband waitin', and no children, either.

Thinking on the topic burnin' inside her, she honestly wondered if maybe Preacher's cousin just might not want to keep things the way they were. Her bein' an old maid and all.

Some folk seemed more cut out for a solitary life. Maybe Miriam was one of 'em.

But how could Lydia stand by and not ask, at least? She just couldn't, not with her own future and the future of her sisters and brothers at stake. She'd seen the struggle Aunt Sarah had over makin' her stitches, tryin' to fit in 'round the Plain women this mornin'. 'Twas no easy task for a fancy Englischer.

Truly, she felt sorry for Mamma's sister, havin' to come to Lancaster like this. Prob'ly against her will.

"Trust the Lord God for His timing. . . ."

Preacher Esh's words were more than a comfort to her just now.

"Jah, that's right, I hope to start teachin' school next Monday," Lydia told Ada King, Levi's mamma, after lunch, when the work had resumed on the red, purple, and green quilt.

"Seems to me I heard something 'bout that," Ada said, a twinkle of discernment in her gray blue eyes.

Lydia was thankful her beau's mother had been discreet 'bout not sayin' where she'd heard the news. Surely, Levi had mentioned something in passing at mealtime 'bout Lydia's hope to teach. Besides, now the whole community had prob'ly heard, 'least they would've if Preacher Esh had talked it 'round, like she was perty sure he had.

Fannie grinned at Lydia across the quilt. She, too, prob'ly suspected there was much more than met the eye between Levi King and Lydia Cottrell. In that affectionate exchange of glances, Lydia thought of Levi and honestly wished she could've given him something more to go on, that she had said she *would* marry him, just not run off with him . . . elope. Even if Aunt Sarah took Lydia and her family away from here, there wasn't anything that said the young lovers couldn't correspond by mail, to keep their affection alive, till such time as they could be wed.

Why she was thinkin' like this, she didn't rightly know. But ofttimes such knotty problems actually had a chance to be mentally solved durin' the process of a quilting.

"There's a healing that often comes from creating an heirloom," Mamma used to say.

Mammi Elizabeth, too, was a believer in the notion that each and every quilt had pieced into it stitches of the quilters' lives. In fact, Lydia was surprised no one was doin' any storytelling today. Were they bein' extra cautious because of Aunt Sarah?

There was only one way to find out. So she asked, "Does anybody know what happened

267

to Redbeet John's Abe's Susannah's center-diamond quilt?" she asked, referring to the ancestral line, as was the People's way.

"Ach, that's one of the saddest things I ever did hear," Emma Flaud spoke up, takin' the bait.

Sarah listened with interest to Mrs. Flaud's account of the Amishwoman whose garden shed, where an array of homemade quilts and samplers and other crafts were displayed and sold, had been broken into by way of a window in back of the small outbuilding.

"Prob'ly nobody could see what the robber was doin'," Mammi Elizabeth interjected at one point. "Sneaky fella, he was."

"That's right, and, sadly enough, many of Susannah's beautiful quilts were taken in the wink of an eye — several thousand dollars' worth."

The quilters *oohed* softly in unison.

Most interesting to Sarah was the manner in which Emma Flaud had characterized the deplorable situation. The poor woman's quilts had been stolen, but the "robber couldn't steal Susannah's joy from her."

Young Fannie spoke up, "No, and she went on to make even pertier quilts after that. I know it's true, 'cause two of her quilts are on my bed . . . and two in my hope

268

chest." Fannie and her mother traded endearing looks, then settled back to the quilting at hand.

Lydia was puzzled at the strange turn of events at the Lapp quilting. Never once did Miriam Esh open her mouth for a Tellin' — didn't seem like she wanted to be there quiltin', even.

Honest to goodness, she couldn't ever remember Miriam actin' so peculiar. It wondered her. Just what had Preacher told Miriam, anyways?

On the drive home after the quiltin', Aunt Sarah said, "I had hoped to speak with Miriam Esh today, but there never seemed to be an opportune time."

"I know. I felt the same way." She went on to say how awkward things had been with Miriam. "Something's up with her."

"Is she normally friendly . . . outgoing?"

"Jah."

"I don't mean to second-guess her, but do you think she was upset because I was present?"

Lydia thought her aunt might be right. "Hard to say, really. We'll just have to wait and see what can be done." She was hopin' that Preacher might be able to talk to Miriam, get her to rethink things, maybe.

"Is there anyone else Amish in the neighborhood who could be foster parents?"

"No one who'd be apt to take all five of us," she replied. "Mamma would turn over in her grave if —"

"I guess you're right," interrupted Aunt Sarah.

They rode in silence for less than a mile. Darkness began to settle 'round them like gray kittens tiptoein' into the warm haymow for the long night ahead.

Lydia was itchin' to share something with her aunt. She didn't know why exactly, but she felt she wanted to all the same. "That boy you saw me with in the kitchen? Well, his mamma was there at Susie's frolic," she said softly.

"Which woman?"

"Ada King . . . and Mammi Elizabeth's his great-grandmother."

Aunt Sarah kept her eyes on the road as she drove. "Does your young man have a name *today?*"

"Jah, it's Levi King."

The road was a bumpy snow-white ribbon, barren of traffic except for two teams. Aunt Sarah passed them slowly, giving the horse and carriage wide girth so as not to spook the animals.

Lydia was ever so glad of that. Seemed to

her that Aunt Sarah was at least tryin' to show some respect for the People.

"Thank you for the quilting experience," Sarah said as the car turned into their lane.

"Well, at first, I honestly wondered how things would be." Lydia didn't want to spoil things and say something out of turn. *"Best to keep disappointments unspoken,"* Mamma had often counseled. "Things are always different when outsiders are present."

"I understand," said Aunt Sarah.

Lydia had a powerful-strong feeling she did.

"What am I to do 'bout Miriam Esh?" Lydia asked Fannie on the phone that night.

"If I were you, I'd go 'n talk to her at her house."

"Without Aunt Sarah?"

"What've you got to lose?"

"Do you think Miriam's troubled over something? She didn't seem to have much of a gut time today."

"I'm *sure* she's bothered, all right" came Fannie's less than evasive reply.

Lydia felt her friend knew more than she was lettin' on. "Tell me what you've heard, *please?*"

"Right now, on the telephone? Do ya think it's such a gut idea, Lyddie?"

"Well, everyone's asleep here. How 'bout you?"

"Same thing."

"Then go ahead and tell what you know. C'mon, Fannie."

"You won't say where you heard this, promise?"

"Won't say a word."

"Seems it's all over Grasshopper Level that Miriam Esh has no intention of bein' your foster mother. It's the last thing she wants."

"Well, why on earth not?"

"I'll tell you why. She's got it in her head that we — all the People — oughta be honorin' your mamma's last wishes, followin' every jot and tittle of her will."

Lydia didn't understand what Fannie was gettin' at. "What do you mean?"

"It's just that Miriam doesn't wanna take over the duties your mamma *'specially* chose for your Aunt Sarah to do."

"I don't get it. How could Miriam even *know* what Mamma was thinkin'?"

"Hard to say, really. Maybe she and your mamma talked a while back before Ivy died. I'm thinkin' — and my mamma says so, too — it's possible there's some reason why Ivy wanted her sister to stay 'round here."

Lydia listened intently. The reason was beyond *her*.

"If'n your aunt stays, it may not be the best years of her life, Lyddie. But who's to say they won't be the most important?"

Maybe Fannie had something there.

"Knowin' Aunt Sarah for this short of time, I can't see how her stayin' will do any of us much gut." Lydia sighed, skippin' ahead in her mind. "If she doesn't have ideas 'bout taking us back to Oregon with her, then I *will* get to start teachin' school. That, in itself, would be a blessing in more ways than one."

"It's what you always wanted," Fannie said. "I'm happy for you if it works out."

Lydia said her good-byes to her dear friend, wonderin' how such talk had spread 'round so awful fast. She was worried now, more than ever, that Aunt Sarah might just up and parcel them out to more than one family, since Miriam was makin' such a stand against helping out. 'Course now, she hadn't heard anything lately 'bout that from her aunt. But it was awful hard to predict just what was twirling 'round in that fancy head of hers.

Oh, she wished she could run on over to Miriam Esh's house this minute. Just what did Miriam know about Mamma's wishes anyhow?

Chapter Twenty-Three

Sarah read all of Ivy's 1989 journal until her tired eyes would no longer stay open. She ended with:

Dad always liked to talk in riddles. After he surrendered his heart to the Almighty, he said his shell-seeking had more to do with knowing God than finding himself.

Clearly, I remember one time when he said, "The outside of one's life is their shell. It can guide one to find the ultimate answer . . . within." Then he looked at me and said, "Ivy, a person is always free to change his shell at any time."

I don't know for sure, but maybe Dad was the one who first planted the seed for change in me. For Gil and me to become followers of Jesus . . . and, later, Plain.

This entry stood out as being rather profound, and it took Sarah back to her own reluctant walks with Dad on the shores of Watch Hill. Still, she found it difficult to believe that Ivy and her husband had gotten the notion to join the Amish from him.

But it was her sister's prayer that her children would "live their lives to the fullest measure, even if I should die prematurely" that struck Sarah as most significant. How could Ivy have known she would be dead within ten years from the time of this writing?

Sarah laid her head on Ivy's pillow, still wishing she were back home in Portland, relaxing in her own lovely bedroom. From her vantage point she glanced around, noting the light from the moon cascading in through the windows. Her gaze roamed over the simple furnishings to the mirror over the washstand, where the tiny decorative pins adorned a smooth linen towel.

Ivy's room was not nearly as offensive to her as it had been that first night, and she fell asleep with the concluding words of her sister in mind. *God is sovereign, in all, over all, and above all. I do put my faith and hope in Him!*

The next morning, seconds before the rooster crowed, Sarah was out of bed and in the shower. She checked her email messages as soon as she was dressed and was delighted to discover another note from Bryan.

Sarah,

Hope things are much better for you there!
*   I don't know how to tell you this, but my spiritual search is over. Don't laugh — I've found God. Or, better put, He's found me.*
*   When can we talk?*

                          Blessings to you,
                          Bryan

Sarah shook her head. Was this some sort of nightmare? No, she was very much awake.

Rereading Bryan's message, she was inclined to pick up the phone, wake him out of his stupor, set him straight about this God business.

Blessings to you, he had signed off.

She frowned at the screen, blown away. What could have happened? This was the first she had ever heard of a religious quest on the part of her longtime friend.

Brushing her hair, she stared at the mirror, only to turn away in frustration.

First Ivy, now Bryan . . .

Was there no sanity, no reason left in the world?

Everywhere Lydia went all day — to market, to the bank, and over to Miriam's —

276

everywhere — she kept runnin' into Levi King. First time, she saw him on the road, drivin' his new open courting buggy with his spirited mare, Bess. She wasn't sure, but it seemed almost that he looked away, not wantin' to catch her eye.

He's worried 'bout what Aunt Sarah saw, Lydia guessed. *He doesn't trust her, either.*

The second time she spotted him, Levi was in line at the bank, closer to the teller than she was. When he turned 'round, she was downright *sure* he purposely walked right past her without a glance.

What's happenin'? she wondered, looking behind her to see if there were other Plain folk in line. None were. So what was Levi up to?

By the third encounter, he ignored her altogether. By now, she was feelin' a bit angry, wonderin' if she oughta put a bug in one of his sisters' ears, tellin' Levi she'd changed her mind. 'Course she wouldn't go on to say just what she had changed her mind 'bout. Anybody knows *that* would be a big mistake, blabbing his marriage proposal 'round! Next thing, the whole church district would know she and Levi were — *had been* — a couple. She couldn't risk lettin' that happen, not if she hoped to have a second chance with him.

The sun had come out a whit stronger by

the time she arrived at Miriam's house. Getting out of the carriage, she tied Dobbin to the fence post, glancing over at the house and wonderin' if anybody was home. Surely Miriam would be home on a Friday afternoon, 'specially after such a long quilting yesterday.

A shelter of trees — a whole lineup of sycamores — banked the northeast side of the large property. In comparison to the farmland that surrounded it, the white clapboard house was mighty small.

Lydia had been a wee thing the first time she'd come here with Mamma for a visit. They'd come to pick up a basket of mending from Miriam, who needed the extra money, and since Mamma needed help with patchin' some of Dat's and Caleb's trousers, the arrangement worked out fine and dandy.

At the time, Mamma was expectin' Anna Mae, she recalled, which would've made Lydia about six years old. Despite her young age, she remembered Miriam's big spread of land, the emerald green level of grassland and alfalfa fields stretchin' out to meet the blue, blue sky. She thought then — *and* now — if ever she was so blessed to own such acreage of land, she would know God had truly shone His kindness down upon her.

Just now, waitin' for Miriam to come to

the door, she realized that what Dat and Mamma had given her and her brothers and sisters, by their untimely deaths, was every bit as wonderful-gut as a spread like Miriam's.

"Well, hullo . . . again," Miriam said at the door.

"Hope you don't mind me comin' unannounced."

Miriam didn't move aside or open the door wider. "What's on your mind, Lyddie?" Miriam was as cold as a dead fish.

"I can't stay long, really," Lydia said. "But I wonder if I could talk to you for a bit."

Miriam eyed her curiously. "Well, now that you're here, I 'spect you might as well make it worth your while." She opened the door, inviting Lydia inside.

Following Miriam into the kitchen, Lydia sat down at the kitchen table.

"I've got some pumpkin pie a-coolin'. Care for a piece?"

Lydia knew she ought to be polite and agree to have some, but she also knew that Aunt Sarah was at home, prob'ly wonderin' where she'd gotten to. "I'll have some pie if I may use your telephone first."

Miriam, smelling a smidgen better than her usual, pointed Lydia in the direction of the phone, around the corner from the kitchen, in the large front room. "Help yourself."

Dialing her home phone number, she hoped Aunt Sarah would answer and not just let it ring. Turned out the line was busy, so she waited, counting to twenty nice and slow, then tried again. This time it rang.

Aunt Sarah picked it up on the first ring. "Cottrell residence," she said, a deep rasp in her throat.

"It's Lydia callin'. Just wanted to tell you I'll be on my way home soon."

"Where are you?"

Should she say? Would it bother Aunt Sarah to know she'd come to Miriam's today, alone . . . without her?

"Lydia, are you all right?" Aunt Sarah asked.

"Jah, I'm over visitin' Miriam Esh. I won't be too long . . . just long enough to taste some of her pumpkin pie."

"While you were gone, I called your preacher, and we had a nice chat."

Aunt Sarah's words struck terror to her heart. "You did?"

"I found his number in the little address book next to the phone. I hope that's all right."

"Jah." Lydia wondered what her aunt wanted with the preacher.

"Well, I'll see you when you get here."

Aunt Sarah started to cough.

"You don't sound well. Are you?"

"My throat is sore. I'll get some cough drops if you don't have any."

"Mamma always said drinkin' chamomile tea with raw honey was the best way to cure a sore throat."

Aunt Sarah chuckled a little. "I must confess that I'm not much for tea."

"Well, it works, so why not give it a try?"

"I'm a captive to coffee."

"Mamma liked hers black as can be, but when she was startin' to come down with somethin', she always drank her chamomile tea. That, and lots of water."

"Thank you for the suggestion," Aunt Sarah said, as though she had no intention of doin' anything that resembled her sister's approach. 'Least that's how it came across over the phone.

So Aunt Sarah called the preacher, thought Lydia, finding no humor in it whatsoever. Truth was, she was perty sure her aunt had asked him 'bout Amish courting customs, checkin' up on Lydia's account of things, and in the process, prob'ly revealed too much 'bout Levi King. If so — and if Preacher's wife had overheard the conversation — the whole of their community would know by dark.

★ ★ ★

Sarah hung up, staring at the black receiver in its matching cradle — certainly the most archaic-looking telephone she had seen in recent years. She wondered where her sister had unearthed such a relic.

Dismissing the rhetorical question, she analyzed her earlier phone conversation with the Amish minister, the somewhat engaging farmer, blacksmith, and preacher all in one — Mr. Esh — of whom she had inquired about a certain young man. Namely, Levi King, Lydia's romantic interest. Never having been one to pry, Sarah had chosen her words carefully, asking only those questions necessary to acquire the pertinent information from someone in the Amish community. A man of the cloth, preferably. Someone who knew Lydia's boyfriend well. Someone who could be trusted to keep such a conversation confidential.

Having had opportunity to further evaluate Ivy's closest friend, Susie Lapp, Sarah was clearly not impressed. And neither would she have been so brazen as to contact any of the other women who had attended the recent quilting. It was Preacher Esh or no one at all. So she had begun: "Is Levi a good prospect for Lydia . . . as far as a marriage partner?" she had asked.

"Jah, I do believe he is that."

"Is he honest?"

"Ever so truthful, he is."

"Trustworthy?" She didn't clarify her meaning, but she *had* seen the passion with which the boy's lips had found Lydia's, holding her niece in his arms with obvious experience.

Again, Mr. Esh had answered in the affirmative. So she had felt some better about the courtship between her niece and the King boy.

"Is there anything else you want to know?" the minister had asked.

Cautiously, she quizzed him on the various dating customs Lydia had mentioned. The older man confirmed the details of Amish courtship. He also mentioned that Lancaster Amish no longer embraced the eighteenth- and nineteenth-century practice of bundling. A prospective suitor — under the covering of night and because houses were cold — was invited to a young girl's bedroom to spend time with her, fully clothed, in the warmest place the house had to offer. Her bed.

"There are Plain communities outside Lancaster where the custom is retained to this day," continued Preacher Esh, "mostly due to the lack of central heating in farmhouses. 'Course, in circles where bundling continues, the young people are taught not to engage in sexual intimacies. They're instructed to remain pure before marriage."

Sarah was taken aback by the discourse. He had told her far more than she cared to know. She was, however, relieved to know that "bed courtship" was a dead issue in Lydia's community. One less worry, at least.

Preacher Esh sighed. "Bundling is discouraged, in part, by keepin' kitchens and front rooms warm nowadays."

"I understand."

"We also teach our young people to save the full declarations of physical love for the marriage union. Both women and men are admonished to do this. And," he paused briefly, "I am certain our Lyddie would not choose to be courted by a young man who did not share her stand in this."

"Well, I certainly appreciate your time," she said, eager to conclude their chat.

"Will that be all?"

"Yes, thank you."

"Then I'll be sayin', 'God be with you, Sarah Cain.' "

Hearing her name spoken with such respect touched a chord somewhere in her heart. The reverend's soft-spoken mannerism reminded her of her beachcomber

284

father, and for a fleeting moment, she wondered if Ivy might not have thought so, as well.

The children arrived home before Lydia returned from Miriam's. At first, Sarah was reticent about greeting them, or if she should welcome them home at all. What was her place here?

Caleb and Anna Mae seemed pensive, hardly smiling as she opened the door for them. Josiah and Hannah, on the other hand, grinned at her, seemingly glad to see her.

Josiah broke the ice. "Teacher had to wash my hair outside right quick at the pump today."

"Jah, that's 'cause ya fell headfirst in the snow and mud during recess," Hannah tattled.

Sarah wondered aloud, "Did you sit in class all afternoon with wet hair?"

"Ach, no!" Josiah explained. "I sat by the wood stove for a spell . . . didn't take too awful long to dry."

Little Hannah snickered, trying to hide her smile behind her hands. "He looked right funny sittin' there, too, drenched as a cat caught in a rainstorm."

"Aw, go on!" Josiah said, hanging up his coat.

Sarah sighed. "Sounds like an interesting afternoon."

"Do ya *think* so?" Hannah said. "Well, I stood up and recited my ABCs in front of the whole class."

"With four other pupils, ya did," Josiah called from the utility room. "Don't let her pull the wool over your eyes!"

Sitting down, Sarah listened as the girl practiced reciting the entire alphabet. When Hannah finished, Sarah nodded, smiling. "You said your ABCs very well."

"Teacher said so, too." Hannah came closer, sitting on the wood bench next to her. "I'm gonna be readin' in a few weeks."

"You'll read soon enough, all right," Josiah said, coming into the kitchen. "Once Lydia starts teachin' us, you'll pick up speed with your learnin', you'll see."

Sarah hadn't thought to ask Lydia when it was that she planned to begin her assignment at the Amish school, so after Caleb and Anna Mae left to go to the barn, she asked Hannah and Josiah. "When does Lydia start as your teacher?"

"Come Monday." Josiah's blue eyes danced with glee. "And if you ask me, I think it's a right gut thing our sister's comin' to school. She'll keep order, that's for sure."

The boy's remark bothered Sarah. "What

do you mean by that, Josiah?"

He shrugged a bit, rolled his eyes, and grinned. "Well, I best not say."

Hannah shook her pointer finger at her brother. "Now, you oughtn't be tellin' on yourself."

Sarah observed the banter between the two children, recalling her own experience with an older sibling. Sure, Josiah teased, but there was none of the cutting sarcasm she had endured as a youngster. "What happened, Josiah?" she asked.

"Today or yesterday?"

"So you've been in trouble more than once this week?"

"Nothin' much to worry 'bout," the boy replied.

Hannah shook her head. "He's a rascal, is all."

Sarah didn't press the matter. "Is your teacher attentive to *each* of you?"

Josiah turned, frowning quizzically. "Ach, she's always watchin' over us."

"Jah, she is," Hannah confirmed it.

"Didja think differently?" Josiah asked.

Sarah shrugged off the question, saying no more. She was relieved to hear that their teacher had been vigilant and hoped young Lydia would be the same.

Getting up, she went to make the hot

cocoa Lydia would have already prepared and served by now had she been here.

Lydia waited patiently while Miriam set a dessert plate in front of her, eager to get on with the reason why she'd come.

"Something's a-botherin' you, child. I can see it all over your face," Miriam said, sitting across from her at the table.

Lydia had come for a completely different purpose — not to confide her concerns 'bout Levi's and her courtship or lack thereof. "I've heard . . . well, there's talk that you know something — 'bout Mamma's plans for our future," she began.

Miriam poured a glass of milk, raising her eyebrows and making a great heaving sound as she sighed. "Before we go any further, I must say that your dear mamma had some strong opinions 'bout what she wanted for you and your sisters and brothers, come her death."

Lydia listened, eager for more. "She talked to you 'bout that?"

"Jah, she did."

That was a surprise. Why hadn't Mamma confided in her closest friend, Susie Lapp? This made no sense at all.

"You may not know much 'bout your mamma's last wishes," Miriam continued.

"I know she loved us with all her heart."

The older woman nodded, her eyes blinkin' to beat the band. "Jah, so there's a gut reason why she wanted her fancy sister to come to Amish country."

"Maybe so Aunt Sarah would go Plain on her own accord, ain't so?"

Chuckling, Miriam placed a hand on her ample bosom. "Oh my, no. I'd say that was the *last* thing on your mamma's mind."

Seemed to Lydia that the woman was talkin' in circles — riddles, really. "I don't understand," she said softly.

A mysterious, almost angelic look passed over Miriam's face. "Sometimes it's best if we sit back and let the Good Lord work in His own way and time."

Well, Lydia wasn't one to argue with that. She'd heard it a-plenty from Mamma. Had seen for herself God's hand at work when a good portion of patience was applied to a situation.

The smooth, creamy texture of Miriam's pie felt wonderful on her tongue. "Mm-m, this is awful gut," Lydia said, changing the subject.

"Glad ya like it. Take some home with you — for the others."

She finished up her dessert and milk, sayin' a quick good-bye and headed out to the horse and buggy, several pieces of pie in tow. All the while she wondered what it was that Mamma had confided in tight-lipped Miriam. And what did the Lord have to work out anyhow?

Chapter Twenty-Four

Long after evening prayers and Bible reading, Sarah sat in her room, concocting an appropriate reply to Bryan's morning email. She had deliberately refrained from dashing off a quick response. Had learned from past business mistakes to think through every point before committing the conclusion to paper — or computer screen, as the case may be.

Bryan,

Good to hear from you.
I've thought about your most recent message all day, and I really don't know how to respond. I guess I hope this is just one of your many one-liners . . . or was it two?
I'll give you a call when you're rational.
                                                    Sarah

Feeling dreadful, as if she might be coming down with a sore throat or worse, Sarah took a warm bath and rubbed her neck and chest with Vicks VapoRub, hoping to soothe her symptoms. Lydia had insisted that she try some chamomile tea after supper. But Sarah was adamant about doing things her way.

By Saturday morning, Sarah's throat was swollen and her temperature had soared. She wouldn't be traveling home anytime *this* weekend. Besides, there was the matter of acquiring foster parents for her sister's children. Certainly, she could not leave here until she accomplished what she had come to do.

Sarah succumbed to Lydia's pleas and sipped the herbal brew her niece brought on a tray first thing in the morning.

"I'm praying you'll feel better soon," Lydia said, standing near the doorway. "I can bring you more tea when you're ready . . . more water, too."

She nodded, unable to squeak out a reply of thanks. This was what she got for walking with the children in the bitter wind three days ago. Sampling the tea again, she took a longer drink this time, wondering how Ivy had gotten hooked up with herbs.

Their dad had been big on them, enjoyed growing several different varieties in a small garden plot just off the back porch. But his interest had flourished long after Ivy married and moved to Bridgeport. Was there a connection? Had Ivy written as many letters to Mother and Dad as she had to Sarah?

Ivy and Dad had always been close. They shared a rapport she had never experienced with either her father or her mother. Ivy drew people to herself. She was a magnet of appealing looks and personality. People had always said the same of Sarah, yet the results had been far different.

Leaning back on the pillow, she breathed in the peppermint vapor exuding from the small humidifier Lydia had set up in the room. Oddly enough, she felt well cared for — almost pampered — like a young girl looked after by an attentive mother.

Lydia was nursing *her* back to health. Ironically, the intended roles were completely reversed.

Sarah dragged herself out of bed before noon to write and send another email message. This one to the real estate broker in Portland, her boss, Bill Alexander.

Bill,

Due to an unexpected illness, I will have to postpone my return for a few days. Would it be too much trouble for you to handle my scheduled closings for the upcoming week? Heidi can easily help you with the necessary info. If you need more clarification, feel free to phone me at: 717-555-0239.

Thanks a million!

Later,
Sarah

"When you're well, would it be all right if we talk 'bout your conversation with Preacher Esh?" Lydia asked, her eyes imploring.

Sarah nodded. "Sure."

"These are for you," Lydia said, offering Sarah two homemade cards. One was from Caleb, the other from Josiah.

"Your brothers must be the artists in the family," she rasped, studying the rather crude drawings of farm animals, birds, and trees.

"They just wanted to do something nice for you, since they won't be servin' you tea or toast or whatnot."

Sarah understood suddenly what her niece was saying. Of course, her nephews wouldn't think of stepping foot in the bedroom of a woman. After visiting in a conservative community for nearly a week, she should have known.

"Please thank them for me," she said in a weak voice.

"I will." Lydia smiled. "Is there anything else I can get for you?"

Sarah pointed to Ivy's diary. "I'm finished

with that one," she whispered. "May I have another?"

"I'll be more than happy to bring *all* of Mamma's journals for you. And . . . I doubt Mamma would mind one little bit."

Sipping the last half of her third cup of herbal tea, Sarah found it remarkable that Lydia seemed quite content to share her mother's diary with an English relative. *Today*, that is.

What had changed the girl's mind?

Anna Mae brought up a lunch tray with the homemade chicken soup Lydia must have made. The girl inched her way across the floor, holding out the tray as she approached the bed.

Not wanting to expose Anna Mae to her germs, Sarah nodded her thanks, accepted the offered tray, and waved her away.

"Will ya be needin' any salt?" asked Anna Mae.

"Thank you, but no . . . this is fine."

Anna Mae pointed to a small silver bell in the upper left-hand corner of the tray. "Lyddie says to ring the bell if ya need anything at all . . . or when you're through with your tray."

Again, Sarah nodded. "I appreciate that. It's very thoughtful of you," she said, almost before she realized that she had complimented the shy girl.

"Denki." Anna Mae dipped, turned, and exited the room like a miniature French maid.

Now that she had refused the salt, Sarah tasted the soup. It was beyond delicious. She must have the recipe for herself. To think doctors were baffled by the mysterious ingredient in chicken soup that supposedly helped cure the common cold!

Even so, if her fever didn't break soon, she would definitely surrender to the modern method of fighting such miserable symptoms — an old-fashioned aspirin!

Caleb and Josiah worked to shovel the heavy wet snow off the walkway leading to the barnyard while Hannah and Anna Mae used their brooms to sweep behind the boys. Indoors, Lydia washed the dishes, scrubbed the kitchen floor, and wiped down several walls and all the appliances. She darned the rest of her brothers' socks, mended rips in dress seams, and, last but not least, made a quick "gratitude list" like her friend Fannie often did, jotting down things she was most thankful for.

Right away, she knew what the number one spot should be. Thinking of Miriam

Esh's revelation — vague as it was — Lydia wrote at the top of her list: *I am thankful for God's providence.*

Lydia was ever so excited to meet with two seasoned teachers — Mary Fisher, from the Esbenshade Road School, and Susannah Stoltzfus, the present teacher at Peach Lane School, who was leaving her teachin' post due to her parents' relocating to northern New York. Both young women arrived long before supper and stayed for a good two hours. They seemed happy to share their ideas, showing Lydia how to plan the school day, fitting in all subjects from vocabulary studies to geography to German. She, in turn, offered them some coffee and cherry pudding.

When all was said and done, Lydia decided to keep the same starting time of 8:30 in the morning, followed by a Bible story and the recitation of the Lord's Prayer. What she *would* change was the appointed time for unison singing. Her pupils would sing three songs from the *Ausbund*, the Amish hymn book, after the prayer. Next was arithmetic, followed by recess at ten o'clock, lasting just fifteen minutes, then the children must return to their lessons. At noon the big rush to the lunch buckets began. If she remembered correctly, most of the children gobbled up their lunches in 'bout five minutes, then ran outside to play for the remainder of the hour. Silent reading followed the long recess. After that, she planned to assign lessons to each of the eight grades, lined up in specific grade by rows of desks. Students would be dismissed at three o'clock in the afternoon to walk or scooter home on nice days.

She thanked Mary and Susannah for their help and encouragement, then went with them to the door to see them off.

"You must let me know how you get along," Susannah said as she headed outside. "Mam can give you our new address at Preaching service tomorrow."

"Jah, I'll write a letter to you soon as I can."

Susannah grinned. "I can tell you one thing — I'll be missin' your little brother Josiah. He's a handful but still lotsa fun."

"You aren't tellin' me anything," she replied. "Denki for puttin' up with his shenanigans."

"Well, what's a teacher for?" Susannah said. "Remember, there's quite a difference between joyful and rowdy, jah?"

Lydia nodded, remembering that Mamma had often said the same thing. "What 'bout

Anna Mae?" she asked hesitantly. "Has *she* caused you any trouble?"

"Sometimes she's off in a world of her own, that's all."

"Daydreamin', wouldja say?"

"That . . . and a bit of mumblin' to herself."

Lydia had hoped her sister might've taken their late-night talk to heart. "Mamma's passing has been ever so hard on her — all of us, really."

Susannah came back to the door. "Truth be told, I'm glad your mamma's sister is here now. Her coming seems to have helped Anna Mae some. She's doin' better at school, 'specially the last day or two."

"Do you think so?"

"I *know* so," Susannah said. "And I hope your aunt Sarah will stay 'round here . . . 'least for the younger children's sake."

"Me too." She paused, thinkin' how to say what she honestly wanted from Susannah. "Will you pray for me . . . that I'll do a right gut job as a teacher?"

"Ach, Lyddie, you'll do just fine. Don'tcha worry none. I have all confidence in you."

She waved as the women scurried through the snow to their waiting buggies. "*Da Herr sei mit du* — the Lord be with you!" she called, the weight of responsibility settlin'

299

over her just then. Yet she could hardly wait to begin, hoping against hope that nothin' would come up to spoil this wonderful-gut opportunity. A dream come true!

After closing the back door, Lydia hurried into the kitchen and noticed Anna Mae had already begun peelin' potatoes. The water was boiling, too. "I see you got supper started," she said. "That's gut of you."

"Thought I'd best help a bit, since our aunt's under the weather," Anna Mae replied.

"How's she doin' anyway?"

" 'Bout the same. She could use a gut dose of cod-liver oil, prob'ly."

Lydia chuckled. "Have *you* had your portion for the day?"

Anna Mae's eyes were suddenly downcast. "I hate cod-liver oil."

"You don't wanna catch what Aunt Sarah's got, now do ya?"

"Can't!"

"What'd you say?" Lydia asked, mindful of her sister's belligerence.

"I *hate* the taste of fish oil . . . and I won't be catchin' no fancy woman's illness neither."

"Don't be *Bensel* — a silly child — Anna Mae." She thought on what she should say next. "Best not to say 'hate,' neither. Doesn't become you."

Her sister made a face. "What you mean to say is that Mamma would be dismayed if she could hear me, ain't so?"

Lydia sighed loudly. *What am I to do with her?*

"Well, *ain't so?*" Anna Mae insisted.

"Sister, don't talk that way."

"What way — 'bout the fish oil or 'ain't so'?"

Ever so frustrated, Lydia wondered what it would be like teachin' her own sisters and brothers at school, as well as tryin' to be a good example to them at home. Somebody had to, 'specially when it came to Anna Mae. The girl needed a firm and steady hand.

Lydia hoped somewhere along the line things might settle down at home with Anna Mae. She just couldn't stand for any of this back talk goin' on, and if Anna Mae didn't respect Lydia's teacher's authority at school, she didn't know what she'd do. For sure and for certain, she must show Preacher Esh and the People — the children, too — that she was in charge. *Antwattlich* — responsible. Jah, on the very first day she must earn their respect.

"I understand you begin teaching school this Monday." Aunt Sarah made the comment from her sickbed when Lydia took more tea upstairs.

"Jah, I do." She felt hesitant to share more, 'specially since she'd withheld the information earlier.

"You have strong leadership qualities, Lydia."

She was surprised to hear such words comin' from Aunt Sarah.

"I've observed you with your brothers and sisters for nearly a week, and I have every reason to believe you will do an excellent job."

"With all my heart, I want to."

"And you will."

I have all confidence in you. . . ." Susannah's words had been heartening, all right. And now Aunt Sarah's, too. Still, Lydia wondered how to bring up the topic that was truly on her mind.

Setting the tray down in front of her mamma's sister, she steadied the mug of hot tea. "I've been meanin' to ask you something, Aunt Sarah," she began. "I've been wonderin' . . . will you stay with us till we find someone to live with?"

The smooth temples knit into an instant frown. "As soon as I'm feeling better, we will definitely talk about that issue, as well as some other things."

She hoped Aunt Sarah wasn't 'bout to spring something on her relating to Levi King, that she'd spilled the beans to Preacher Esh. But it was easy to see her mamma's sister was quite *grank* — ill. So certain things would just have to wait.

Meanwhile, she'd be prayin' ever so hard 'bout Anna Mae's contentious spirit, Aunt Sarah's phone conversation with Preacher Esh, and Levi King, too. Just not in that order.

Lying in her sister's bed, Sarah sipped her tea, remembering that at their father's funeral, her contacts had slipped around in her eyes, due to her tears, making it nearly impossible to focus on the minister who stood behind the pulpit. She had not wept so much out of sorrow. It was regret that caused her emotional state that day. Regret due to her seeming inability to connect with either of her parents, or they with her. And Ivy had made no attempt to reach out to her at the funeral, but that was many years ago . . . before her sister's supposed spiritual enlightenment. Why she thought of that crucial autumn day at this moment, she did not know.

She reached for the homemade cards her nephews had created for her. Holding them in her hands, she suppressed the urge to weep.

No doubt her physical state was affecting her emotions at the moment. Nothing more.

Get well she must. The children down-stairs — Ivy's brood — deserved a home where they were encircled and nurtured by Plain folk. Not a blubbering, too-modern aunt, impaired by a vacant soul. A mere shadow of the woman she had once been. Yet she could do little to move ahead with plans while nursing a bad case of the flu.

As for Lydia's plea for a chat, she would put it off for as long as possible. Perhaps the girl would forget, though it was rather un-likely. Sarah did not relish the thought of di-vulging her conversation with the Amish minister. How humiliating for Lydia to hear from her aunt's lips that Sarah had ques-tioned the girl's choice of a life partner.

Preacher Esh had certainly been resolute. Young Levi King was, in his opinion, ideal husband material for Lydia. An upstanding, chaste young man.

Sarah was chagrined to recall the ques-tions she had posed to a complete stranger. Why had she felt the necessity to probe?

She gazed about the bedroom, looking hard at the simple furnishings, the barren windows, the lone chair near the bed. But it was the row of wooden pegs along the opposite wall that summoned her attention. There, her various purchases from last Monday's visit to the outlet stores hung neatly. Yet the thrill of the hunt, the ecstasy of possessing the lovely new garments, had faded sometime during the week. Precisely when, she did not know.

Chapter Twenty-Five

During the Sunday morning ride to the meetinghouse, Lydia thought ahead to summer and berry-pickin' days. She could scarcely wait for the warm days of runnin' barefoot through the meadow out back. And she figured by the time summer came, things just might be worked out with Aunt Sarah. There was another reason for her daydreamin', though. Levi King.

Surely by June or July — ach, she hoped so — they'd be back on better terms, maybe even long before then. She secretly wished there might be a chance to see him at church today after the common meal to be held in the meetinghouse basement. With her whole heart, she prayed Levi might speak to her, let her know there were no hard feelings between them. Yet she couldn't blame him for thinkin' so, if he did. Not after the way she'd put him off right after his heartfelt marriage proposal and all.

If only he would think back to their kiss, how she'd *let* him pull her close, didn't push away from him one iota, allowed him to snuggle with her much longer than ever before. If he did, he'd most surely know that she loved him ev'ry bit as much as he loved her.

"Whatcha think's come over Aunt Sarah?" Caleb said unexpectedly as ol' Dobbin waited calmly for the light just one block from the meetinghouse.

"What do you mean?" Lydia replied.

"She's different somehow," Caleb said. "Not nearly so vexed as when she first came."

Josiah laughed. "Well, now, she's *sick*, ain't she?"

"That's not what I'm sayin'," Caleb spoke up. "Mamma's sister isn't the same as when she came here a week ago, I tell ya."

Lydia listened, moved by what her brothers had observed. What *she* herself had also noticed.

Little Hannah tugged on Lydia's coat sleeve. "She's even startin' to look more like Mamma, seems to me."

"No one looks like Mamma 'cept Lyddie," Josiah insisted, grinning at her.

Lydia felt she oughta say something. "Well, now, haven't we been prayin' for our aunt?"

"To stay with us for always?" Hannah asked.

"No, to find what she's searchin' for," Lydia said.

"And just what might that be?" Anna Mae said at last.

Lydia turned to face her younger sisters behind her in the backseat of the carriage. "Why do *you* think Aunt Sarah came here?"

" 'Cause Mamma wanted her to?" little Hannah asked.

"Maybe that's it."

Anna Mae frowned and shrugged. "Seems to me she's here to find love."

"And not just *any* kind," Josiah said.

"It's God's love she's after, prob'ly," Caleb said softly.

Lydia smiled back at her sisters, then turned to face the road. "Jah, I'm thinkin' all of you are right, most likely."

Sarah spent the morning drinking several glasses of water and dozing off and on. She had given in to taking an aspirin every four hours to control the fever she knew she had. Along about noon, she put on her bathrobe and slippers and plodded down the long staircase to the kitchen, where she found a note from Lydia directing her to a large plastic container of leftover chicken soup.

P.S. Heat up what you want to eat. We'll be

back from Preaching service in time for afternoon milking. Hope you're feeling better soon.

— Lydia

Her spirits were lifted by the cheerful note, and after a half cup of the hearty soup, she felt even better. Still a bit weak, she made herself some herbal tea and headed back to bed. There, she nursed her symptoms by nestling down with several more of Ivy's journals.

Halfway through a diary marked, "In the Year of our Lord, 1993," Sarah came upon an interesting account. A mutually shared recollection between herself and Ivy. The entry was untitled and there was nothing to characterize it or set this writing apart from any other day in the life of an Amishwoman. It was merely the retelling of an extraordinary afternoon that happened so long ago Sarah had nearly forgotten. . . .

August 22, 1993

Today, while sorting through my dresser drawer, I came across an old letter from Dad.

It was odd, really, how I stumbled onto it. The children and I had just returned from

309

an afternoon picnic in the daisy-filled meadow out behind the barn. I had the urge to ret out some old papers and things. That's when I discovered the letter. For some reason, Dad had felt a need to remind me of one particular day along the shores of Watch Hill, years back.

He wrote that Sarah had been seven and I thirteen the day the most amazing thing happened. We had been strolling along the beach, tagging along with Dad as he inspected one seashell after another, when out of nowhere a beautiful long-necked swan came up out of the water, heading straight for us.

Of course, I remembered the incident ever so clearly . . . how the graceful creature seemed eager to make friends with us. Dad fished around in his pockets and found small packages of crackers he often carried with him to feed the sea ducklings. We'd never seen such an enormous swan, and what a neighborly one, at that!

The more crumbs Dad tossed, the closer he came. Soon he was eating directly out of Dad's hand. Other folks who observed the situation from the dock must've thought it somewhat miraculous, too. Three fishing boats shut down their motors and drifted toward the shoreline to snap pictures. Dad waved to them, all the while talking softly to *the swan, who seemed to trust us completely.*

At one point, Dad, Sarah, and I sat on a long piece of driftwood, fully expecting the enormous bird to turn and swim back into the broad inlet. Yet he remained.

I was brave enough to extend my hand with a piece of cracker in my palm. Sarah was too afraid to try, and even after Daddy encouraged her to "keep your hand flat as can be," she refused.

The encounter with the swan was truly a special gift. Dad believed almighty God wanted to give us a "one-and-only moment in time." The lesson we gleaned from the experience was the incredible knowing that the swan met us in our world, making our place his. Making one world between us.

I wonder if Sarah remembers that afternoon . . .

Reluctant to move past this particular entry, Sarah closed the journal, keeping her finger between the pages. She reveled in the memory, so aptly penned by Ivy, who, not more than a few months before the swan event, had entered her teen years.

A one-and-only moment in time, Dad had referred to the rare episode.

The sun had shone its diamond-shaped brilliance on the shore as seagulls seemed to hang in the air above the water. Children scoured the seacoast for shells and other tokens washed up by the tide. And that day Sarah had found her first and only double-sunrise shell and offered it to Daddy. He swept her up in his arms and carried her home, more than pleased for both the shell gift and the personal rendezvous with a swan. Best of all, neither Ivy nor Dad had criticized Sarah for being afraid to feed the bird, she now recalled.

Holding the journal close, she whispered into the stillness, "Yes, Ivy, I do remember."

After the Preaching service, Susannah's mother caught up with Lydia and gave her their New York address. "Susannah wanted you to have this."

"I promised her I'd be writing," she told Nancy Stoltzfus.

"Just give us a little time to get moved and settled before you do," Nancy said with a broad smile.

"Oh, I will." Lydia collected her sisters, allowing Caleb and Josiah to head outdoors with the men, while the women set the long tables in the basement of the meetinghouse. She made note that Levi King and his three brothers were also in attendance, and once she caught him lookin' her way, if only briefly.

"Too bad Aunt Sarah had to be sick today," little Hannah said as they helped by turning the plastic plates right side up on the tables.

"Jah, 'tis," Lydia said.

"She's missin' out on the common meal," Hannah said innocently. "Lookee, all kinds of gut food."

"What makes you think Aunt Sarah would enjoy eatin' with us Plain folk?"

Anna Mae had an answer. "Ach, she might like it just fine, if she ever decided to become one of us."

"I doubt that'll happen . . . ever." Lydia straightened her apron and went to help the older women with the serving platters. "You best not hold your breath hopin' for it, hear?"

"You don't know for sure, now, do ya?" Anna Mae had followed her, insisting on continuing the conversation.

"We'll talk 'bout this later." *When we're not bein' overheard or observed,* she thought.

"I have a gut mind to ask Aunt Sarah right out . . . what she's planning to do 'bout us," Anna Mae blurted.

"Please, not now," Lydia said, glancing 'round to see if anyone was listening.

"Maybe it's a gut thing she *did* get sick." Anna Mae spun on her heels, nearly bumping into Miriam Esh.

What an awful thing to say, thought Lydia.

"Hullo, Anna Mae," Miriam said with a smile. She wrapped her arms 'round Anna Mae, whose face turned a blazing pink and whose wide eyes told Lydia just how awful bad the plump woman must be smellin'. "How's everyone at your house?"

Lydia went on over to chat with Miriam, rescuing Anna Mae from the woman's clutches. "Aunt Sarah's down with a sore throat and strong fever."

"Is she drinkin' lotsa chamomile tea and honey?"

Lydia had to chuckle. "*Now* she is."

The men and boys were beginning to file in, ready to be served cold cuts and Jell-O salads. Lydia was actually glad when Miriam turned around, the woman's body blocking Lydia a bit during the silent prayer, which Preacher Esh and Bishop Joseph signaled with a few coughs. Then came the hushed silence.

Peeking, Lydia located Levi's bowed head quickly enough, watching him during the men's prayer. When the blessing was done, his eyes fluttered open, and he looked across the room at her, as if he'd known where she was standin' all along. His smile was ever so cautious, but it made Lydia's heart sing just the same.

Chapter Twenty-Six

The Peach Lane School had been standing smack dab in the middle of Peach Lane since the late 1830s, a few years after the Public School Law was decreed in Pennsylvania.

Lydia arrived at six-thirty on Monday morning and, for the first time, noticed the many rounded and crumblin' bricks. More than a century and a half of wind, rain, and snow had gnawed away at the old schoolhouse. The little white porch dipped and creaked under her snow boots; so did the wood floor inside. The walls sagged a bit, too, marked by patches of new brick here and there, and the student desks wore obvious signs of ink stains, chipped edges, and carved initials. Near the teacher's desk, an immense woodstove also bore years of wear.

How odd, thought Lydia. She'd never noticed any of this before today. But then, she had never been appointed to the task of schoolteacher in the red brick school, either. Now she was the teacher solely responsible for eight grades and thirty-six students — four of them her own brothers and sisters.

Just now the room was bone-chillin' cold, and she had only two hours to tend the fire, make the room cozy but not *too* warm for busy minds and active bodies. There was a fine line between too snug and too cool, she recalled from her own years as a pupil here. Part of being a good teacher was to heed that line, so her pupils would neither doze off nor shiver in their boots.

She quickly reviewed the schedule for the day, eager to pull on the heavy rope at the back of the classroom when it was time. Only once in her life as a student had she ever been allowed to ring the old bell that hung in the wooden belfry above the schoolhouse. Today began a series of days, weeks, and hopefully months of pealing the bell, alerting the children that school was in session. Hard work with little pay. Yet the People had given her the honor of molding the lives of their future preachers, bishops, farmers' wives, and mothers of a growing Amish community. She hoped her assignment as Peach Lane schoolmistress might also help certain children — 'specially too-curious teenagers — remain true to the covenant community and not wander away into the world.

Sarah had managed to come downstairs

to oversee the children's breakfast, but it seemed that Lydia had covered all the bases — notes left in prominent places for Anna Mae and little Hannah, advising them as to what foods to offer their brothers. She was scarcely needed today and was rather glad of it, since her fever had broken in the wee hours, leaving her quite weak. Wishing for a long warm bath, she greeted the children, keeping her distance as they ate scrambled eggs and bacon cooked by Anna Mae.

Josiah was the one to inquire of her health. "Are you some better today?"

"She *looks* better," volunteered little Hannah, smiling from the table.

"Well, thank you, dear."

"Guess Aunt Sarah won't be walkin' us to school today," Anna Mae said, referring to her as though she were not in the room.

She spoke up quickly. "I'll walk with you again in a few days."

At that, Josiah and Hannah spun around. "Then you'll be stayin' longer . . . with us?" Josiah asked, his face earnest.

"For a while longer, I guess." She had not begun to think through the logistics, however.

"I'm glad you're gonna be our half-mamma, at least," Hannah remarked.

"Me too!" Josiah agreed.

Caleb poured another glass of milk, and Anna Mae reached for a second piece of buttered toast. "Would you be able to help us out and fold some of the clothes?" Anna Mae ventured timidly. "Lyddie hung them out this morning awful early, so they're dry already. Right stiff, really, so they're warming up in the front room."

"I'd be glad to help with that," Sarah replied. She wondered how Lydia had managed to do so much at home and still rush off to teach school. Resolving to take much of the domestic load off her niece's shoulders, Sarah would begin by cooking and baking today.

"Just what's a half-mamma, anyways?" Josiah said, a piece of bacon hanging off his chin.

"Don't know, really," Hannah said. "But that's kinda what Aunt Sarah is, ain't so?"

"Best not say 'ain't' today at school," Caleb warned.

"Jah," Anna Mae piped up. "It's Lyddie's first day teachin', ya know."

"Best be on your gut behavior," Caleb said. "I doubt Lyddie's gonna put up with much from her own brothers and sisters."

"No . . . prob'ly not," Anna Mae said, looking rather worried.

Sarah stood in the doorway, leaning against

the wide wood molding, listening to the children's comments, finding humor in their apparent oblivion to her.

Suddenly Josiah got up and went to wash his hands and face at the sink. "Does Lyddie know you're stayin' on longer?" he asked, his gaze fixed on her.

"She'll know soon enough," Sarah replied.

Hannah jumped off the wooden bench. "Can I tell her at mornin' recess?"

"No . . . no, I want to!" Josiah insisted.

Caleb and Anna Mae exchanged somber glances, saying nothing, sitting motionless.

"Lydia will hear the news from me when she comes home." Sarah turned toward the stairs. *I'll stay only long enough to locate a foster parent,* she thought.

"Can't we say nothin' at school 'bout it?" Josiah called from the kitchen.

Sarah turned to face them, feeling rather breathless. "That's right, you can't say *anything* at school."

He grinned back at her. "You were a teacher once, too, ain't?"

She smiled. "Who told you that?"

"Mamma did," Hannah said, coming toward her.

"Better not get too close," she said. "I want all of you to stay healthy."

319

"Honestly, you *do?*" Hannah asked.

"Of course I do."

"Aunt Sarah's a wonderful-gut half-mamma," Josiah said, tugging on Hannah's apron.

Sarah chuckled a little, bursting out with it so fast she couldn't stop it.

Well after the children had left for school, Sarah's cell phone rang. "Hello?" she answered.

"Hi, Sarah. Are you ignoring your email messages?" It was Bryan.

"Oh, sorry. I haven't even checked lately. I've been sick in bed."

"Allergic to farm work?"

"I'm fighting off the flu."

"Who's winning?"

"Let's put it this way. I've guzzled enough chamomile tea to relaunch the Boston Tea Party."

"Boston, hmm, nice place."

"So . . . what's on your mind?" She had no intention of addressing the issue of his strange pronouncement — that he'd found God.

"I've been thinking a lot about you."

She was silent and wouldn't admit to having thought about him, too.

"Still hanging out in Amish country?"

"I plan to be here a few more days . . . or so."

"May I drop by for a visit sometime this week?"

"That's not necessary, Bryan."

"But I *want* to talk to you." His voice was sweet. Too sweet.

"Not about this religious kick you're on, I hope." She shuddered, pulling her bathrobe snugly around her shoulders. "You have me worried."

"We have some catching up to do, and since I'm in Harrisburg . . . less than an hour away, I couldn't resist calling."

She thought about the prospect of seeing him. "How long will you be in the area?"

"Two days, then I fly home." He was silent, then — "It's important that I see you again, Sarah."

An inner voice urged her on. Yet the feeling was foreign, this feeling of *wanting* to be with him. "Give me another day to beat this bug. I'll call you tomorrow night."

"Okay . . . I'll wait for your call."

They said hurried good-byes and hung up.

She had to get well and see Bryan, possibly on Wednesday, and somewhere between now and then, she and Lydia must have a heart-to-heart talk, as well.

Sarah reached for an aspirin and a cup of chamomile and drank it straight down.

The morning was going along wonderful-gut for her first day, and Lydia was pleased. "Time to tidy up for lunch," she told the children at noon.

Josiah raised his hand as he sat at his student desk. "I forgot my lunch bucket."

"Ach, you did?"

"Jah, and it was 'cause you weren't home this mornin' to remind me," he said, solemn faced.

Little Hannah and two other first-grade girls cupped their hands over their mouths.

"What 'bout Anna Mae, your sister?" Lydia replied. "Didn't *she* remind you to bring your lunch bucket?"

Josiah raised his hand again.

"What is it?" she asked, beginning to feel uneasy, bringing family matters into the school day.

"Can I come whisper somethin' to you?"

"*May* I whisper . . ."

"Jah, that's what I meant."

She motioned for her second-grade brother to approach her desk. "What's on your mind?"

He leaned over and whispered in her ear, "We got to talkin' to Aunt Sarah, that's why

I forgot my lunch bucket."

"You can share some of my sandwich. Maybe Caleb and Anna Mae will share with you, too. We won't let you go hungry."

He wasn't finished whispering by the looks of it. "Aunt Sarah's got something to tell you when you get home."

Lydia was all ears. "Why do you say that?"

"She told us so . . ." His voice trailed off. "But I best let *her* tell you."

Motioning to his desk, she said, "And you best take your seat."

Josiah's words played tag in her head all through the lunch hour and throughout recess time. After playing hard outside, several of the older girls stood at the back of the classroom and helped rebraid the hair of the younger ones, standing one in front of the other. In a few minutes, many sets of braids had been smoothed and tucked back into tightly wound buns. Boys, meanwhile, ran broken and bent combs through their own tousled hair, putting it in order.

Soon afternoon recitations were under way. Monday was always arithmetic day, so each grade stood and recited for twenty minutes at a time. At three o'clock on the dot, school was dismissed.

Caleb grinned at her as the last pupil filed out the door. "I like havin' you for our teacher, Lyddie," he said, waiting for her to gather up her books and things. "Will you be drivin' home, or should I?"

She agreed that he should. "Go ahead and hitch up Dobbin now. I'll come in a minute."

Anna Mae, Josiah, and Hannah came wandering back inside to warm themselves by the woodstove while Lydia cleared her teacher's desk. "I'm ready for a snack," little Hannah said.

"I wonder if Aunt Sarah'll have any cocoa waitin' for us," Josiah said with a sly grin.

"If not, we'll make some ourselves," replied Caleb.

Anna Mae laughed. "That'll be the day — when I see my brothers cookin' in the kitchen."

"Now, now," scolded Lydia. "Let's head on home."

Josiah hung back, waiting for her to close the door on the woodstove. Its dying embers would be stirred to life early tomorrow morning once again. "Aunt Sarah's got gut news for ya," he whispered as they made their way to the door and closed it securely.

"Is that so?" she said, playing along.

"And I think you'll be mighty pleased."

The way he said it, she was perty sure what that news was. It wouldn't do to hear an unpleasant report of Aunt Sarah's chat with Preacher Esh . . . possibly talk 'bout Levi King. Ach, she hoped she was right, what she was thinkin' just now.

Sarah mulled over her phone conversation with Bryan Ford. He had seemed exceptionally confident. Perhaps a little *too* upbeat.

"We have some catching up to do," he had said, sounding both urgent and amiable. She didn't care to imagine what he might have on his mind.

Still wearing her robe and slippers, she crept into the bathroom and drew the water for a midafternoon bath. Without the aid of antibiotics or decongestants, she was beginning to feel better. Quite a bit better, in fact.

After her bath, she dressed quickly, noting the time. The children would be arriving home soon, most likely by horse and buggy, as she had heard Lydia leave just after six o'clock this morning. *I'll simmer some milk for hot cocoa,* she thought.

On the ride home, they happened to pass Levi King. He was sittin' high in his racy black open carriage, brand-new last year, given to him by his father. Levi waved to the younger children, even called a warm "hullo!" to

Caleb, but didn't begin to look Lydia's way. Not this time. Her heart sank, yet the fact that he was riding alone gave her good courage. No one else had taken her place in his heart. Not yet.

During the supper hour, Sarah encouraged each of the children to practice table manners. But Josiah promptly explained for her benefit that "a gut, loud belch is the People's way of showin' a cook just how tasty a meal is."

Sarah tried to keep from grinning, the boy's response was so adorable.

" 'Please' and 'thank you' are Englischer words," he continued. "And we wouldn't wanna be soundin' like fancy folk nohow."

"I see," she replied, not seeing at all. In fact, she was even more puzzled as to why her sister had chosen *her*.

Before retiring for the night, Sarah read the last entry in one of Ivy's earlier journals, six months after Anna Mae was born:

It's nearly midnight and my youngest is still restless. Tiny Anna Mae needs lots of attention, it seems. She's clingy and colicky, more so than either Lyddie or Caleb were at this age. Yet I am determined to be a loving, caring mother to this wee one, so needy she is.

I received a short letter from Sarah today. She's looking ahead to her practice teaching this spring. I'm surprised, really. Sarah has never been inclined toward children.

Gil and I were talking this evening after supper. We've come to this conclusion: We must get rid of even more clutter in the house and the barn. He says if we don't free ourselves of things, we'll spend our whole life tidying up.

Sarah, weary from the day and the lingering effects of her illness, had felt uplifted somewhat by the children's reaction to her staying on a few more days. Their eyes had brightened when she greeted them after school and served the mugs of hot chocolate on a tray, complete with oatmeal cookies, which Lydia and Anna Mae had baked on Saturday.

Slipping under the sheets, she thought of Ivy's journal entry. Her sister's pointed opinion regarding Sarah's inadequacy with children had been emphasized once again. She sighed, staring across the room at the wisps of light floating in the window.

What a dichotomy that Ivy had continually felt that way, yet named Sarah as guardian for her offspring nonetheless. It never ceased to boggle Sarah's mind.

Pushing that thought aside, she pondered the final paragraph in Ivy's diary. Somehow, the extremely modern Ivy Cottrell, former teenage prom princess and socialite, had turned a corner in her life. How *had* she managed to free her life of things — of chaos — as she had written?

Lydia, tired as she was, couldn't wait to write in her diary before going to bed.

Monday night, January 31

My first day as teacher at Peach Lane School!

Honestly, I don't see how I did it, getting up at three-thirty this morning to do the washing, without the help of Anna Mae or anyone else. I do believe Mondays will be the hardest day for a young schoolteacher like me. When things are settled — and I hope they are soon — I hope not to have the clothes-washing duties, along with the added responsibility of getting the fire in the wood-stove going at the schoolhouse. Maybe Preacher Esh or another nearby farmer might help with that . . . 'least on Mondays. Aunt Sarah is pitching in a lot more now that she's feelin' better. She'll prob'ly take over the laundry duties for us.

328

I'd never be so forward as to declare it, but I felt exhilarated on my first day of teaching. Seems to me the Lord God helped me do a right good job, too. Wasn't so hard to manage all eight grades, either, as I put some of the older pupils to work helping the younger ones. Everything worked out so well. Even Anna Mae was on her best behavior. Glory be!

Josiah, bless his heart, could hardly keep the secret that Aunt Sarah's planning to stay on a bit more. He was nearly bursting at the seams on the ride home in the buggy after school. It was quite interesting, though, the look on Aunt Sarah's face when I was sipping her hot cocoa, listening as she shared her news. I don't know how she's going to go 'bout it, really. Finding a foster family in this community, what with most parents juggling seven or more children, well, it'll be a difficult task. If it's God's will for us to live with someone other than Mamma's sister, He'll provide for us.

I'm praying ever so hard these days. Levi King's still on my mind and in my heart.

The cell phone rang around nine-thirty, waking Sarah. She reached for it quickly, so as not to startle the house full of sleeping children. "Yes?" she answered.

"Sarah, it's Bill Alexander. You sound sleepy."

"I am." She reminded him of the time differential.

"It's early there, right?"

She smiled. "We're a farm family . . . we get up with the cows. Sometimes earlier."

"Oh, a *family*, eh?"

Too tired to explain, she inquired of the closing she knew had taken place that afternoon. "How did things go?"

"Smooth as molasses . . . or is it pudding?"

She smiled. "Glad to hear it. Send me the check."

"You must be planning to stay there a while longer."

"I haven't decided exactly how long."

"Well, can you give me a heads up when you think you might return?"

"Sure."

"Before I forget, Heidi's got everything lined up for your closing on Wednesday and Thursday."

"Super. Thanks, Bill. I appreciate it."

"Hey, you okay? You sound sick."

She wondered if he'd noticed her raspy throat. "Actually, I'm on the mend. I plan to be up and at 'em full force early tomorrow."

"They got you plowing fields yet?"

"Not *this* week." She chuckled softly.

"Don't forget the real estate business. We need you, Sarah. You're the best."

"Hey, I like that — has a nice ring to it."

"Well, I'm not kidding," Bill said before they hung up.

She turned the power off on the cell phone, eager for a tranquil night's sleep.

Long past midnight, she thought there must be a phone ringing somewhere, though in her sleepy haze, she questioned ever having turned hers off. Groping in the darkness, she put the receiver to her ear and heard the voice of Megan Holmes. "Please, Teacher? It won't take me long. I'll hurry. *Please?*"

"All right, Megan, one more time. But be very careful," she said, now standing behind a long line of noisy children, bundled up for a wintry recess, waiting impatiently to get back inside the school building. They were jostling one another, vying for position, overly anxious for the door to open.

Just then, she thought she must have dropped the phone when Meggie's screams awakened her. She sat straight up in bed, her heart pounding nearly out of her rib cage. The silence in the Amish farmhouse made her ears feel clogged, deafened.

Sarah drew a deep breath and reached for a glass of water and, out of habit, another aspirin. As she swallowed both water and pill, she realized that while she knew the precise location of Megan Holmes's grave site, she had no idea where her own sister's body was buried.

Chapter Twenty-Seven

Sarah was ravenous at breakfast and took a second small helping of scrambled eggs, along with her oatmeal. After Lydia left for school, Sarah followed Hannah around, helping her gather up her lunch bucket and books for school.

After everyone was out the door and on their way, she cleaned the kitchen thoroughly, baked some bread, and took a roast out of the freezer to thaw for supper. Feeling far better than she had in days, she sat at the table and reached into the small shoe box that Lydia had brought downstairs before breakfast. "These were Mamma's favorite shells," her niece had said with a big smile. "Ten of them . . . gathered with Grandpa Cain, when Mamma was little."

"Oh, really?" Sarah replied, surprising herself with immediate interest. "I'll take a look once the house is quiet." Which is precisely what she planned to do at the moment.

Lifting the lid off the box, she peered inside. There she found colorful seashells, smooth and pearlescent. *Lydia wanted me to see these . . . why?* she wondered. But there was an instinctive quickening of her senses. She knew, possibly, that it was a type of reward from Lydia for Sarah's willingness to stay on "a while longer."

Smiling, she picked up the first shell — a snail shell, also called moon shell, which she knew from the occasional walks with her father. She examined it, stroking its glossy fullness, its rounded borders, enjoying its opaque rose color, the smoothness in her hands. A whiff of salty ocean air tickled her imagination. She was a girl, back in Watch Hill, a few blocks east of her parents' summer cottage.

Her father had once said, *"Human beings often despise aloneness."* This bit of wisdom he had shared while holding a gossamer shell in his hand. *"We avoid isolation at all costs. Yet we must reconcile with solitude, learn to embrace it, so that we can hear God's voice."*

God's voice . . .

Was he referring to the still, small *inner* voice he often mentioned? Was it an audible utterance? Had Bryan heard it, too?

Embrace the solitude. . . .

She pressed the snail's shell to her cheek. Its coolness soothed her. Was the lack of God's voice in her life evident to others? And what of Ivy and Gilbert and their children? When, *how* had they managed to hear — listen to — such a divine pronouncement? Was "hearing" an outgrowth of their purposeful solitude, their abandonment of things, the embracing of a simple, uncomplicated life? Or the reverse — the *reason* for having heard?

She stared at the milky-colored shell. *"Treasures from the sea teach us heavenly lessons,"* her dad had said repeatedly when she was growing up.

God's treasures . . .

The phone rang, startling her. Carefully, she returned the moon shell to its cradle in a wad of tissues and got up to reach for the wall phone. "Cottrell residence."

"Hullo, Sarah" came a somewhat familiar voice. "I met you at the quilting last week . . . at Susie Lapp's place. My name is Miriam Esh."

"How are you, Miriam?" She was careful not to sound too exuberant.

"Well, I'm doin' just fine, I reckon, and how are *you* gettin' along?"

She did not know if the woman was referring to her physically, or otherwise. "We're fine," she said cautiously.

"I understand Lyddie's at Peach Lane School, teachin' the youngsters."

"And enjoying it, too, from what she says."

"Wonderful-gut news." Miriam paused. "Well, now, the reason I telephoned you was to see if you might like to join some of the womenfolk again. We're gettin' together Thursday at my house to sew a new binding on an old quilt."

"It's kind of you to ask."

"So you'll give it some thought . . . 'bout coming?"

"Yes, I think I *will* come," she replied, glad that the work frolic wasn't scheduled for tomorrow. She fully intended to meet with Bryan Ford in the morning.

"I could ask someone to stop by 'n pick you up, if you'd like."

She thought of riding in an Amish buggy — her first time. The notion made her nervous. "If you give me directions, I'm sure I can get there on my own, thanks."

Miriam obliged her. "Watch for a hitchin' post on the east side of the road, and that white picket fence at the corner of such and so" was the gist of it.

Sarah smiled to herself as she said goodbye. What a folksy way of telling a person how to locate a place. Her father, unpretentious man that he was, would have enjoyed it. Of this, she was certain.

At midmorning, Sarah was surprised by a visit from Susie Lapp. The woman came with two hot dishes.

"One's hamburger casserole, the other's Texas hash," she said as she strolled into the kitchen, wearing a cheerful countenance.

"Well, thank you," Sarah said, thinking of the rock-hard roast on the counter. "We'll enjoy this tonight . . . the children and I."

"I made some corn fritters, too." Susie seemed more relaxed today. "Thought you might enjoy 'em."

"I'm sure we will," Sarah said, pouring some coffee. "Care for a cup?"

"Oh my, yes . . . black coffee would taste awful gut 'bout now."

Sarah wondered if Susie was headed off to another house — perhaps to deliver more food to a friend. She did not inquire, however, settling down at the kitchen table with the woman her sister had deemed her closest friend.

"I was rude to you when first we met," Susie said, her eyes downcast. When she looked up, Sarah saw that her eyes were glistening.

"There's no need to apologize."

"Oh, but there *is*." Susie sniffled, then — "Your sister — Ivy — would've been appalled at my behavior. I'm sorry, Sarah."

Unaccustomed to entertaining expressions of regret, Sarah scarcely knew what to say.

"I heard you're comin' to Miriam's for another frolic . . . Thursday."

"That's right."

"Maybe we can sit together at the quiltin' frame, you and I." Susie did not make eye contact with her this time. She sat quietly now, sipping her coffee.

"I'd like that" was all Sarah said.

Sarah went around to each of the children's bedrooms — even to Caleb's and Josiah's — tucking them in for the night. As she moved from room to room, she realized this was the first time she had done such a thing since her arrival.

Hannah leaned up and kissed her cheek unexpectedly. "Well, aren't *you* the quick one?" she said, hugging the little girl.

"Mamma *always* kissed and hugged us."

"And she told us how the Lord God heavenly Father loves us and sends His angels to watch over us while we sleep," volunteered Anna Mae.

"I think your mother must have loved you very much," she replied.

Anna Mae leaned up on her elbow, propping her head up. "You didn't know her too awful gut, didja, Aunt Sarah?"

She pondered the question, wondering, *Did I ever know Ivy at all?*

Hannah spoke up, her tiny face pensive. "You're sisters, ain't so?"

Sisters . . .

Uncertain about her response, she said, "Your mother and I were never close the way you and Anna Mae are . . . not sisters who are also friends."

"Well, why *not?*" Hannah pressed, sitting up.

"We just weren't," Sarah answered softly. "I really don't know why."

Anna Mae's comment was even more thought-provoking. "Maybe Mamma wanted you to know who *she* was . . . by knowin' *us.*"

The sting of tears prompted Sarah to get up quickly and turn off the light. "Maybe so," she whispered. "Good night, girls. Sleep well."

"God be with you, Aunt Sarah," they said in unison.

In some inexplicable way, Hannah's and Anna Mae's words seemed to belong to the moment, so much a part of this night that her sudden feeling of aloneness might have been the very invitation God had been waiting for.

Embrace the solitude . . . so God can speak to you.

She did not linger long enough in her stark solitude to hear a divine voice, however. Closing the door gently, Sarah slipped quietly down the hall to Ivy's former bedroom. She had an important phone call to make.

"Are we still on for tomorrow?" she asked when Bryan answered.

"Sarah . . . hi! You must be feeling better."

"Much better, thanks."

"Great. So where should we meet?"

"How does right here sound? I want to show you around the farm."

"Where exactly *is* this place?"

"Nestled deep in the heart of Lancaster County, on the outskirts of Strasburg." She gave him directions to the Cottrell farmhouse.

"When's a good time for you?"

"How would you like a hearty home-cooked breakfast?"

He laughed softly. "You're feeding me a line, right?"

"No . . . I'll feed you cholesterol. Bacon-flavored."

Their mutual laughter melted some of the cold hesitancy that had resided in the back of her heart since their college breakup. She could hardly wait to see him again.

Chapter Twenty-Eight

The fact that today was February 2, Groundhog's Day, struck Sarah rather humorously as she dressed for the day. She took time to brush her hair more thoroughly than she had in the past few days, hoping to put a shine in it, while the children milked the cows.

Bacon and eggs were planned for breakfast, just as she had envisioned, although she assisted Lydia and Anna Mae in making an extra large batch. Lydia never questioned her as to why so much food, but during cleanup Sarah mentioned, in passing, that "an old friend" was stopping by for breakfast.

"Who's coming?" Josiah asked, offering a quizzical look.

"A man from Boston," she felt comfortable saying.

"Have a gut time," Lydia said, then she left to meet the car that was driving into the lane — one of their non-Amish raw milk customers.

Sarah watched through the kitchen window, marveling at Lydia's ceaseless energy. The young woman kept up so efficiently with everything. *She gets her dash from the Cain side of the family,* she decided.

Wouldn't be long, by Amish standards, that Lydia would manage her own household just as efficiently. Ivy had trained her oldest daughter well.

Turning from the window, Sarah helped Hannah out the door. She cautioned Josiah not to leave his lunch on the kitchen counter again. "You'll definitely need this along about noontime," she said, handing over the gray metal box.

"Denki, Aunt Sarah." He surprised her by hugging her arm, then turned pink in the cheeks and headed for the utility room with the others.

"Have a nice day at school," she called to all of them as they rushed out.

She did not search for candles or any other romantic trappings as she prepared the table for a quiet, intimate breakfast with her friend — though it would have been most appropriate for this quaint countryside setting.

Bryan was prompt. He rang the front doorbell, something she was not accustomed to. No one in the Amish community, at least no one she had encountered in her time here, had ever used the front door for entrance. Everyone came in the back way.

"Please, come in," she greeted him, opening the door wide.

"You look lovely, Sarah." Their eyes met and held.

"Thanks." She was the first to break the gaze. "May I take your coat?"

Quickly, he removed it. "Wow, what a gorgeous drive out here." His eyes darted about, taking in the room. "There's something nostalgic . . . terribly peaceful about this place."

"The house or the landscape?"

"Both." He sniffed the air comically. "And something smells delicious."

"Follow me." She led the way to the kitchen, draping his coat on a chair as they passed through the front room and past the corner cupboard, where many colorful china cups and saucers and other glassware were on display.

Once he was seated — she had him sit at the head of the table — she poured some coffee for both of them. They engaged in casual chitchat. "So . . . when are you heading back to Portland?" he began.

"I don't know yet."

"What will happen to the children — your nieces and nephews — when you go?"

She placed a platter of eggs and bacon in

the center of the table, then sat down to his left, facing the window. "I *do* have a plan. At least, I'm working on it."

His grin warmed her heart, and he reached for her hand. "Before you tell me your plan, do you mind if I say a blessing for the food?"

He wants to say grace?

"Go ahead," she said.

"What do Amish do?" he asked, suddenly.

"Silent prayer, before and after the meal."

His dark eyes searched hers. "That's really quite unique, isn't it?" He didn't wait for her to respond but squeezed her hand gently, then began to pray audibly. "Dear heavenly Father, I thank you for the food set before us. Bless Sarah for preparing it, and . . . grace us with your presence at this table. Amen."

Bless Sarah. . . .

She wondered when he had learned to speak to God so comfortably. The prayer, his hand on hers, his placid demeanor — all this took her off guard. "Have some breakfast," she said when the prayer was finished, reaching for the platter. A good excuse to release his hand.

He took a sizeable portion of eggs and two strips of bacon. "When did you start cooking?"

"Things can get very hectic in a house filled to the brim with five children."

"Sounds like a good enough reason to me."

"And, too, the children have so many chores — the boys work outdoors and in the barn, and the girls clean and sew and, in general, do the inside chores. Cooking is something I actually enjoy . . . again. At home, I never have the time."

"Helping out here is the reason you came, right?"

At all costs, she would avoid the topic of Ivy and her will and what that entailed. "I'm surprised that the children, as grief-stricken as they were, kept going as they did before I arrived." She also explained that a number of Plain friends and neighbors had looked in on them periodically. "The Amish take care of their own. I've come to know this first-hand."

Their chatter took on a familiar cadence — the way things were naturally between them. It was Bryan's allusion to a "life-changing experience" that caused her to be more circumspect, put up her guard once more. "Do you mind if I share something personal with you?" he asked, keeping his eyes on her.

Sarah felt the coldness creep into her.

"Sure, Bryan." But she wasn't at *all* sure she wanted to hear what he had to say.

He hesitated for a moment, seemingly unsure of how to begin. "I guess you could say I feel like I've finally come home. I can't really explain it. I realized I'd been running from something . . . or rather *Someone.* Sounds hokey, I know. But I have a *feeling* I've never had before. Forgiveness. Peace."

He paused again. "All my life I've been searching for a reprieve from nagging guilt. And I finally found Christ."

She had no idea why Bryan was saying this. He was the kindest, dearest man she had ever known. Guilt was *her* department. She fully associated herself with blame. She was no stranger to it.

But Bryan . . . what had *he* done?

"I think you're a good person," she said, sighing. "Why do *you* need God?"

He reached for a piece of toast, buttered it, and spread rhubarb preserves on top. She could tell he was arranging his thoughts.

"We *all* need God," he said. "We're all in need of redemption and forgiveness —"

"So this is about religion?" she interrupted.

"Not really . . . not in the sense that you mean. It's about a person. A Savior."

She wouldn't snicker, but Bryan definitely

seemed a bit out there. But she couldn't help feeling somewhat intrigued in spite of herself. At the same time, she felt *distanced* by his experience. Like she was *losing* Bryan somehow. Losing him to God?

"I want to apologize to you, Sarah," he said, catching her off guard. "Sometimes I've been pretty headstrong about things. I suppose just keeping in touch with you, persisting in our friendship, is one way I've been stubborn, not always caring whether you even wanted me in your life. But about other things, too. About insisting on a large family. I think my stubbornness about children may be why you've kept me at bay, and I understand now. I hope you can forgive me."

Of course, she could. But it seemed his apology was closely connected to his recent religious experience. "I've never believed the way my parents did. I didn't want to clutter up my life with that sort of thing."

"My life *was* cluttered before I let Christ come in," he replied softly, yet very firmly.

The silence between them was suddenly charged with discord. Sarah felt it and shivered slightly. "That's your business."

He wiped his hands on the paper napkin, studying her with a penetrating gaze. "I'd hoped you might feel differently."

His words tumbled over in her mind, even as she got up to pour more coffee. With an unspoken agreement to disagree — at least for now — their conversation turned to lighter topics through the early morning hours, stretching into midmorning and beyond.

She showed him around the two-level back barn, the lower stalls where the mules and driving horses bedded down for the night and the upper level haymow. Bryan insisted on climbing up the long ladder to the top and marching around in the dry straw strewn on the timbered floor above her. She laughed at his antics, playing with three kittens that wandered over to ask for some petting.

"Tell me about your nephews," Bryan said, reaching for the rope swing high in the rafters.

"Caleb's fourteen, rather quiet, and on the verge of manhood. From what I understand of Amish customs, he'll start attending social events when he turns sixteen. Then the dating and courtship begins."

"*That* young?"

"I know. I was surprised, too."

He was poised to swing down but paused, holding on to the taut rope. "What about the other boy?"

"Josiah is eight and a big talker."

"And the others?"

"Lydia will probably be married within the year. She runs a tight ship around here. She's the new teacher for the one-room school down the road."

"How old is Lydia?"

She smiled. Bryan was really into this. "She'll be seventeen next month."

"Who else?"

"Anna Mae is eleven." She didn't comment on Anna Mae's emotional problems. "And Hannah is the baby . . . six years old."

"That's some age span," he said. "I'd like to meet them."

"They'll be home in a few hours. Stay around, and I'll introduce you."

The grin that burst upon his face seemed to spread to his torso, and he reached high above his head and seized the rope. He came sailing down past her, then up . . . up to the far, lofty beams on the opposite side of the barn.

Sarah watched as he came swinging across again — almost close enough to touch — then up to the haymow where he found good footing and let go of the rope. He dropped down to sit on the edge of the hayloft, his long legs dangling in midair. "It's lonely up here," he said.

She headed for the haymow ladder,

climbing it for the first time.

"Watch your step," he cautioned.

She reached the top of the ladder and planted herself beside him. "What are you doing here with me anyway, Bryan?"

"I came to visit."

"No . . . I mean why do you keep coming back?"

He sighed. "I *know* you, Sarah. I knew you before the accident. Underneath all the pain of your life, I know there is a part of you that will flower someday. I want to be there when that happens."

"I don't know what to say," she whispered.

"Say you love me, too."

"I can't . . . not now, Bryan. There's so much for me to work through."

"Talk to me, Sarah."

Sighing, she began to open her heart. "Ivy's death — her children being orphaned and hurting, and me visiting here — well, it has been a real struggle."

"Making the decision to come must have been difficult for you."

"More than anyone knows."

He reached for her hand. "I love you, Sarah. Is it all right for me to tell you again?"

"I'm not a good risk," she admitted, shaking her head. "I'm not worthy of your love."

"Let me be the judge of that."

"Oh, Bryan, my sister's world has spilled over into mine. I don't know when or how I can ever find contentment with the past."

"Grieving Ivy's death would be a good starting place . . . to peace, my darling."

An overwhelming sadness encompassed her, and she did not fight back the tears. Bryan reached for her, holding her tenderly, silently. And in the serenity of the sweet-smelling haymow, at last Sarah mourned for her sister.

When the children arrived home, Bryan greeted them enthusiastically. Sarah marveled at his relaxed approach to both Caleb and Josiah, as well as the girls. He seemed reluctant to say good-bye after supper. Tall, handsome, and strong, Bryan Ford was infinitely more than was evident on the outside, Sarah decided with a certain tingle of discovery. He was also one of the most patient men she had ever known — especially with youngsters. No wonder he had talked of wanting a half dozen back in college.

Chapter Twenty-Nine

Sarah drove the younger children to the Peach Lane School on Thursday morning. "I'm going to Miriam Esh's house today," she told them as they rode along. "I'll be back when school is dismissed."

"Does Lyddie know you're goin'?" Hannah asked, sitting up front.

"She knows about the quilting. Why do you ask?"

"I thought Lyddie might like you goin' to quilt at Miriam's, that's all."

Josiah spoke up from the backseat. "What 'bout Uncle Bryan? Does *he* know you're going to Miriam's?"

"*Who?*"

"Your friend from Boston."

She smiled. "Why did you call him 'uncle'?"

Josiah explained. "Dat and Mamma taught us not to say older Englischer's names just plain . . . just so."

She glanced in the rearview mirror, noting Josiah's boyish grin and tousled hair. "*Uncle* Bryan doesn't know about the quilting, no.

But I think *you* had better run a comb through your hair before we get to school."

Caleb said, "Ach, his hair always looks like that."

"Well, maybe it's time Josiah was more careful about his personal hygiene. I'll bet your mother wanted your hair clean and neat, right, Josiah?"

Anna Mae was next to give her opinion of her brother's hair. "Mamma was forever gettin' after him 'bout it. Ain't so, Josiah?"

The boy seemed to enjoy the attention. He folded his arms across his chest and sat smugly between Caleb and Anna Mae. "Seems to me I *can* do better . . . if I want to."

"You best be wantin' to," Caleb scolded.

"Jah, listen to your big brother," Hannah said, turning around and staring at Josiah.

They continued bantering, not so much picking on each other but chattering about the fact that it was Groundhog's Day and wondering if the furry creature would see his shadow or not.

Anna Mae was silent now, staring out the window. Sarah saw her brush a tear from her cheek. Poor girl — she seemed to be hurting just as Megan Holmes had been, when Meggie first came to Stonington Elementary School.

The wispy second-grader had been an island unto herself — a loner — and by the end of the first week, Sarah found herself becoming strongly attached. Her heart went out to the girl. Easy to understand why. Here was another "little Sarah," a youngster continually tormented by her inability to fit in with her peers. Meggie demonstrated some symptoms of autism, as well, so it was natural for her to withhold herself from the other children. She had very few friends, and the ones who claimed to like her often ridiculed her, along with the others. No wonder Megan Holmes had a fear of connecting. So it was Sarah, her teacher, whom Meggie trusted above all.

The Peach Lane schoolhouse came into view, its tall white belfry standing out against the blue sky and the patches of melting snow on the playground.

"Here we are," she said, flicking the automatic lock, opening all the doors. "Does Lydia let you go outside for recess when there is snow on the ground?"

"Jah, just depends how cold 'tis," Josiah spoke up. "Susannah Stoltzfus did, too, when she was our teacher."

"Are you extra careful during recess, especially in the winter?"

"It's the best time to build snow forts,"

Hannah said with glee.

"But is Lydia always nearby, watching over you?" Her four nieces and nephews were staring at her skeptically.

"Why're ya askin' us all this?" Anna Mae said, holding her little sister's hand.

"Are ya afraid something might happen?" Josiah asked.

She said, "Well, no . . . I *hope* not."

"You can ask Lyddie 'bout how she keeps watch so ev'ryone's safe," Caleb said, his voice strong.

"No . . . no, that's not necessary. Just be careful, all right?"

They waved and turned to run across the school yard, past the white picket fence, toward the narrow, sagging porch.

Please, please be safe. . . .

Sarah knocked on Miriam Esh's back door, waited for more than a few minutes, then realized from the sound of the chatter inside, she should apparently just enter.

Susie Lapp was talking as Sarah came into the kitchen. "I just wish more young folk would keep to the Old Ways."

"I know whatcha mean 'bout the unclean talk and whatnot amongst our young people," another remarked. "Seems to be gettin' worse with each new generation, not to mention the low courtship and moral standards of the young. Parents have been ignorin' such things far too long."

"We're just lackadaisical sometimes, I'm afraid," said another.

"Well, here's Sarah. Hullo!" called Miriam Esh, putting down a dishcloth and going over to greet her. "I'm awful glad you came." She went around introducing Sarah to the women, ten or more.

The discussion regarding Amish young people ceased once all of them were aware of Sarah's presence. They began work on the old quilt binding as soon as coffee was finished and cups were washed and put away "for later on."

Sarah recognized the task at hand to be far less difficult than the quilting bee she had attended last week. Today's stitching involved the easy slip stitch her mother had used when hemming a dress or skirt. In her estimation, with this many hands, the binding would be finished in a few hours.

When the babble had died down some, Miriam said softly, "I feel a Telling comin' on." Exactly what Miriam meant by that, Sarah was soon to discover.

"Seems there was once a smithy with a horse that was a slowpoke, not so old as he was downright slow in the head. But that little horse was also well trained and obedient. The horse would do for the smithy anything he said."

The women listened, some seemingly more interested than others. Sarah kept her needle busy, looking up every so often as she sat with Susie Lapp, intrigued by the process of sharing a story in this setting.

Miriam continued in a low voice to tell her tale of an Amish blacksmith and his beloved horse. "The animal was out in the pasture one summer day, chewin' on some grass, just a-grazin' with all the other horses. Several mules fed alongside the horses in the meadow, too.

"The smithy — a long piece of grass between his teeth — stood, leanin' on the fence just observing things, minding his own business, when a clap of thunder rumbled out of the sky. Near out of nowhere it came.

"Quick as a wink, more and more hair-raisin' thunder-smacks exploded from the sky, and the blacksmith started roundin' up his animals. He'd had himself a look at the clouds and knew, sure as rain, a big storm was a-brewin'. And fast!

"He got his straw hat a-fannin' and a-wavin' at them horses, calling for them to head for the barn, getting 'em going in the right direction and following them, too, making a beeline for safety.

"A single powerful bolt of lightning split the sky, silver and sizzlin'. And, well, if it didn't up and strike that slow little horse of his.

" 'Nee — no . . . no!' the smithy hollered, running out of the stable, past the barnyard, toward the clearing. When he got to the pony, the animal lay on the ground, dead.

"Some folk still say the reason the poor creature got hit by the only thunderbolt for miles around was due to the horse's dawdling. Others say the smithy was at fault for neglecting to take better care, not seein' to it that *all* the animals were safe from the storm. But the story has nothin' whatever to do with any of that, really.

"Truth was, the smithy blamed himself for his horse's death. Clear to his own dyin' day, he did. And folk who knew the blacksmith say his own guilty conscience took him in the end. For sure and for certain, he never forgave himself for what happened. Had he done so, the very deed of forgiveness, workin' its way and will in him, would've freed him from the ropes that bound him to his mortal wound.

"A farmer in Wisconsin quit farmin' after his barn burned to rubble. Instead of lettin' the brethren come and raise a new one, he was bitter and ended up losin' everything. Somewhere in Virginia, a schoolteacher let discouragement overtake her and stopped instructing her pupils. Over in Ohio, a mother mourned hard her daughter's shunning, givin' up hope the girl would ever come to her senses and return to the People. The woman can't seem to forgive herself for whatever part she surely must have played in the rebellion of her dear girl.

"Jah, it's always the same when we can't — or don't — forgive others or ourselves," Miriam said, sighing, tears glistening in the corner of her eyes. "My grandfather was the one who had the little horse with half a brain that got struck by lightning," she said. "I first heard this story at the knee of my own father."

The womenfolk put down their needles and clapped a little, nodding their heads, eyes bright. "I never tire of that one, Miriam," Susie Lapp said, smiling at Sarah.

"Me, neither," said the elder Elizabeth. "I think you tell it better each and ev'ry time."

Miriam did not say thank you or show any visible reception of the praise. But when the woman looked her way, Sarah began to wonder just how *well* Miriam Esh must have known Ivy Cottrell before she died.

★ ★ ★

On the drive home, Sarah replayed the story of the blacksmith and his horse in her mind.

I have found forgiveness and peace . . . a reprieve from guilt.

Bryan's words, coupled with Miriam's story, continued to echo in her head. She longed for freedom from the pain of her own guilt. She wished she could forgive herself for Meggie's accident. Forgive Ivy for her obsession with being the only child, missing the parent-baby relationship she'd had for six beautiful years with Mother and Daddy when Ivy was their one and only. When the playroom door shut out the rest of the world, and she alone was the cherished child.

Sarah remembered that Ivy, as a teenager, had once told her that she desperately longed for the "old days," before Sarah had come along and spoiled everything. This, Ivy had shared with utter disgust in her tone. Yet somewhere, through the years, Ivy had changed radically. She had found and accepted God's forgiveness — had heard His voice.

Sarah knew her sister had found peace, as Bryan had so boldly announced at the breakfast table yesterday. Because Ivy's place of peace was alive and evident on the faces of each of her five children.

Lydia heard a sound on the porch of the schoolhouse. All the children, even her sisters and brothers, had gone home for the day. It had turned out fairly warm, and because it was Groundhog's Day, the children bemoaned the fact that since the sun had shone all day, the groundhog had prob'ly seen his shadow. Alas, another six weeks of winter.

She was organizing her desk when the door at the back of the classroom inched open. Levi King walked in, removed his black felt hat, and turned to close the door, locking it. He approached her desk, almost like a shy little boy in trouble with the teacher.

"Sorry if I startled ya, Lyddie."

"Hullo, Levi . . . s'nice to see you again."

He stared at the floor, then sighed, breathing in like he was tryin' to muster up the strength to talk to her. *Really* talk. "Things haven't been right for me for the longest time . . . ever since last week, well, when your aunt caught us together."

"For me, neither."

He switched his hat from one hand to the other. "I'm still hopin' you think of me as a friend, at least."

She felt weak in the knees, so she sat down at her desk. "Jah, at least . . ." She didn't want to say much more. Didn't want to spoil the chance of hearin' whatever Levi wanted to say to her.

"Has your aunt Sarah made up her mind 'bout staying on here or not?" He sounded more bold just now.

"I have a feelin' we may not be leaving, if that's what you're askin'."

"Ach, that's gut news!"

"She's hopin' to find someone to take us in, and between you and me, I'm thinkin' it's Miriam Esh. But you won't say anything, will you?"

He promised not to. "I've prayed awful hard 'bout us, Lyddie."

"I have, too. Ever so much."

Just then, he came 'round the desk and pulled her to her feet. "I never stopped lovin' you. Not even when you put me off."

Honestly, she tried to say something dear back to him, but he had her in his arms, holding her tight as she'd ever been hugged by a boy or a relative, neither one. "Levi, I . . ."

"Don't say nothin', please, Lyddie. Don't say nothin' but what I want to hear."

She leaned her head against his chest, listening to the quick pounding of his heart. "I won't ever hurt you again," she whispered.

"Then you *will* marry me?"

She sighed, looking into his face. "Come the wedding season, jah, I will."

"You'll make me the happiest Amishman in Lancaster County!" He leaned down close to her face, kissing her forehead, then his lips brushed hers lightly.

She gave in to his embrace, returning his kiss. With all her heart, she did.

Chapter Thirty

Searching through Ivy's journals, Sarah found — at long last — the one entry she had been anxious to read.

Pentecost Sunday, 1991

It's truly hard to say, but I do believe, as I think on it, that my father's love for God and all of creation was one of the reasons I turned to the Lord when I did. Looking back, Gilbert, too, was hungry for what his heart was missing. One night, the two of us sat down together, opened up Dad's old Bible, and read the passages in John's Gospel. We clasped hands and prayed the sinner's prayer found written in the flyleaf of his well-worn Good Book.

Daddy would've been mighty happy if he were alive to know what happened that wonderful-gut night. Honestly, I felt clean inside. Gone was the tension of sin, along with my need to dominate those around me, especially Sarah. I've set my mind to sharing this experience with her, though it may not be well re-

ceived. My sister has every right to be put out with me. Goodness' sake, I kept her under my thumb for so long. No wonder she as much as renounced our sisterhood. Still, I won't give up on trying to reach her.

Sarah and Lydia cleaned the kitchen together after supper. Lydia seemed especially eager to share more stories of her first days of teaching. Then suddenly, she asked, "Did you teach all the subjects when you were a schoolteacher?" asked Lydia.

"Only the curriculum the public school system required for second grade," Sarah replied.

Lydia turned to face her, leaning against the counter. "Then you had *just* second-grade pupils in your classroom?"

"Yes."

"Did you ever wish you had older children in the room to help the younger ones?"

"The way the school was set up, we had occasional teachers' aides come several times each week. But older students never assisted."

Lydia described the process by which the Amish schools were generally run, sharing their philosophy of education. Pupils' studies were based on the belief that the future generation must be preserved for the church by semi-isolation, essential for the devout practice of their faith.

"The beliefs of Amish children must be protected, it sounds to me," Sarah said.

"Jah, so much so that parents sometimes go to extreme measures to make sure of it."

When the dishes were washed, dried, and put away, Sarah and Lydia sat at the table again. "Days ago, you asked me a question, Lydia — about an accident your mother referred to in her journal. I want to give you a satisfactory answer . . . now." Anxious to open up to her sister's daughter, Sarah felt the urgency ignite within.

"Don't feel you *have* to share with me, Aunt Sarah."

She shook her head. "No, it's time I told you. . . ."

Lydia nodded, her face earnest.

"The day of the school accident, the weather was exceptionally cold," she began. "I remember dreading having to fulfill my recess duty. There was snow and even a few icy patches on the playground, too, which most schools now use as a measure against having outdoor recess."

She continued on, reciting the details of the day of Megan Holmes' accident. Then she felt she should tell Lydia about Meggie herself. "She was such a needy little girl, and she trusted me implicitly. I must admit, I loved Meggie dearly — even as I might have loved my own child. But I made a dreadful error in judgment that day. It cost Megan her life. . . ." Her voice trailed away.

Lydia's eyes were more serious now. She leaned her elbows hard on the table.

"The recess bell rang, signaling the end of play. Meggie, who was impatient to line up with the other children, stood shivering at the end of the line, jumping around, trying to keep warm. She must have known she would have to stand there for a long time, being the last child to wait for the school doors to open." Bowing her head, Sarah inhaled deeply. "Meggie was always fidgety."

Lydia touched her hand. "There's no need to grieve yourself more, Aunt Sarah."

"I *need* to tell you what happened." She forged ahead with her sorrowful story. "Meggie pleaded with me repeatedly to run back to the playground and go down the slide. 'Just once more, Miss Cain? Please, *please?*'

"Judging by the crowd of children at the door, I assumed she had plenty of time. Reluctantly, I gave my permission — 'Be very careful,' I cautioned her.

"I lost track of the moments — perhaps they were only seconds, I don't know — but when I heard a child's scream, I turned to see Meggie lying on the ground only a few yards behind me."

Lydia gasped, covering her mouth. *"Himmel,"* she whispered.

Choking back tears, Sarah continued. "Meggie — my precious Meggie — must have slipped on a ladder rung near the top of the slide. Falling, she had torn her coat as her little hands groped for safety. In one horrifying moment, Meggie fell, hitting her head on the frozen ground. She died instantly."

Lydia wiped her eyes. "No one could save her?"

"Oh, I tried to revive her, but there was no pulse."

A ghastly silence invaded the kitchen. Then Lydia said in a near whisper, "Was that why you quit teaching and moved to Oregon?"

Sarah let out a long sigh. "What followed the accident was an ongoing *living* nightmare. Meggie's parents acquired an attorney and threatened to sue the school for negligence. There was lots of talk, a growing swell, that I, the playground teacher in charge, should be suspended. Empathy from a handful of people in the school community grew to a frenzied rage. In the end, I resigned."

Leaning back in the chair, Lydia crossed

her arms. "After Mamma died, I didn't understand why you took so long to come here. Now I think I do . . . a little."

"I was frightened to be around children," she confessed.

"No wonder . . ."

Sarah looked into the face of Ivy's firstborn. "But my visit here with you has helped to change all that, Lydia. Truly it has."

Miriam Esh answered the phone on the first ring the next morning. "Hello, Miriam. It's Sarah Cain."

"Well, Sarah, what can I do for *you?*"

"I was wondering — may I stop by for a quick visit?"

"Come right over. We'll drink some coffee and sit a spell."

"Thank you, Miriam," she said before they hung up.

Ever so much, she thought, with a smile.

Sarah was eager to get right to the subject, but Miriam was more interested in how she and the children were getting along. "Don't you just get a chuckle over the young man Josiah? My, my, he's the funniest little fella."

"All the children are delightful," she replied. "They really are."

"Sounds to me like you've come a long

way in just two weeks." Miriam stirred two lumps of sugar into her coffee.

Sarah drank hers black. She was grateful to be able to immerse herself in its aroma, blocking out some of the offensive odor exuding from Miriam. "It's important that I do the best thing for my nieces and nephews. They must stay here in the Amish community. I certainly don't fit in with the Plain customs and ways — never will." She paused, then continued. "You, Miriam, are the best answer for Ivy's children staying together as a unit."

"Well, now, Ivy had *other* ideas, you know."

"If my sister had thought things through more carefully — perhaps if she hadn't been so ill — I'm sure she would have named you their legal guardian in the first place."

"Well, I don't know, really." Miriam sipped her coffee, then said, "But it seems you've made up your mind 'bout all this."

"As fond as I am of Lydia and her brothers and sisters, I believe they'll be far better off with someone Amish. Someone kind and loving, too, like you."

"Since you seem sincere 'bout this, I must be tellin' you something." Miriam's eyes glimmered. "Ivy came to me a few weeks before she died and asked if I'd make sure her children stayed together. She said to me, '*If things don't work out with Sarah, will you raise my children?'"*

"Then you *were* Ivy's backup plan?"

Miriam chortled, lashes fluttering. "I guess you could say that."

"Well, I'm relieved, to say the least. When can you move in with the children?"

"I could start moving things over this weekend."

"Tomorrow?"

Miriam nodded.

"I'll tell the children. I'm sure they'll be happy with this news." Sarah paused, measuring her words. "I want to do whatever I can to make the transition smooth for you."

Miriam said she would plan to have some of the brethren come and move her things, store some of her furnishings in the farmhouse cellar, and rent out her little house to someone in the community. It was settled, rather effortlessly, in a matter of a half hour.

Sarah felt better than she had in years, having cleared the air with Lydia the night before, telling her why she had dragged her feet about coming in the first place. And she had done Ivy's highest bidding by contacting Miriam, keeping the Cottrell family intact. What's more, she had found a portion of peace she might have missed had she not come to Lancaster County.

371

On the drive back to the farmhouse, she felt the urge to pull the car over to the side of the road. Getting out, she surveyed the sweep of land — acres of the richest, most fertile soil in all of America — stretching out for miles in every direction. Ivy had often referred to the area as "God's country." Their father, too, had said the same of New England, especially his seaside haven in Rhode Island.

Sarah stared in wonderment at the beauty around her as the sun made its gradual ascent toward the loftiest spot in the sky. Far as her eyes could behold, she embraced the miracle of God's creation.

Is this what drew my father to the divine Creator? she wondered.

She amazed herself and began to talk to God. "I've resisted you all these years," she began, her tears falling freely. "If it's not too late . . . for me, I want to entrust my life — my future — to your safekeeping."

The cry of her heart was directed to the master Creator of shell homes for millions of tiny sea creatures — the Lord Jesus, mender of broken hearts and Savior of mankind. A great peace, a calmness settled on her, and deep within she knew and understood that she, too, was one of God's beloved treasures. For the first time, she heard the still, small voice. Unmistakably so.

Chapter Thirty-One

The minute she returned to the house, Sarah phoned Bryan. "I'm sorry to call you at work."

"No problem. What's up?"

"I . . . well, I think I understand what you meant when you were here."

"Please tell me about it." His voice, his compassionate response, gave her nerve to continue.

"I talked to God today, Bryan. I know now about the still, small voice. I guess you could say . . . I'm a Christian."

"Oh, Sarah, I'm so happy for you. I prayed this would happen."

They talked animatedly about getting together for another visit. "Sometime soon," she said.

Bryan agreed. "I'll call you tonight. We'll talk more then."

She wanted to tell him she loved him. After all these years. But words so dear were better said face-to-face.

Sarah decided to wait until after supper to talk with the children. Josiah and Hannah were a bit upset about the possibility of a coming snowstorm. "It ain't springtime yet, after all," Josiah piped up.

"Ach, we're gonna be stuck with more cold weather," Hannah said. "Lots of it!"

"That's 'cause the groundhog had to go and see his shadow," Lydia teased.

"Seems to me he sees it *ev'ry* year!" Anna Mae remarked. "I think it's the dumbest thing anyone ever thought up."

Sarah was glad to see Anna Mae entering into the table chatter. She observed her throughout the meal, hoping that the decision she had come to wouldn't set the girl back emotionally. Miriam was a wonderful woman, a *good* woman — though she needed to bathe more often — but maybe her becoming responsible for a family might cause her to change her habits of hygiene. For the children's sake. And, too, Sarah would be checking in on all of them from time to time. She had already assumed she would fly in and visit often.

Lydia and Anna Mae got up to clear the table, bringing over an angel food cake for dessert. "Anna Mae baked this just for you, Aunt Sarah," Lydia said.

Anna Mae stood at Sarah's side, close enough to touch. "I want you to have the first piece." The girl grinned, showing her gums slightly.

"How nice of you," Sarah said, holding her plate while Anna Mae cut into the spongy white dessert.

Without another word, Anna Mae scooted onto the bench next to Sarah. "Hannah's always the one sittin' beside you," she said softly. "Is it all right if *I* do?"

"Of course, dear," she said, taking a bite of the cake.

"How's it taste?" asked Anna Mae, watching her every move.

"Delicious. Absolutely melts in my mouth!"

Anna Mae leaned her head on Sarah's arm. "I'm ever so happy."

Sarah fought the lump in her throat and folded the young girl in her warm embrace.

"She likes huggin'," Josiah said, chuckling.

"Lots of hugs," Lydia added.

"We all need a nice long one every so often," Sarah said, dreading the revelation of the news she must give. Tomorrow, Miriam Esh would begin moving in. All hugging aside, Ivy's children had to be told the truth.

"Somebody saw Levi King drivin' his fastest horse down to the school this-after," Josiah said, looking mighty sheepish.

"Aw, that somebody must've been seein' things," Lydia said.

Caleb was grinning now. "Oh, they saw a-plenty."

Lydia would never let on. Her get-together with Levi was no one's business but her own. Caleb and anybody else could just think what they wanted. Come next fall, everyone would know. She would be published to marry Levi by late October.

Right now she had her mind on other things. She wondered if Aunt Sarah had made her decision 'bout staying. She had a strong feeling their aunt was goin' to tell them something important tonight. She was perty sure, 'cause Aunt Sarah had that same expectant look on her face that Mamma often got.

It was all well and good, the children teasing Lydia about Levi King in their roundabout, good-natured way. But as each of the children finished his or her dessert, Sarah realized that what she must do could no longer be delayed. Time was of the essence. They — *all* of them — would need time this evening, while they were still together with Sarah, to talk things out. Little Hannah would cry; Josiah might, as well. Caleb would sulk in silence, and Anna Mae might rush upstairs to her room. Lydia, bless her heart, would be strong for her brothers and sisters; possibly even give Sarah moral support out of her genuine need to nurture. Lydia was a true gem of a girl.

"There is something we must talk about tonight, children," she began. "I've made a difficult decision. . . ."

Josiah's eyes were big as saucers, but he said nothing. Hannah put down her fork and wiped her mouth on the napkin. Caleb coughed softly, as if signaling their silent after-the-meal prayer.

Lydia sighed audibly.

Anna Mae grabbed Sarah's arm and squeezed. "Don't say that you're leavin' us," the girl at her side said breathlessly. "Please don't let that be your decision."

Sarah's eyes began to cloud up the way they had at her father's funeral. Her contacts slid annoyingly.

"We love you, Aunt Sarah. Honest, we do." Hannah began to cry.

Caleb got up from the table and shuffled outside, head down. Josiah, too, stood up, mimicking his older brother, but he paused behind the bench, resting one knee on it. "Seems to me, Mamma made a mighty big mistake askin' you to come here."

Her vision blurred completely, but she heard the tears in the boy's voice and the feeling of heaviness in the room. She remembered at that moment her mother telling her something so long ago she wondered if, possibly, she had dreamed it. *"When you were born, you looked like a Sarah to me. That's why I gave you the name. Sarah means 'princess,' after all."* Never again had Mother repeated herself.

Sarah with an h, she thought. *What an excellent choice.*

Mother had empowered her twenty-eight years ago by bestowing such a name on her young life. Stupidity and heartache had kept her from receiving the name-gift her parents had so graciously given.

Until this moment, she had never felt like royalty. Lonely and searching, she'd had little connection with family. Tonight, as she composed herself and was eventually able to look into the faces of her sister's beautiful children — her own flesh-and-blood family — a deep serenity filled her spirit.

"No, Josiah," she said, finding her voice, "your mamma was a very wise woman. She did *not* make a mistake. . . ."

Epilogue

Sometimes, I s'pose a person must look through someone else's eyes to see the truth — the goodness, too — that is in front of them all along. That's what must've happened to our aunt Sarah, 'bout herself *and* the way she viewed Mamma. Both.

On the day Miriam Esh came over to stay with us, Aunt Sarah made a phone call to her boss, tellin' him she'd be flying back to Oregon, but only to pack, put her house up for sale, and drive 'cross country with her own car. "I'm going to live in Amish country with my family," I heard her say with a ring in her voice.

So Miriam *did* come and stay for a couple-a weeks, and Josiah gave her some of Mamma's homemade soap. Not so surprisingly, she took the hint!

When Aunt Sarah returned, Miriam was ever so glad to step aside and go back to her little house on the big spread. I figured out why Mamma had confided in Miriam and not Susie Lapp. Mamma knew Miriam could easily substitute for Sarah. Susie, a busy grandmother and older woman, wouldn't have been a right good choice, considerin' everything.

Before Aunt Sarah flew to Oregon, preparing to be our full-time stepmamma, she asked me to take her up to see Mamma's grave. There, she and I stood alone together on Glendorn Hill, silent as the sky, looking down at the spot where Mamma lay buried. "I'm so glad we came here . . . together," Aunt Sarah said. After drying our tears, we hugged each other close, staying a while longer, as we looked over the valley below, acres of farmland widening out to the horizon. Truly, 'twas a promising sight. And Aunt Sarah said so, too.

Spring finally came to Grasshopper Level, and along 'bout the time the locust trees out behind the barn blossomed, in early May, all of us skipped barefoot through the daisy-filled meadow and had us a sunny wedding day. With the help of an English minister, Uncle Bryan married Aunt Sarah beneath the bluest sky I've ever seen. Hannah, Anna Mae, and I made a yellow-and-white daisy-chain for Aunt Sarah's head covering. It was one of the happiest days of my life, for sure and for certain.

Not for the longest time have I seen the

picture of Meggie on display in Uncle Bryan and Aunt Sarah's bedroom. Truth be told, I believe Aunt Sarah's forgiven herself, with a lot of help from on high. She and Uncle Bryan take turns reading the Bible to us of a mornin'. At nighttime, too.

I still catch Anna Mae mumblin' to herself, but not near like she used to. She and Aunt Sarah are like two peas in a pod most of the time, a-huggin' and talkin'. I even caught them napping once together, Aunt Sarah's arm flung over my sister. I wouldn't be one bit surprised if Anna Mae — all of us, really — are God's second chance for Aunt Sarah.

Well, come next November, I'll marry Levi. I'll keep teaching at the Peach Lane School till a few days before our wedding. A dowry was set aside for me, all planned by Mamma before her passing, Aunt Sarah told me.

As for me marryin' and makin' a home with Levi, I have every confidence my brothers and sisters will be well cared for here. My leaving will free up a bedroom for Anna Mae, who's comin' up on twelve real soon. That'll make an empty spot in Hannah's room for Aunt Sarah's baby . . . if and when that happens. And by the way Uncle Bryan and Aunt Sarah seem to fall into each other's eyes, I 'spect it won't be long before there'll be another little one living in Dat's country farmhouse. Speakin' of bedrooms, Mamma's old room is all spruced up modern with wallpaper and curtains, even some cut flowers!

Uncle Bryan shorted out the electrical system the other night. Guess all that fancy computer equipment of his takes up plenty-a power. Anyway, we had us a candlelight supper like the Old Order folk often did in the old days, before gas lamps. 'Twas lots of fun, though, and Uncle Bryan held Aunt Sarah's hand and told us stories of growin' up in Boston, ridin' the subway, and walking 'round Boston Commons. Things most any father would tell their children.

Bein' this happy seems like a wonderful-gut dream to me sometimes. Honestly, I wouldn't be one bit surprised if Mamma and Dat have *some* idea just how blessed their children are. Best of all, we'll see them in Glory some sweet day. When that time comes, I'll remind Mamma that I kept my promise with the dear Lord's help.

Surely goodness and mercy shall follow me. . . .

Author's Note

I am grateful for the patience and wisdom of many people during the writing of this book.

There was ongoing prayer support, careful editing, and love from my husband, Dave, paving the way for Sarah Cain and Lydia Cottrell to come alive in my heart and on paper.

I offer my heartfelt appreciation to my editors, Barb Lilland, Anne Severance, and Carol Johnson, whose faith in my work gave me courage for the journey.

Numerous references offered a wellspring of inspiration, from such authentic works about the Amish and their way of life as — *Amish Women*, by Louise Stoltzfus, *The Amish, In Their Own Words*, compiled by Brad Igou, *The Amish Quilt*, by Eve Wheatcroft Granick, *A Fruitful Vine*, by Carrie Bender, and *Amish Society*, by John A. Hostetler. If there are inaccuracies in my portrayal of the Lancaster County Amish, gleaned from any of the above-mentioned resources, I bear sole responsibility.

I wish to thank my prayer partners, family

members, resource gatherers, loyal encouragers, and manuscript readers who prayed, assisted in research, and sent Lancaster County-based news clippings, books, brochures, and other regional information. They cheered me on during the lengthy process of the writing and are the following: various unnamed Amish and Mennonite friends and contacts, the Mennonite Information Center in Lancaster, Pennsylvania, my dear "Pen Women" friends, John and Ada Reba Bachman, Doran and Elise Bartle, Jerry and Shari Bieber, Carole Billingsley, Dale and Barbara Birch, Julie Buxman, Becky Byler, Glenda Cooper, Roswell Flower, Verna Flower, Bill and Beverly Fry, Susan and Tabitha Gordon, Tom and Anne Gray, Don and Jeannette Green, Sandi Heisler, June Heimsoth, John Henderson, Bob and Aleta Hirschberg, Herb and Jane Jones, Iris Jones, Eline Lardie, Connie McKenzie, Martha Nelson, Steve and Nancy Oates, Mona Paulson, Susan Pelham, Steve Rabey, Barb Reinhard, Alan and Pam Ronn, Len and Barbara Rosner, Barbara Saladin, Laura Taylor, Judy Verhage, Rhoda Welsch, and Dave and Linda Woodward.